change baby

✺

june spence

RIVERHEAD BOOKS

a member of Penguin Group (USA) Inc.

New York

2004

Riverhead Books
a member of
Penguin Group (USA) Inc.
375 Hudson Street
New York, NY 10014

Library of Congress Cataloging-in-Publication Data

Spence, June, date.
Change baby / June Spence.
p. cm.
ISBN 1-57322-286-0
1. Women—North Carolina—Fiction.   2. Conflict of generations—Fiction.   3. Mothers and daughters—Fiction.
4. North Carolina—Fiction.   I. Title.
PS3569.P4454C48   2004   2004043778
813'.54—dc22

Printed in the United States of America
1   3   5   7   9   10   8   6   4   2

This book is printed on acid-free paper. ∞

BOOK DESIGN BY AMANDA DEWEY

For Ruth and Ozella

change baby

✻

avie goss

My mother, Mabry Goss, had been ill for some time, but she kept it to herself. At seventy-three years old, she felt she was holding steady, though her heart was congestive and her lungs porous and simmering inside her chest—she carried their bloated weight with little complaint. The doctor harped on her smoking, and so she did not go to see him any more than she could help it. He'd made the dire predictions years before. She would not give him the satisfaction, would not permit him to lord and gloat while she sat helpless in a paper smock.

Her concessions were gradual. She was scaling back her gar-den, planting fewer rows of vegetables, and scattering handfuls of zinnia and marigold seeds with a wholly uncustomary abandon. She'd always been strict and relentless with the yard. She admitted only to tiring more easily, which seemed ordinary enough, given her age. Her gravelly cough was long-established, but I didn't know that it was now strangling her awake all night, that she nodded off in the flowerbeds and sometimes church, and collapsed, gasping, into armchairs after hauling laundry from the basement or the Sunday paper from the edge of the driveway. Her dwindling strength wasn't something I was ready to think about, and she wasn't about to make a point of it, not even to procure more visits.

"You couldn't have been expected to know," she reproached me afterward, meaning, I think, to console. "You weren't here."

Fire flushed out her secret, but it was hidden too at first, lingering in the walls while it gathered momentum.

It was important to her that I understand—and let it be known—that the fire was not caused by any lapse in her vigilance, a pot put on to boil and forgotten, or worse, and what people would at first conclude: a cigarette not properly tamped out. It had never been her habit to smoke in the bed, or even in the bedroom, she insisted, nor was she careless in the disposal of ash; she ran her ashtrays under the tap. Nor would she subject any minor-aged children to her smoke, now that it was out about how bad that was. If she hadn't been able to quit the cigarettes, she said, at least she was not a fool about them.

No, the fire had other origins. She'd have figured her furnace for the culprit, but instead it was a nest of frayed wires smoldering like a grudge inside bedroom walls packed with old cedar shavings near to ash already, a slow burn of age and filth warming the plaster.

She'd been noticing that the bedside lamp flickered and that the alarm clock lagged behind, but the electrical outlet behind her nightstand that must have been growing steadily hotter went undetected for days. She'd catch a vague odor—not of burning but of something gone sour. Then a curious humming woke her in the night. Unable to locate the source, she let it mingle with the groaning and settling of old frame and floorboards, the low warning chitter of the furnace. She'd trained herself since my father died not to startle at night sounds; there'd be no sleep in an empty house otherwise. The dark was full of noise, the air dry and alive, her sheets crackling with static. This is dream stuff, she reasoned, and old nerves bristling, but she was already pulling harder than she knew for breath.

She soon began to cough and sputter, so she propped herself upright for ease. The humming that had meshed with other sounds asserted itself again. It became a buzz, a vibration she could feel along the headboard. She tried to switch on the lamp, but it hissed, and something popped inside the bulb. She reached to unplug both clock and lamp, and her hand brushed the hot metal of the socket plate, searing her fingerpads smooth.

Still, she hesitated, acknowledging *burn* but not *fire*. She put on a decent robe and slid her feet into satiny pink scuffs. Embers were drifting to lodge in dark crevices and spread, but at first she escaped no farther than the kitchen, where she iced her fingers and swallowed two tablespoons of grape cough syrup. Her mouth filled with a sour tang, and she cleared her throat again and again and finally spat, then retched into the sink, but she could not quell the itching deep in her gullet. Tentative plumes of gray fog were now snaking out of the bedroom, carrying an acrid, coppery stink.

Whose fault, this? It was a failure of maintenance, she supposed. She'd been putting off the necessary arrangements, no longer sure exactly whom to call on and what to ask for. Some type of inspection had long been in order for all the pipes and wires, for the many little motors that whirred unseen, but she'd hesitated to make any broad inquiries. Feared they would expose her ignorance and thus cause her to be fleeced by unscrupulous tradesmen.

She'd fretted constantly over whether it was time to paint again and if the roof would yet hold, and meantime her strength and attention were diverted into beating back the constant dust trod into her rugs, the oily grime seeping into countertops and linoleum. It was her every waking minute, something to do with that house, its cleaning and upkeep. Or going to the market every time she turned around, for there were never enough eggs, and stale flour was no good for the baking, and the refrigerator fluctuated so that either the milk curdled or the lettuce froze. Cans of potted meat and boxes of saltines were stacked high in the pantry to buoy her through inclement weather or in the event she could no longer drive and must look to others to bring her what they would, when they could.

She called the fire department and asked them to come but not to blare their sirens, which request of course they did not heed but blared away. She went to wait in the yard, by now taking desperate gulps of air between ragged coughs that doubled her over. There was nothing visible from the outside to indicate the house was burning, but she could taste the dirty smoke from where she stood.

She'd meant for the house to outlast her and did not intend to leave it until that wet heart of hers quit flapping. She wasn't one to hurl entitlements at the Lord, but she felt she had this one thing owed her. She'd wanted to die before her husband—or at least she had not wanted to be left behind—and that had not been granted. She'd wanted to keep her children close by her, and *that* had not been granted.

She backed away from the house until the grass ended and her feet broke through the dry clumps of soil in her garden. The man had tilled too early, it had rained too much since, and the mud had formed a brittle crust. It would have to be tilled again before she could put in anything, but the man was unreliable. There was no telling when she could get him to come again. If it occurred to her that she would not be in any condition to work a garden this year, she directed her anger instead to the man who had come and tilled too early.

She sent up a fierce prayer for breath and strength, spat as much as she could dredge, and set off walking, dragging her crepe-soled scuffs through the gravel. It had been a foolish choice to wear them, but she hadn't intended to do anything but wait in the yard. Now she found herself walking to the house of her oldest friend, Zephra Overby. It used to be a matter of crossing fields, but those had long ago been sectioned into plots, and streets had been cut through. She counted driveways as she teetered along the lips of ditches. She wouldn't make it as far as Zephra's; the fumes and smoke breathed in sleep would be enough to put her in the hospital and keep her there for thirteen weeks.

It was this Mabry was walking toward: she held a picture in her mind of Zephra standing in the doorframe, her arms outstretched. It was an image culled from distant memory; Zephra was many years younger, as was Mabry. And Zephra's arms would have been reaching not for Mabry but for the infant she carried, a squalling, wriggling weight Mabry was desperate to pass to her. The infant wasn't me, but another baby girl—Mabry wouldn't be my mother for a very long time yet. But the picture did not waver: Zephra would know what to do. Her arms outstretched.

When I was little the talk used to flow around me unchecked, but I picked up more cadences than words. Two voices woven together, Mama's and Zephra's—two women I moved easily between and found the same comfort in. Then the low, guarded tones of my daddy as he breached their talk, just passing through. I played quietly beneath the kitchen table, dodging the women's legs. I was promised a whipping if I gave in to what my hands ached to do—pat the shiny percolator as it burbled from the stovetop or take hold of the matchbox—but I was never whipped. I was often held, inspected, and admired, my dresses hemmed, the snarls worked patiently out of my hair. I was gently or sternly admonished, as the situation required, but never whipped.

In a house long ago emptied of siblings and made over by new money, I was neither spy nor witness to my own family. Born too late, I was coddled as an only child, too well fed, heedless, and unimaginative for dredging up the past. I seemed to have missed out on something, but in time the stain showed in me, too: genetics is just curse gussied up by science. I came to believe in this when things went bad for me and feel the truth of it still, though less forcefully since I stopped drinking; the literature stresses personal responsibility. Besides, as the books are so fond of saying, "Feelings are not facts"—I seemed to confuse the two quite often, and to my own detriment. But it occurs to me that feelings are the embryos of facts, soft and half-formed, little buds becoming digits, limbs.

My mother called me her "change baby," arriving at the brink of menopause; she said she'd laughed like Abraham's barren old Sarah, doubt and delight all mingled, when she learned she was to be blessed at the impossible age of forty-nine. They spoiled me, her and Daddy both. They had the means by then, no longer tenants but landowners. Regina, North Carolina, had been a farming town, but by the time of my raising it was fast becoming what it is now, a bedroom community with residual patches of brightleaf tobacco, to me little more than a blur of white blossom caps along the flanks of a speeding car as me and my friends flung our dregs of soda into the ditches and bewailed the lack of things to do besides ride aimlessly, singing to the radio. Go on diets of Tab, grapefruit, and popcorn. Pluck our eyebrows and brown our legs with baby oil and iodine. I thought settling in Regina meant aspiring only to marry young and drive an hour to Raleigh to work someplace you could wear lipstick and hose, quitting when the babies came. *If* your husband could afford it. I carried vague notions of ascent. I trusted that once I got out of Regina, the future would cough up its gems.

I was intended for college, which I accepted as my birthright, not knowing or caring how judiciously they'd saved for this purpose. I got as far as Raleigh, and after graduation I made one big leap, then migrated northwesterly in fits and starts, a tight cluster of tacks on a board if I were to chart it like a salesman's territory or the progression of a not-too-aggressive disease. At the age of twenty-four I found myself in the northernmost point of Ohio, staring down Canada across a vast, glittering lake, frozen through.

When Mama's house caught fire and my sister, Dahlia, called me home, it wasn't out of goodness that I obliged. I did have visions of redeeming myself through selfless tending labors, but if I'd really understood what would be required of me—perhaps it's better that I didn't. I was ready to come back, anyway; I was tired of people finding my accent charming or laughable, tired of the interminable drives home, and completely unwilling to endure another bleak winter. That was my story, and it was enough of the truth to suffice. I could go on about the winters if pressed: my sandblasted face; the dirty heaps of snow; the trees and power lines bowing under ice; the salted asphalt leaving brackish puddles that ate the paint off my car; the pilling sweaters and scratchy mufflers I wore, the slippery Gore-Tex underwear and the fleece-lined baby-bunting cap; the gray, gray skies and no reprieve. I had never gotten used to any of it. I was homesick, and I was heartbroken; I needed to be with my mama.

I was sober by then, though my thinking wasn't yet. My head still felt stoppered and dull, mule-kicked. Even in my diminished state, though, apparently I was the only one capable of looking after Mama's affairs. Dahlia said as much in her histrionic summons: "You're not a baby anymore and I can't do this. I can't be left with it, do you understand?" She brought a paperback romance and a sack of hard candies to Mama in the hospital, cast some panicky glances at the monitors and the view of the parking lot, and fled when I got there.

I rested on a crippling foldout cot in Mama's hospital room. She wasn't able to speak because they'd intubated her, a small blessing in that it meant she couldn't berate me for not taking her straight home. Though her eyes sparked under fluttery lids and her fingers cramped desperately around mine, I could pretend I didn't know what she wanted. After six hours of half-sleep, balled up tightly as a fist, a limp pillow over my face to block the winking red lights and the nurses' constant visitations, I gave up, scuttled out of the building, folded my sore body back into the car, and drove to Regina as the sun rose.

I hadn't dared let loose in front of Mama when I'd seen how sick she was, so I wept myself dry at the state of the house. A gray and stifling pall dusted every surface with ash, though most of the actual damage had been confined to her bedroom. Everything within it was blackened, or wet, or both, and the walls were gouged by the fireman's ax. The dresser's bird's-eye maple finish, where I'd once discerned faces and animals, was obliterated, and the matching bedframe was charred too brittle now for use. I snipped a clean square of the ruined chenille spread and pocketed the soft, nubbled fabric that had once cloaked both my parents' bodies in sleep. Then a panic shimmied through me as I considered how close to an orphan I'd become, and I got the hell out of there.

I figured both my mother and the house to be ruined beyond repair, and I banged on Zephra's door to tell her so.

Zephra, unflappable even after being pulled from a sound sleep, listened to my ravings for a few indulgent minutes while she put the coffee on, pulled a couple of cereal boxes down from the shelf, and gave the milk a tentative sniff before setting it out. When she'd had her fill of my nonsense, she stopped me. "You need to get hold of yourself, and quick," she said. "You're no good to anybody like this. May as well have Dahlia here." Her words were more bracing than a slap.

"First thing is, where are you planning to sleep?" she asked. "Because you can't stay at your house until it's fixed up a little, and it's clear there's no sleep to be had where your mama is."

"I-I hadn't thought—"

"And why are you stepping so tender?" she demanded.

"Am I?" I sputtered. "My tailbone hurts, I guess. I've been in the car a long time, then I tried sleeping on a cot." Last winter's fall on the ice didn't help, but no one here knew anything about that.

"You'll sleep here, of course," she proclaimed. "Long as you need to. Now that that's settled, I'm going back to bed. You can go ahead and make your phone calls, it's not going to bother me."

I looked at her blankly.

"You've got to make arrangements, don't you? Get somebody over to look at the house? Talk to your Ohio people?"

"My 'Ohio people'?"

"You are a wonder and a marvel. Don't you need to call your boss? And I'll bet you've got a boyfriend waiting to hear from you." I shook my head so vehemently against this, she laughed and said, "Well, call somebody to water your plants, at least. I think you're going to be needed here awhile." And with a swish of her housecoat, she disappeared into her bedroom.

I got hold of myself and made the calls.

Heartrending tasks aside, it felt good to be home. I couldn't rail anymore against Regina and its single stoplight. Now it had three, and some of the old farms-turned-subdivisions had turned as tree-lined and exclusive as the nicer Raleigh neighborhoods. Our own block was a hodgepodge of tenant, ranch-style, bungalow, and mobile dwellings of variegated clapboard, vinyl siding, brick, and one odd, moldering stucco. But even here a regulatory influence was making itself felt—driveways paved, dogs fenced.

At its core ours was still a tenant house, retrofit with plumbing and electricity, two small bedrooms appended like afterthoughts to the original bare essentials of sitting room, eating room, sleeping room. The house's extensions had been absorbed in the original expansion: the lean-to propped up and insulated to accommodate a bathroom, the back porch enclosed to make an oblong parlor. Even those additions were old by the time I was born, begun before my father got the deed to the place in the fifties. Each new layer obscured the original shape, hiding what it was beneath a glossier shell that the fire had only scorched. I might have gutted the place if I'd had the means and Mama could have stood it, or razed it entirely and begun again. I had little nostalgia for old houses and their skittery wiring. But instead I called a contractor who'd worked with my father in his carpentry business long ago, hoping his loyalty would give me some leverage on costs and timetable.

I went to Raleigh each morning to stroke Mama's hand and confer with the nurses. I returned to Regina each afternoon and usually went straight to the house to monitor the progress, alternately coaxing and harassing the poor contractor in my zeal to have things ready by the time Mama was discharged. I did all the painting myself. I'd decided to repaint the whole interior, not just her bedroom. There were empty hours to fill; my body savored the exertion, and my mind needed the blank precision of gliding the roller, lining up thick stripes of enamel. Under my ministrations, Mama's house would come clean again, the walls a dazzling mineral white, but recognizably home. With the barest whiff of bleach and fresh paint, the windows sealed, it would soon hum the neuter breath of the oxygen pump: clean, a little cold.

The sitting room furnishings had not been harmed, but since the wall adjoining Mama's bedroom had been replaced entirely, they were still covered with protective tarps. When I finished priming the new drywall, I unveiled the television set, thinking to doze briefly in front of it and comfort my pulsing lower back. I saw she'd hooked up the VCR I'd sent her last Christmas in a fit of guilty largesse over not coming home. I'd never shown her how to use it and had half-expected to find it still sealed in its box, reproachful. An unmarked videocassette protruded from it. Curious, I nudged it back in and pressed Play.

There was no sound, just black-and-white images etched with

lines, quick cuts of people strolling up and down a thoroughfare, nervously sidling up to the camera and greeting it with winks and tortured grimaces. Men in overalls and snap-brimmed fedoras leaning against Model As or leading mules. Women in gauzy rayon dresses and cotton shifts, stout farm women and sleek-girdled town girls. People eating ice cream cones, playing checkers. An endless parade of schoolchildren marching solemnly by, and when bidden by some silent, unseen presence, breaking into raucous horseplay, mussing hair and knocking hats aslant.

I stopped the tape. I didn't recognize it as old footage of Regina, and I wasn't much interested in the generic Past for its own sake. I was more interested in resting my spine to the soothing background bicker of a soap opera.

Later, I sorted through smoke-glazed pictures to see what could be saved. One frame held a yellowed cross-stitch that read:

Do nothing that you would not want to be doing
when Jesus comes.
Go noplace where you would not like to be found
when Jesus comes.
Say nothing that you would not like to be saying
when Jesus comes.

It was a throwback to what I imagined had been stricter, more pious times in our house, before I was born and everything went lax: church attendance encouraged but not compulsory, flexible curfews and generous allowances, closet bulging with clothes. I'd found it easy to be good under such conditions, or rather, easy not to be bad, which is not quite the same.

A tinted oval portrait of long-dead grandparents came clean as I burnished the convex glass with a chamois cloth. They were the Gosses, my daddy's people, from Virginia: Linwood Senior with his pomaded hair and wire spectacles, Charity Goss in a high buttoned collar, her cheeks dabbed with tubercular flush. I knew little about them except that they'd managed to have eleven children, of whom my father was the youngest, and that due to some injustice he'd inherited nothing. When I was a child their faces regarding me somberly from the dim nineteenth century had a mild chastening effect.

Not so my mother's mother, Avalon Petty, for whom I was named, and I was grateful that her picture was also intact. It was a grainy, sepia-toned print, and the lines in her still-young face were already evident. Her hair was severe, braided tightly and pinned in flat coils on either side of her head, but she was smiling, an anachronism in those old photographs. She'd also died long before I was born. I used to think the accident of my late birth had deprived me of grandparents, but Dahlia and William, my more suitably timed siblings, hadn't known them either.

In several other frames the glass was blackened and smashed, glanced by the firehose, and the photos inside ruined. Still salvageable was a picture of my parents, young and handsome, each holding a child: a newborn and a toddler in white eyelet gowns. Daddy wore a tie but his shirtsleeves were rolled up wiry forearms. He held the tiny baby aloft. The toddler straddled Mama's slim hip, one chunky leg in mid-kick. I knew the toddler was William, who as a young man had some falling-out with Daddy and cut himself off from the family, and the baby aloft was Linwood Junior, who was born sickly and lived only a few short months.

I found myself wondering why Dahlia wasn't in the picture; she would have been in her teens by then. There were intimations she'd had a troubled youth and a marginally less troubled adulthood. Regarding Dahlia, I had been privy only to tightly pressed lips, rueful shakings of the head, low conversations trailing off midsentence.

I located her in a separate portrait, obliterated by smoke to little more than a silhouette. Thinking it could be restored, I brushed away the loose soot and put it in my bedroom—*her* bedroom first—to puzzle over later. I didn't linger; I gave the stale room a perfunctory coat of white and left it to air.

The nurses kept Mama swaddled up good in foam blankets bound and tucked tightly around her. Still she was cold, she complained, and swimmy-headed from the oxygen piped up her nostrils through the cannula she'd plucked away until they threatened restraints. She'd jerked a tube out of her arm as well, but that proved too awful to try again after it was finally threaded back into her flat veins, which seemed to have retreated deep into her skin, barely pulsing. When the nurse worked at the needle, jiggling it back and forth in the flesh trying to rehook those submerged veins, Mama was cowed and nauseated, and she had to shut her eyes against it. My mother, who flinched at nothing, who had reported waking up in the middle of her own knee-replacement surgery five years before and watching in detached fascination the flayed meat of her leg, the surgeon paring the kneecap like soapstone until the pain caught up, escaping her throat, and the mask descended.

It proved useless to pull out the tubes, and she was a reasonable woman, so she checked herself when she startled out of a nap, quelling the impulse to rip them from her. She'd been too sick to fool with the ventilator tube—a blessing, she admitted, now that it was out. They'd been as gentle as possible, and still the blunt force of its insertion left her throat raw and scraped.

She was glad she hadn't bothered it, she said. She was comforted by my reminder that what she wanted most she could have if she cooperated; she could go home. With a lot of fussing, granted, neighbors milling through her house, their casseroles clotting up the sink. What she wanted at least as urgently, I knew, was a cigarette, which she was never supposed to have again and which nobody was liable to get for her. "You know I'm feeling better if I feel good enough to smoke," she joked. "When I feel good enough to eat again I'm going to get fat."

My father never gave her grief over the smoking, though she knew he didn't care for it. Tobacco had been their livelihood, and only a hypocrite could decry the thing he made his money from. She didn't think he had been a hypocrite about that. And he had taken a dip of snuff on occasion, a fouler habit, in her estimation, though not one to shorten the breath. She pondered switching over, she said to tease the frowning doctor. She could twirl the little twig along her gums to ease her cravings, keep a can handy for the brown spit. It was only nasty if you meant to kiss, and who would she be kissing now? It tickled her to consider the widowers her age from church, toothless and haggard. They needed nursemaids, she said, not sweethearts.

People from the church showed up regularly to pay their respects and were doled out to her carefully, ushered into the sickroom singly and in pairs for brief visitations. "It's good of you," she said again and again, humbled; there were so many she hadn't kept up with, and then all the new members, young people she barely knew, yet they came, bringing slim vases of carnations and cards that entire Sunday school classes had signed. They clasped her hands and offered prayers. Their visits cheered her some, but she watched always and only for Zephra, her oldest friend, who did not come or call. She said she didn't expect William, doubted she'd ever lay eyes on him again, and Dahlia, well, she'd done the best she could, and Mama was content for her to do her visiting by phone, for the present.

"She's not taken ill, is she?" Mama asked the minister, who assured her Zephra was doing fine.

"She sends her best," he improvised, but my mother knew better than that. Zephra's best was bedside.

I'd moved back into our house as soon as the electricity was running again, but I still stopped by Zephra's house fairly often. I thought she seemed lonely, and I knew I was. She'd deflected my offers to bring her to the hospital, saying, "I just can't see her like that," but I thought she would surely come now that Mama had improved so and was asking for her.

"We can call her," I offered, but Mama demurred.

"She don't answer that phone, and can't half hear if she does. I'm not up to a shouting match."

"Well, I can let it ring, and I can holler," I said, picking up the phone.

"Leave it!" she spat. I dropped the phone back into its cradle.

The dayshift nurse hovered in the doorway. Those who dealt with Mama most often had learned it was best to take me aside first and explain what needed doing so she could hear it from me.

"Mama, they've got to catheterize you again, " I reported. "You remember what that is?"

"Another blame tube," she complained. She wouldn't say damn. "Quit giving me so much broth and Kool-Aid, I won't need it. And anyway, I can use the pan."

"Not as much as you need to. Sheets are damp," the nurse explained gently. "By the time you call for me and I get it under you, it's too late. But you've got to keep your bladder emptied. If you try to hold it, you'll end up with an infection." She peeled back the layers of blanket, eased my mother's frame aside, worked the sheets out from under her, and deftly slid in fresh ones, an economy of sure motions. I watched, hoping for some measure of this grace when it came my turn to look after her.

Oxygen thinned the wheezing. One arm tube brought glucose, another softened pain, lulled the racking in her chest, and made her loose and light of bone. And now another tube to drain her bladder. She winced at the intimate sting, but in an instant the catheter was inserted, the bag discreetly hung, and her bedclothes snugged around her again.

"You're doing so remarkably well, considering all that's happened," the nurse consoled. "Don't let this get you down. This is nothing." Mama thanked her; she'd been unfailingly polite to all the nurses, even when she was pulling out tubes the moment they left the room.

"You don't have to report back to me all the time," Zephra asserted bitterly when I told her Mama was improving and would soon be coming home. "We're not even kin." I pressed her on this point, and she said to ask my mother—her cousin, I'd thought. I used to think they were sisters. You assume a certain kinship, and time had clarified that only somewhat.

"I'd have thought you'd be glad to hear it," I said to her, a little sullen.

"Of course I'm glad," she said, "but she won't get but so much better, you know."

I knew. Keeping Mama alive was now a complicated business, requiring backup oxygen and bronchodilators, steroids and antibiotics, a restricted-salt diet—all to manage what couldn't be cured. No cure, and Zephra wouldn't see her. She was mad, I realized, and I assumed it was about Mama's smoking. Getting sick was something she'd done to herself, was one way of looking at it, when you'd rather be angry than sorrowful. I'd been mad with Mama, too, but had spent it fussing with the insurance people and the contractor, scrubbing yellowed baseboards and linoleum, priming the new drywall, slicking everything with paint, smashing ashtrays, and setting up the crank-style bed to keep her upright and breathing. After that the house reeked of bleach, not smoke, and I worried a little that it wouldn't seem like home to her—but I didn't feel angry anymore. Not at anyone.

"She's had to quit now," I told Zephra, hoping to placate her into a visit.

"If she was able, she'd steal a puff next chance she got. Blow up the house with that oxygen after all the work you did."

"She won't be able to. She knows she can't smoke anymore. There's no one who would give them to her, anyway."

"A fine way to give it up," Zephra mused. "Just before you're dead of it."

Yet somehow it was all right for Zephra to grow a few acres of tobacco for others to wheeze on, though I resisted saying so. I also knew Zephra still took a secret dip of snuff, having glimpsed the coffee can lined with foul brown sludge tucked away in her pantry. I saved the knowledge to prod her with later, in case Mama got worse and Zephra wouldn't budge. I knew she'd set her mind hard enough to wait until the brink, but they'd been as close as sisters, closer.

But not sisters—not even cousins. What, then?

"Ask your mama" was all Zephra would say about that.

As homecoming day approached, the respiratory therapist worked to get us acquainted with the home routine. She reviewed with

Mama the technique of pursed-lip breathing to force out more air than she took in. It made her face squinched and disapproving—not a significant change of affect from when Mama faced medical advice.

The therapist showed us the proper settings on the demo concentrator, a bedside device that would pluck extra oxygen from the air and funnel it up Mama's nose through the cannula—or "that hateful thing," as she referred to it. She complained about her raw nose, and the therapist described the nasty tracheal catheter that some patients had to rely on instead and suggested she dab petroleum jelly on her nostrils. "Be glad your daughter doesn't have to pull a tube out of your throat and suction out the clogs," she offered by way of comfort.

There would be a portable tank for use in the car that could also be wheeled around outdoors when Mama felt more mobile, but for indoors there'd be a generous length of tubing for the concentrator. The distance was short enough that my mother probably wouldn't have to rely on a potty chair but could reach the bathroom—a good thing, since I could see by Mama's expression that she had no intention of using a potty chair.

I was advised to administer a series of hard thumps between her shoulder blades as needed to "loosen secretions."

"Honor thy mother," Mama warned, so we didn't practice just then.

After she had a little nap and got some soup down and kept it down, and after the church ladies had come and gone, I sat by her bed and stroked cream into her papery skin, careful not to rub up a bruise. My mother, never delicate, now fragile as petals, bone-brittle, her fine wheeze like breathing through wet felt. If her lungs grew too sodden, pneumonia would set in, and she'd be back in the hospital quick as a flash. One errant germ could wipe her out, one tiny cloud of dust. I shook myself clear of such thoughts.

"Zephra's still getting over her bug," I lied, though Mama had quit asking for her. "She sent over some peanut butter candy, though. Do you think you'd eat a little?"

Mama shot me a look, piercing and skeptical, though I'd thought it entirely plausible that Zephra would make up a batch of something that didn't need cooking.

"Can't stand the sweet right now" was all she said.

"Mama," I broached gently as possible, "Zephra says we're not really kin. She's not your cousin?"

She closed her eyes. "I'll tell you in a little while." I waited, and when her exhalations came less ragged, signaling sleep, I tried to slip my hand out from under hers, but she clasped it back with some of her old strength and began: "The grippe killed her people. That poor girl was switched here and yonder and everywhere before she came to help me tend my baby."

In epidemic times, she told me, people kept an eye out for their neighbors' chimney smoke. Its absence meant those inside were stricken or worse, and the ones not swooning with heat or crippled by diarrhea would go over to check. No smoke at the Overby house. Zephra was found still fastened to her dead mother; the fevered milk hadn't gotten her.

The young and robust succumbed to this flu; it was somehow better at killing them than old people or infants. Their skin turned mahogany in spreading patches, and blackened feet signaled the end, when they drowned in their lungs' dense fluid.

Zephra's father had staggered into the woods, ill with grief, not flu, and drank turpentine when he found the still abandoned dry. Half-blind when they found him, he complained his joints were freezing up, but he asked for Zephra and didn't drop her, though he twitched and jerked and moaned. It was told she went to sleep in those spasming arms. To a baby gone long unrocked, it might have soothed. Her father quieted soon after and did not come to.

Neighbors took her in and raised her, an act of Christian charity that at the same time afforded them an extra field hand. Mama said, "She liked to never learned reading, they worked her so." The last family Zephra stayed with before she went to Mama had sons, and when she "came into her womanly time," as Mama put it, "they weren't really her brothers, you see. She had to keep smart."

"Keep smart," echoed my sister, Dahlia, chuckling, when I relayed what I'd learned. "That was the total extent of my sex education." She was calling regularly from her home in Cobb, Virginia, to check on Mama, but was clearly in no hurry to come again herself. She'd lived in Cobb for as long as I could remember, sharing a little apartment with another widowed cafeteria worker. I'd never been to Cobb. Never been invited.

"Had you known any of that?" I asked her. "Had you known Zephra was a hired girl or nanny or something?"

"She was just always there," my sister said. "I didn't think to ask *what* she was until I started catching the whispers."

"Whispers?"

She snorted disdainfully. "Some people called Daddy 'The Mormon,' with his two wives."

Not *my* daddy, I thought, and: You hateful bitch. Almost immediately, though, her suggestion lost its juice; I could understand how such things hid in plain sight, so old now nobody thought to point to it much anymore. Nothing deliberately secret, just better forgotten, an anachronism, like the potbellied stove that for years huddled uselessly in a corner of the kitchen, our backs to it as we cooked and ate. Until it was finally being dismantled and hauled off to make room for a china hutch, I barely considered it. I was ten years old at the time, and nobody had thought to say to me, "This is how we used to live." But I don't know whether that was because they no longer cared to remember or simply that I'd shown no curiosity. Before they removed that stove, I'd idly pulled the curved doors and pried at the heavy lids, peering into the sooty maw of it, but it contained nothing of value that I could see.

zephra overby

I told you to take that up with Mabry. I'm not going into all that.

Zephra carefully kept her back to me as she dusted her pots of plastic violets placed all along the kitchen sill, a task she called her gardening.

"Mama drifts in and out sometimes," I complained. "She did tell me you were an orphan and that you lived all over till you came to help with Dahlia."

Well, there you have it. I can't do nothing for her now.

"Was my daddy a Mormon?" I asked pointedly.

Not hardly. And you can just say what you mean instead of going all around it.

We went all around it anyway. I couldn't ask her straight out what she was to my father, and what she offered me instead was the story of my mother:

Mabry won't but sixteen, younger than me. Didn't know a thing. She was already carrying, and folks didn't talk since she'd married quick, but the doctor counted weeks and was unkind to her for it.

Zephra assisted with the birth, offering small comforts, but the doctor waved her away. The chloroform descended, a cloying rag to smother Mabry only briefly. The infant clambered down her spine, rung by rung, and frothed her bowels. She thought she would soil herself, but only blood came. Her muscles jellied by the vapor, she couldn't push. He seemed to put the whole of his arm up her, as if she were calving. It must have shamed her to be so open and for him to reach into her and pull with the full force of his disapproval, as if he would tear out the sin.

Birthing split her wide, cracked her open, and with the baby sorrow came gushing forth. She lay there stricken, and for a time they let her, latching the baby to her as it needed, letting it drain what pooled in her breasts like infection. When Mabry should have risen and gone back to the work of the home and the fields but could not, Zephra stayed on.

I think she lost too much blood, was part of her ailment. I looked after her and the baby, and after a while I was like family. She needed a rest after the birth, anyway, and I was glad to leave my situation.

Won't none of the men in that other house but was sorry. They acted like they never seen a girl, always putting the feel to me, trying to spy me at the bath. And the mama so crazy and jealous, when she wasn't praying over me she was slapping my face or trying to snatch the hair out of my head. They worked me like a mule on top of that. Fine by me. I learned to drive a row straight as a man's, and if my dress was streaked with guano, it helped stave off those hands. I'd as soon been in the fields every minute than cornered in that house. Mabry was a balm compared to all that, pitiful as she was in her birthing time. When Linwood asked me to sit with her until the doctor was fetched, I left nothing behind that I would have to go back for.

The people that had took me in had no use or money for doctors; my woman, she knew what to do. Bid me truck off the other children and come back quick, keep a pad under her, let her pull on me. Catch the baby, blood brown and slick. Dip my finger in his tiny mouth to clear it, and he lets out a cry. Pass a knife through flame. When the cord quits pumping, tie it off and cut it clean. Ball thread will do. Wrap the afterbirth in paper for the husband to bury. She had a belief about that. He had to bury it, no one else. What the doctor could do was to put silver drops in the baby's eyes, but my woman didn't want that. She wiped the eyes with her first milk.

Queer ways, but nothing like the doctor's with his twilight sleep. I don't question that the birthing hurts and when you're put out you can forget that, but then the mama can't push. I had Mabry up and walking before the doctor came. She was still early in her pains. I told her it was all old hat to me and not to fret. She asked me how long, and I said let's walk to pass the time and help the baby drop down to where it would come. When you can't walk anymore, I told her, we'll know it's getting time. She put her arm about my waist and we strolled up and down the rows of fodder corn like we was shopping a dress.

Mabry chattered away, trying to keep ahead of the pains. She said, you sure are a nice girl, do you go to school how old are you who's your fellow? I told her I had no need of a fellow, though I had a young man to take me walking once before the man who made to be my daddy put him off with his wild talk. He cast aspersions so wouldn't nobody have me. And Mabry said that was a shame and what did I reckon moved people to act so? Anyone with a brain in his head could see I was a fine person to come and help her. She was grateful not to be let alone, and she clung to me.

The baby might be coming now, she said, on account of her just having had a shock. It was the news of her mother dead from birthing. And the child, too. Did I think that the shock would hurt *her* baby? I knew what manner of vile things my woman could tell her: that grief will mark your child; he will lack a smile, maybe even lack a mouth, or his eyes will forever leak tears. But I said no, no; she was a strong girl, and her child would be stout.

Linwood came back with the doctor, who put Mabry in the bed at once and told me not to stay underfoot; go and fix them something to eat. I went to the kitchen with some ill feeling toward that man and stirred up what leavings I found in a pan to make cush. Easiest thing to make, and so good. Tear up some old cornbread and biscuit, add a little grease or milk, break an egg in it, bake it up brown. I thought better of fixing it for the men and put the pan aside. More fitting for the mama when she's hungry again, I thought. Something soft and easy on the stomach. I made a new batch of biscuits for the men, and fried and sugared some green apples. That was all else I could find to fix. I saved back some of the apples for Mabry, too.

Doctor had her in that twilight sleep when I got back to the bedroom, but she was pitching in and out. Eyes never quite closed as in true rest. Confused and hurting when she came to. Calling for her mama. I let her hold on to me. He would put her back under it seemed like to make her be quiet, but if she couldn't yell she couldn't push. He had something for that, too: bent tongs to clamp around the baby's head and pull her on out. Made me feel sick for him to do that, and I had caught my woman's baby as it slid out from her in a bloody gush.

Mabry's child had a blue cast, but Doctor shook her and rubbed her with a towel until she turned pink and wailed. Poor little mashed head, dents along her temples where the tongs had squeezed. There is a method for rounding out the head, but I was afraid of any more pressing on that soft skull. In a few days, though, the red marks faded, and she looked all right. That was Dahlia. She was an easy baby, didn't fuss more than was reasonable. We all doted on her, calling her Dolly or Doll; could be why she turned out so willful.

The custom for new mamas was nine days' confinement, though few could keep still that long with so much to do, and it was a prideful thing to say you were up and keeping house in less. "I don't want to be no trouble," Mabry said when her nine had come and gone, "but I can't get out of the bed just now. Every time I try, I lose all ambition."

"Quit trying for now," I told her. "You're still diapered like a baby your own self." I'd wrapped her up good and made her keep still. It wasn't a bit of trouble to look after her so far as I was concerned. There was a place for me, my very own, there in that house. It was just a curtained-off corner at first, a pallet on the floor and a nail to hang my dress on, but it was clean and mine, and my sleep was not fretful. Staying there was pure ease as I saw it. Nothing but to boil diapers and cook and sweep, and still some hours free to get out in the yard and keep up the garden they'd just had time to start, and later I'd join Linwood in the field. I'd be going with that hoe, just chopping, and the vegetable patch would get too small to hold me, so I'd set out to work those long rows beside him.

If the baby fussed while Mabry needed sleep I walked her out-of-doors. Her squirming weight was light and pleasing, but my arms wanted work. I showed Linwood how to hold her right, not let that sweet little head go flopping, and pointed them to the shade. It was in my mind how my daddy had wanted to hold me, and I thought that when the Gosses didn't need me anymore, it would be a joy to have this child know them both so good. Though I didn't much like to think of when they wouldn't need me anymore.

When the nine days and nine more had passed, my woman sent one of her sorry sons to fetch me back. I ran into the house and latched the door. My heart was knocking on my ribs. The boy that come for me was one I had to outrun; I knew he would have me on the ground before we ever got back, and his father would soon have his turn. That was horrors enough, but it seemed to me all the worse after living in kindness. "I'll not go back with him," I said to Mabry. "I'll find some other work just as soon as I can if you'll put me up a little longer."

She didn't press me for why. She wrapped a shawl around her nightdress and stepped onto the porch. "Tell your mama I'm poorly yet," I heard her shout. He gaped at her, wordless, for her hair was loose and wild, her nightdress just skimmed her knees, and she was barelegged and barefoot.

She came back inside, shut the door tight, and latched it again. She took hold of my hand. "He'll have a lonely ride back, poor thing," she said softly, "and on an ugly mule to boot."

"It's the mule I pity," I answered, and we laughed as if all the troubles of the world had passed us over. Even so, we watched from the window until he was gone from our sight, and I kept myself busy indoors the rest of the afternoon.

"You know we're glad to have you stay on," Linwood told me that evening; I knew Mabry had taken up the matter with him. "It's just that we can't offer you more than room and board." I said it suited me to stay as long as I was of use. I was not but seventeen.

At feeding time I'd get the baby settled and try to work the snarls out of Mabry's hair, so fragile and fine. I'd seen that before; all my woman's strength was sapped by birthing and nursing so that the matted strands of her hair would stretch and snap and fill the comb. And Mabry was so tender-headed she'd cry and wake the baby or put her off the breast, so I set aside the comb and soothed her scalp with my fingers. Her milk, I feared, would be thin until her blood had time to build up again, so I spoke frankly with her man.

"Mr. Goss," I said, "we can get by with just a little more meat, but there has got to be a cow." Makes me laugh now to think how I called him Mr. And he got the milk and the meat both, though it stretched him to do it. One thing he couldn't stand to do was buy "on time" at twenty-five cents or more to the dollar, but the preacher loaned him enough for a heifer and some extra, and he wouldn't take interest. Linwood hired himself out all day to meet the debt and raced home to help me in the fields before dark. I was proud that he could leave it to me.

Mabry healed up and grew stronger, but she'd had to keep to the indoors a long time and could hardly bear the sun to beat down upon her. "Linwood'll just work himself to death," she would say and try to pull herself out from under. She would start tearing up at the smallest thing. She'd spill a jar of buttons and weep and rail, entirely persecuted.

Mostly she held for me a sister feeling, but the part of her that wasn't well was deviling her, and caused her to suspicion me. When Linwood had to stay out all night by the curing barns, she took a notion and forbid me to go to him, not even to bring his supper. And though she was nursing still, she fixed up a sugar tit and made to leave me with the baby all night and stay with him herself. Then she must have got scared the baby would favor me too much, because she ran home within the hour and snatched her back quick.

I thought then my time was up, and I gathered my things, but Mabry cried and begged my pardon. I saw she couldn't help the way her thoughts flew around, and I relented. "Your blood's still low," I told her. "It'll take time to get back right again. But look at all you got: your good man, this pretty baby." I promised she'd have no cause to doubt me, and though my time with those other folks had left me little honor to swear by, none could fault my loyalty.

Well, perhaps my woman could. I'd left her to get on the best she could in that house of sorry men.

It was some happy times, some less so—but all better than what I'd come from. Linwood was the only proof I'd seen of good men walking this earth. He was not a demonstrating man, but was thoughtful of his words and actions, and I respected him. He asked me straight out one day was I a saved Christian, and though I dreaded losing my place or getting the hard sell, I admitted I was not.

He said that was my own business, but he'd be praying on it. I told him I had no objection to that, so long as no like action was required of me. I'd had to shut myself of God to bear living in that other house. The man who'd made to be my daddy had always been flinging Jesus' name around, even as he was pulling at me. My woman had put me in with the devil's set for inviting such wickedness, when all I'd done to invite it was to be alive. I'd long ago decided the only grace coming to me was what little I could grab for myself.

I carried a satisfaction in pulling myself up every morning and working flat out until my night's rest was full-earned, not troubled by dreams. And when I considered it, I could see plain that even the longest days were made up of small graces. There was the cool dark of early rising, none but me stirring before the sun burned through; how sweet the quiet. There were my hands working dough, the smell of rising biscuit, salt meat frying. There was driving the plow blade through roots and stones until the furrows ran true; me and the mule's understanding about that. I didn't fool myself that I was pretty, but it suited me to be stout. The cords in my arms were near like a man's strength; the hard soles of my feet naught could pierce. The sun turned my skin to clay but did not stagger me.

I looked for Linwood to say my pleasures showed pride, not grace, and pride goeth before the fall, some such piety. But he studied on my words, took care with them before he made to reply.

He finally allowed that he counted some of that as his grace, too, and he was a godly man. So it must be I was a godly woman. A godly woman. I felt the key turning in my gullet, new air rushing in. He said, "Your work is your prayer. When it comes time to reap, look you on all that green. The Maker has heard you, and there's your answer." That air was swooning as pure oxygen, and I fought to keep my head.

That was all well and good, I said, but what about when His answer was blight, not green? Or a flattening hail? Or a drop in the market so the yield was worthless and put you in debt and left your children hungry? We had much to argue about before I would give over to it. And I do believe the more contrary I was the more Linwood enjoyed it. Those talks bent our days into a shape other than work and worry.

The worry was mostly over Mabry, who in the baby's first months was having some good days and more bad. Even a good day became something to dread, because she could whip herself up into a feverish state. Might wake up singing, laughing, loving on the baby, wanting to do up my hair, make a pie, paper the kitchen, sweep out the yard, just tearing from one thing to the next. Leaving it all half done, but you better not try to straighten up behind her or caution her to go easier, because she was sure to flip the other way. Best you could hope for then was she would wear out quickly and take to the bed. Before she did there'd be a fuss and ugly words said.

When she got too wound up Dolly would startle and cry. And if Mabry couldn't hush the crying, her nerves got more jangled. More than once she thrust the poor child in my arms and screamed at me why not just go ahead and take her, take all that was hers, since that was what I wanted and why I'd made it so the child favored me over her.

When Linwood tried to soften her, Mabry turned on him, too: "Oh yes, take up for your sweetheart. You think I can't see how you two carry on?"

Her accusing always stung. It was false, but there was cunning in the choice. She'd read my hidden heart and shone on it the ugliest light. For I did love him.

But she was sister to me. I thought only to serve them both.

"When you're ready to speak reason, we'll all pray together," Linwood admonished her, all dignity, and made to step out, but Mabry laughed at him.

"If you pray with Zephra like you did me," she taunted, "you'll soon have her belly big!"

And that might be a day that had started out good. On a day bad from the word go—well, she wasn't fit for this world, and I thought she might fold into nothing if she could just ball herself up tiny enough. I almost favored her ugly talk over the quiet of her bad days, though when she lay still I could at least tend to things properly. If more than a day passed in this manner, I'd coax her limbs flat, peel off her damp gown and wipe her down with a soapy cloth, change the bedding right out from under her, wriggle her into a fresh dress, spoon broth between those slack lips, bring the baby to suckle.

To stir up the quiet I crooned wishes and nonsense to her. "When you're better," I tempted, "we'll go on a picnic and bring only jelly cake. I'll learn you to swim and you can learn me to read better. Cool water will hush the baby's fussing all the summer long; it's only heat fuss, for she's a good baby, fat and well loved. I'll learn her to swim, too, so you'll not fear of her drowning. When her hair comes in fuller, I'll rag-roll it, and we'll sew her the fanciest dresses and take her into town to show her off. When she's walking and talking good, we'll all go to singing school, and if your tone-deaf husband don't flunk out, we'll make a traveling quartet and live in hotels and sing for our supper, and for our breakfast and dinner, too. . . ." She'd sigh and blink in what I fancied was agreement to each of these fool ventures, fat tears rolling like pearls I would catch in the washrag.

It's not for me to say whether Linwood did wrong by bringing in folks to pray and lay hands on her. He'd not sought my counsel in the matter. I was for patience. If you prod the body's wounds, that keeps them raw. Even too much loving care will rankle them. It was the same with her spirit, hurt from the double blow of her mama's death right up next to her own hard birthing. But the scripture calls madness a demon, and the preacher was for casting it out of her with prayers unrelenting. And for all Linwood's kindness and caution, he was a practical man in need of a sound wife, and he was weak to the hope of restoring her in one fell swoop.

That preacher's throng had methods worse than Doctor's.

They penned her in, confounded her with hollering and hymns, and shook her till her wits skittered around like dry seeds in a gourd. I wouldn't add my prayers to the mix, yet and still it was not my place to step in. Mabry's screaming shut the wind out of my throat; all I could do was scoop up the baby and outrun the sound of it. I never ran so fast or so far, and by then I'd had much to escape.

To this day, I don't know whose rows we crouched in until dark. It was sweet corn, not fodder, and when Dolly began her hungry fuss I stripped an ear, chewed the kernels to a milky mash, and pushed some into her mouth. She worked her pink gums and swallowed. That's how I learned she could go off the titty if she had to, and I don't know, that calmed me some.

Mabry was up out of the bed next morning, wearing a fresh dress, her bird's-nest hair smoothed down. She quietly set to straightening up the house—none of the old tearing around. She'd start one thing and finish it, right slow and deliberate, and then she'd do another. Cooked us a good dinner that very noon. I fed the baby a soft dumpling while Mabry looked on. She said nothing, but she put her on cow's milk soon after.

Since Mabry was going about a wife's business again, Linwood loosed his watch over her. He praised God for the lightning cure, but to me she seemed a beaten thing intending to duck further blows. I was already missing her before she up and run, the fight in her so broken I don't know what strength carried her off. Or else it was hid from me. Where did she find the nerve or money to board a bus and quit the county she was born in, had never once stepped out of? Somehow she got hold of the nerve and money both, and there was no word from her for near two months.

It wasn't fitting for me to stay on with her away, but Linwood's need of me held more weight. I did hope his broadcast goodness would cool any hateful talk. And yet and still, if my ruin was final, I figured I couldn't be *more* ruined, so I meant to stay and keep the baby right on until—what, I didn't know. I wasn't looking ahead. I was playing house. Pretending it was my house, my little girl. My good man.

How Mabry got by during that time she wouldn't ever say. Whatever she did, it shook off that crippling sadness. All I am certain is she was in Richmond, for the letter she finally sent held that postmark and enough else so that Linwood could find her and fetch her back.

Two things about Mabry when she came home. One, her looks had turned stylish. She was wearing lipstick and a new dress, and her hair was cut to where it barely reached her shoulders and marcelled in shiny-dark waves that were crisp to the touch. There were fancy names for her new coloring: Ashes of Roses for the gray-pink dress; Chestnut Number Twelve for the hair; Tangee for the mouth. Up alongside her I knew I was a dull thing, coarse and workaday, already running to fat; still, the very sight of her was cheering.

The other thing new about her was, she was smoking cigarettes, one right behind another, a habit I knew Linwood didn't favor, but by the time they were back home they must of already settled it, for not a word was spoken. She was like a rich relation come from the city to visit, with that dress and hair, tapping ash into a jar lid. It seemed to steady her, and I did like the new smell she gave off, soot and sweet and burning brush. It gave her natural cause not to try picking up the baby right away—and, too, it was some time before Dolly would come to her on her own. They were shy of one another, though neither could tear her gaze away.

We were all shy of one another, scared of what had happened and what would yet come. The fact was that Linwood and Mabry were reconciled, and yet neither was for putting me out, nor was I for going. Once we knew that to be so, it seemed whatever followed we would have to make up from scratch.

avie goss

Mama cried when she saw her near-empty closet. I'd had to throw out most of her clothes—they'd sopped up too much smoke to come clean—but she admired the linens I'd bought, and she didn't ask after her old bed.

When she was settled, I rolled the TV cart into her bedroom so we could watch together. The tape I'd watched a snippet of was still in the recorder.

"What's this old movie?" I asked.

She had the bed cranked nearly in half and was sitting straight up, still wearing her turquoise nylon windsuit, her homecoming outfit, though she'd unzipped the jacket and thrust her stockinged feet into scuffs. She hadn't wanted to put on her nightgown yet, reasoning there might yet be visitors. A knitted afghan was draped

artfully across her lap, and she batted my hands away when I tried
to spread it over her for warmth.

She looked at the screen a minute, then held out her hand
for the remote. "A lady from the Chamber of Commerce gave me
a copy," she explained. "It's Regina. They found a bunch of old
reels and made a tape." She goosed the Fast Forward button.
Schoolchildren stampeded, townspeople fled. She slowed it back
to normal: in front of an old barn of sparsely chinked slats stood
children and adults, black and white, passing broad sheets of tobacco leaves from hand to hand, sorting careful piles, making swift
strokes to gather them and tie them onto racks. "That was up the
road a ways," she said. "That was the Pitchers's barn. Right there's
your daddy." She gestured with the remote and thumbed the Pause
button, but the man she indicated was hunched purposefully over
a stack of the wrinkled leaves, his face hidden shyly beneath the
brim of his hat. "He didn't want any part of that moviemaking,"
she said.

She advanced the tape again. A mule was dragging a narrow
cart lined with canvas, filled with tobacco leaves, a small girl sitting atop the pile. She was clapping her hands, chortling soundlessly. "You know that one, don't you?" Mama said, smiling. I
studied the girl's smudged cheeks and dirty clumps of hair, her
scrawny arms thrust out of a sleeveless jumper. Her mouth gaped
open in a shout, the mule oblivious, lugging her patiently. Her
hands made fierce little fists, and I knew her.

"Dahlia!" I cried. My sister, long before there was ever me. A
scrawnier, scrappier girl than I'd ever been. "Are you on this, too?"
I asked Mama, excited. She shook her head, no. "Is Zephra?"

She frowned. Zephra had still not come by or called, and I was
sorry to have reminded her. "I thought I spied her in one of the
downtown scenes, but I'm not sure it's her. She was skinnier

then." She sped up the tape. The schoolchildren marching again, the checkers game, men in softball uniforms lingering at a storefront. Inside, tall barrels of corn, tightly packed bales of cotton, piled sacks of buttermilk mash, crates alive with baby chicks. A window lettered DRY GOODS and READY-TO-WEAR, men through the glass thumbing shirts stiff on cardboard frames. A woman seated at a counter sipping demurely at her Coke. "There." She slowed it. The woman wore a filmy dress with a lace collar. Her hair was parted on the side and hunched up high and full of waves, her mouth black with lipstick. She gave the camera a brief sidelong glance and those dark lips broke apart in a grin, then she swiveled abruptly on her stool to face the other way.

"*That's* Zephra?" She'd always been an old woman to me, stout and plain. I couldn't reconcile Zephra's sunlined face with the young, pretty one on the screen—except for the smile, its abrupt ease.

"Could be," Mama said. "I had a dress looked like that. She might have worn it to town."

"Has she seen this? She could recognize herself, I imagine."

"I don't know if she'd recognize herself like that," my mother said tightly. "You'd think she was going to meet a lover, looking like that."

"Maybe she was," I ventured, and Mama puffed her lips dismissively.

I was interested. "I'll ask her," I offered. "Can I show her the tape?"

"Let her come here if she wants to watch it," she snapped. "See if that will bring on a visit." She stabbed the remote with her thumb, and the picture lurched and went black.

When Mama napped I prepared her lunch: Chicken salad sandwich, tomato soup, and chilled grape juice—no ice, a bendy straw. She woke and yanked out the hated cannula, almost by reflex. I gave the bed a fierce crank to set her fully upright. I fit the tray of food neatly over her lap, tucked a clean napkin in her collar. Then, "Tell me about Richmond," I demanded, no preamble. I hoped to ambush her into full disclosure.

She didn't blink. "Nothing *to* tell. It's a nice enough city, I suppose. I haven't been there in years."

"You left Daddy," I said. "You went to Richmond. Why did you go there? What did you do? How come I don't know about any of this?"

"How come you don't know?" she echoed. "Seems to me you know plenty."

"I want to know your side."

She set her quarter of sandwich, barely nibbled, gently back onto the plate. "My *side* is I went to Richmond a long time ago. It was a lovely city, but I never did go back. You don't need to hear it from me." Her breath accordioned then, a tuneful wheeze. "She has no right—" Those wet-pocketed lungs turned to creaky bellows. She pursed her bluish lips and whistled stale air. Her face was blanched gray-white. "Not going to go *through* all that."

She gripped the tray as if bracing herself and tilted the soup onto her stomach, gasping as it splashed her, though it was only lukewarm and didn't scald. She continued to gasp, sharp little bursts.

I rummaged frantically in her nightstand for the inhaler and helped her fit it to her lips. Her hands fluttered weakly at first, but then she grasped it and managed a huff while I assembled the nebulizer.

The vapor reeked of camphor shot through with something green. Chlorophyll, I thought; cut grass. It eluded me. Whatever it was loosened her constricted airways as she sucked it in. I heard her breath soften and slow and watched the blood warm her face until it was flesh again.

Once the spell had safely passed, my pulse thrummed fright and contrition. It was wrong of me, unforgivable really, to cause her to suffer one of these episodes. To compound my crime, she'd woken up from her nap almost hungry, and now she felt too sick to eat. She needed every calorie she could stomach, but even the small cans of supplement that tasted like melted vanilla ice cream repulsed her now. I sponged her clean and helped her into a fresh shirt. The soggy sandwich went into the garbage. She did manage about four ounces of grape juice before lapsing back into sleep.

I burned to know more about her foray to Richmond, but it seemed Zephra had told me all she knew, and to interrogate Mama further just then was to risk another spell. For simplicity's sake I told people she had emphysema, but really it was a grab bag of respiratory ailments that also included bronchitis and asthma, and I saw then how she could deflect me with it.

Mama's breakdown and desertion. My daddy the Mormon, with his two wives. I needed more than these little scraps of story. My parents' lives seemed to me to have played out far in advance of my birth, the exciting parts, anyway, leaving me to grow up with the false impression that they were amiably dull old people for whom I was the liveliest entertainment.

What shoddy entertainment I must have been. I'd caused little trouble, but shown no exceptional talents, and had not even distinguished myself from their other children by leaving Regina; both had already done so long ago. It was only away from home that I'd become even remotely interesting, but I kept those parts concealed from her, carefully editing all accounts of my adult life. I did so intending to protect her but found it hard to accept that she might have similar motivation for her own silence, or merely a right to her own private past.

And wasn't her past her own? Not where it flowed into mine, I decided. Some of what Zephra disclosed about Mama, her moods and fits, were only shocking to the touch; when I grabbed hold and looked, I could recognize them. I'd known her to go on cleaning jags, or be out in the garden before sunup, or bake a cake at midnight. Those were her ups.

And her downs? As a child I must have been shielded from them by the inordinate amounts of time spent with Zephra, countless afternoons after school, and often I spent the night with her, though we lived so close by I could have walked home in minutes. I'd believed my comings and goings were at my whim.

The pretexts and diversions probably originated with Zephra. Once, just before starting the third grade, I stayed with her for a solid two weeks at the end of summer break. Zephra was making my school clothes, all of them, and said she wanted me on hand for fittings. I don't believe I set foot in my parents' house that entire time, yet I never suspected a thing, even when Daddy came to Zephra's to walk me to school on the first day. I may have been given to understand that Mama was ill during this time, but I don't remember much being made over it.

I loved to stay with Zephra. She let me select any brightly colored box from her freezer for our supper, didn't care what I watched on television or for how long, and let me scrabble in the dirt with the rough kids without fretting or interfering. Also, she overlooked mild cursing—"just no GDs"—and proclaimed that our Sundays were for sleeping in, not dressing up for church.

I grew up believing that my parents overprotected me while Zephra granted me freedom; in truth the three must have jointly conspired to ensure I wouldn't see things they thought might hurt or confuse me. I don't think they labored too hard to conceal Daddy's drinking, which had mellowed to an occasional binge. He'd get a little silly, a little weepy, and go to bed. Or else he'd retreat to his woodshop for hours. I was allowed to sit with him, and when he got a little loaded he'd set my mind on fire talking about the universe:

"It just goes on and on. You can't get your mind around the thing. There's no end to it, like God's love. It knows every little bit of you, every hair on your head and every lie you ever told. It swallows up all you did and all you mean to do. Just ponder how small we are and lost inside of it. Ponder that. Where is heaven, do you reckon, in all that space? Is it in the black or in the specks?"

If his drinking garnered comment at all, either or both women would say he was acting a fool, but I don't believe I was ever sent to Zephra's over it. Perhaps the women felt it was instructive for me, a cautionary against overindulgence, or maybe they just didn't find it objectionable enough to shield me from it.

How would they have explained, I wondered, if Mama had again taken flight? Her propensity for rash action must have diminished considerably over the years, tempered by age and leveling medicines and, I think, some measure of contentment. Her highs were surely never again so strenuous, nor her lows so devastating, as when she was young and newly married and a first-time mother who'd just lost her own.

I don't remember missing her when we were apart. But sometimes she would suddenly appear at Zephra's house, dressed up in her navy suit and matching pumps, wearing the choker of fat fake pearls I so coveted, and my heart would leap at the sight of her. She'd ask me sort of shyly was I ready to come home yet, and I always found that I was.

• • •

I wasn't sleeping well, sometimes not at all, and late that night after Mama's spell I languished in half-dreams, sensing low growls and rumbles, the earth's plates shifting, fissures spreading across the ground. Then something punctured the air: a car backfiring, gunshots, a maniacally barking watchdog. I jerked back into consciousness when my name broke through, and the sounds assumed their natural shape: Mama's percussive coughing.

She couldn't dredge anything up, and it was strangling her. I rolled her onto her stomach—she was light as paper—and did as I'd been instructed: chopped the knobby dip between her shoulder blades with the meat of my hand, not expecting I could use the force I did, and after endless blows it shocked and gratified me to feel the choking thing in her shake loose.

Code Red days, when heat-trapped smog from Raleigh traffic rendered the late August air inhospitable for miles, kept Mama indoors and tethered to her oxygen. She complained of feeling imprisoned, and my vigilance wasn't helping any. She'd just gotten the better of a cold that threatened pneumonia—all her colds from now on would carry such deadly potential—and I was anxious about leaving her. For a couple of interminable weeks I had limited my outings to the grocery store and post office. I hovered over her constantly, ready to descend with the inhaler or dial 911 if she so much as cleared her throat.

"You're giving me the claustrophobia," she said, and when she caught me watching her while I thought she slept, she wailed, "Get out of my room!" like a wounded teenager. Worse, I kept the new insulated windows shut tight and the air conditioner running constantly. Stubborn thrift had often kept her from turning on the air conditioner at all. She didn't like the indoor climate, refrigerated, costly: "Still as death in here." She longed for a breeze.

When the heat began slackening, early mornings and late evenings cooling to tolerable, at her urging I finally cracked the windows open, praying whatever pollen or leaf dust or mold spores seeping in through the screen wouldn't rouse new allergies or spells of asthma. She sat on the edge of the mattress, her back to me as she drank in the fresh air.

Bored and restless, frenetically willing to be of service, I asked her for the umpteenth time that day if she needed anything. "To be left alone!" she spat. The view from her window was of her neglected garden, a tangled riot of weeds and bright spikes of perennials, fat, browning blossoms.

I don't know if it was a desire to do something for her or to further rile her that had me out in it the next morning hacking at the vines and brush. About all I'd ever had to do with that garden was to carry out the kitchen scraps for compost. Coffee grounds, eggshells, orange rinds, potato parings, apple skins, and fish spines—all our leavings were heaped on, raked over, and left to cook in the dirt all winter. That was what she'd required and all she'd permitted of me yardwise, except for raking leaves. I couldn't hoe or weed properly, she'd said. I didn't know a weed from a seedling and would chop indiscriminately, wasting her time and money when she preferred to do it herself anyway. No call for me to tear up my hands when hers were already broken in.

Now the black soil was ashen, leached by a season of weeds. I grasped fistfuls of wiregrass and wild onion and probably some cherished stalks of heirloom somethings, and I pulled until my lumbar twinged in warning. I wrenched a few bulbs and roots from the dirt, but mostly just tore the stems. Knowing she watched from the window, I invaded the shed, heretofore forbidden to me for its ancient and sinister concoctions: bonemeal, guano, Paris green. I emerged wielding her prized hoe and began notching the hard ground with it, soon welting my palms on the burnished handle.

The progress was far slower than I'd anticipated, the roots dense and unyielding. I didn't know what to do with what few weeds I did manage to unearth. It seemed like they'd just take root wherever I threw them. I bagged a small pile and retreated indoors, scalded and sore, long before noon. I wasn't used to all the hunching over, and my neck and shoulders seized up and wouldn't loosen; a deep red ache throbbed down in the center of my back. I hadn't set out as early as I should have, and the sun had quickly burned through the mist, then my scalp, then my shirt.

"I don't know as I want you messing in there," Mama scolded when I came in.

But by evening she'd relented some: "You got to see to it early, before the heat of the day. I'll call for you at six."

Before bed: "Mind you don't tear out my peonies with that wild chopping. Those bushes with the glossy leaves. Done bloomed back in June. Grass and vine is all you want to pull, then we'll see what we've got left."

Next morning she suggested plastic baggies to wear over my shoes. "You ought not to muck up your fancy running sneakers," she admonished, and later: "You'll want gloves to save your manicure."

I laughed at that; she must have been thinking of my seventeen-year-old prom queen hands, soft and tipped with pink glaze. Now my cuticles were bloody and flayed, the nails peeled nearly to the quick, but they were wrecked from stress, not gardening. My hoe-blistered palms would soon match those ravaged fingernails, I thought, and that pleased me somehow. I taped over the raw spots and kept hacking.

"Suit yourself. You tear up your hands and then you can't do nothing. There's a hat in the shed; at least you can keep from looking like a wild Indian."

I found a wide-brimmed straw hat mildewed and ragged, a leaking bag of Sevin Dust stored in its cap, and decided lotion and sunglasses would be enough protection. When I staggered in pink again, she met me at the door with aspirins.

"Run some cool water over your head. Only a fool would go without a hat in that sun."

In my suffering, I almost didn't note the extraordinary occurrence of being met at the door by Mama. Though she wasn't confined to her bed, such a distance required her despised and shunned walker—and she'd actually used it, was even now leaning heavily against it as she proffered the aspirins. For smaller trips, to the bathroom, say, she'd been stubbornly traveling hand over hand, clamping the tops of chairs, side tables, and windowsills, guiding herself along the narrow lip of molding down the short hallway until she could grasp the bathroom knob and follow the door's swinging arc, which deposited her onto the toilet. Most of the time. Fortunately the bath mat cushioned her landing when she missed, but I lived in fear of a broken hip. That would be the ruin of us both.

I pretended not to notice this glad new fact: Mama was now moving throughout the house—in medically sanctioned ways! Thrilled as I was, I dared not comment directly on her use of the walker lest it be returned to its former position as nine-hundred-dollar clothing rack. Now if she wanted water while I was outside, she could reach the kitchen sink with the aid of that walker, its rubber-tipped legs checking her slide across the linoleum. Once there, she could pour herself a glass, and even sit at the table to drink it. If I'd been within earshot I'd have fetched it for her so swiftly as to render her painstaking efforts pointless. I'd been helping to keep her in bed that way, I realized. She must have felt ridiculous trying to do for herself when I could manage those little tasks with such ease. But she needed to do for herself.

And I needed her help with the garden. My scalp peeled, and I started wrapping a bandanna around my head and plunking the filthy hat on top of it. It seemed like I was managing to clear no more than a square foot of earth per outing, and I felt miserably hot, itchy, and bored, ready to scrap the whole project.

Too, I was ignorant of growing things. I'd been grandly envisioning the harvest of fat tomatoes, an assortment of frothy blossoms, maybe some fancy blue corn, but when I went to the nursery, I could find only withered shrubbery, packets of expired seed, and a couple of pots of early chrysanthemums in workaday yellow. I was too embarrassed to confirm it with anyone, but I surmised the true growing season was over.

I grew dispirited, even a little pissed off. "Why did you let me do all that worthless hoeing?" I asked Mama. "There's nothing worth growing this time of year, and what's left looks like shit!" She shot me a look. "Like crap," I amended.

"Do you think I would let you tear up my patch for naught? I thought you wanted something to do."

I shook my head. I didn't want makework; I wanted to do something useful, *I wanted to do something I could do.* But I had no skills, no stamina, and not even the commonest sense. I'd never even finished touching up the paint indoors, and now that Mama was back home, I couldn't. The fumes were too risky. And why could I remember nothing useful about this thing my mother loved so much? Had I cared so little?

"It's my fault you're not able," she lamented. "The garden was just for my pleasure by the time you came along, and I never made you work it. But you can cut the grass—any fool with two working lungs can have at that."

"Thanks for the boost," I said.

"No, you see, that's helping me. I have to pay that man twenty dollars! And he doesn't half do it. I asked him to cut it shorter so I wasn't having him to cut it every time I turned around; I don't care that he's sloppy. But he cuts it long and wants his twenty dollars. If your daddy could see what's become of it, I don't know."

"He wanted the yard perfect," I agreed, and could see Daddy with painful clarity in his ballcap and clean, pressed overalls, pushing that red mower he kept waxed to a lacquer gleam, the strips of lawn lined up precisely.

"Linwood got almost peculiar over that grass; got him a stick and poked up anything resembling dandelions, just fussed with it all the time. I put my labor to flowers and vegetables, instead. I just never cared a thing for the grass. For me, anything green will do. I'll strow seeds on the bare spots come fall, and that's the end of it."

I remembered how Daddy would slip over to Zephra's while she was at our house and cut her grass, too. He didn't think she kept hers up as well as she should.

"It was something to do," she mused, "just enough to keep him busy without the doctor getting on him. It hurt him not to work the tobacco anymore if he couldn't put his hands elsewhere. Linwood needed him something to tend."

Our lawn was a glossy jade carpet for as long as he kept it, and he often teased that his extreme ministrations were necessary on my account, for I was a tenderfoot whose soft skin would shred on anything coarse. He called me Tenderfoot with such affection I equated the nickname with Princess.

"But you know he gave out under the sun, and field or yard, it was all the same to me. If he'd been in the field, I wouldn't have seen him go to his knees and press his face to that foolish grass, is all." Her throat made a grating noise. She pursed her lips and sucked in air, pushed it out fiercely. She reached for her walker.

"There's things to plant and grow fall and winter, and then there's making ready for spring," she said stoutly. "I can show you what all to do. There's always something needs doing in a garden."

It was a hot morning, one I'd deemed too stifling for Mama to be outside lording over—I mean supervising—me, so I knew she'd be pissy and I put off going back inside to her. There was only washing up and fixing lunch to do, then the whole of the afternoon would stretch out before me, hours of being cooped up with her, not daring to nap unless I wanted another sleepless night of listening to the low drone of the concentrator. Her whistling exhalations were irregular enough to keep me alert if I didn't fall asleep quickly.

I was resting in the grass under the shade of the pecan tree when a gray sedan came up the drive. An old man's car, I thought, but a young man climbed out. I guessed him to be in his late twenties, though he dressed in an old man's clothes, too, a little shabby, deliberately conservative gray slacks and a short-sleeved white oxford shirt with shiny maroon tie.

When he reached the front steps I called out, not wanting him to knock and disturb Mama, though if he was a salesman she could handle him. She never bought anything from solicitors but would invite them to pray with her, even telemarketers. It was a remarkably effective deterrent.

He came over and I squinted up at him. His straggly, sand-colored hair needed cutting, but I liked his squared-off glasses. They were meant to look plain, a little nerdy even, but they flattered him, giving his face solidity and seriousness. His slacks were pure thrift-store, the fabric pilling and the legs cut too long, hems bunching at the tops of his sneakers. I noted the wallet-sized Bible wedged in his shirt pocket, a green-bound Gideon New Testament, and braced myself for the worst.

"You must be Avie," he said.

"Must I?" I sputtered inanely. Isolation was degrading my social skills. People hadn't been coming by as often as when Mama first got home.

His smile was shy and genuine. "I'm Saul Puckett? Youth pastor over at Witness? I've come for Pastor Joe to look in on your mother. I'm going to be the interim minister while he's on mission, so I'm doing a practice round."

"Still converting the heathens?" I said, more snidely than I'd meant to.

"I think they're digging wells, actually. It's more of a service project."

"I get it. Give them water first, then promise them wine." I didn't know why I was acting this way. I wasn't really looking to spar with God Boy. He looked to be fresh out of the seminary.

He laughed gamely. "Something like that. Is your mother up for some company?"

She'd seen him coming in time to change into her good robe and dab on some peach lipstick. I left them to talk or pray, or whatever interim-pastors-in-training did, while I cleaned myself up. I was a sight: dirt-streaked and braless. Worse, the sweat had rendered my T-shirt translucent. I wondered briefly if he'd gotten a charge and gave myself a punitive scrub with cold water and a washcloth. I couldn't afford to think too far along those lines. I had no capacity for it. Nowhere safe to take it.

I put on a modest bra with nipple-minimizing padding, slipped a prim polo shirt over my head and buttoned the collar up to my throat. I shook the crumbs of dirt out of my hair and pulled it into a tidier ponytail. There: the sexless spinster Goss girl. *Looks like she would of got married by now if anybody would have her.*

He was holding Mama's hand when I rejoined them in the parlor. I could see at once it wasn't creepy, just a natural way of his out of fondness he clearly had for her, and too, I think they'd just prayed together. Except for the medical professionals, and then me by a sort of default, I realized nobody else really touched her. Not with any ease, anyway—swift handclasps from even the minister himself, cheek brushes by her casserole-wielding church ladies. But Saul held fast to her hand as if it were not in him to recoil from her age and illness, and I had a thought I did not like one bit. It made the nastiness rise up in me to rebuke it.

I said, "I'm sorry, am I interrupting something?" My tone was more insinuating than it should have been, and then I was the creepy one. But they both gazed back at me with sweet and deadpan faces, expectant.

I turned back to the kitchen, ashamed, and mixed up a pitcher of lemonade. I iced it and poured it through the strainer into our two surviving crystal goblets. My penance was to deliver them intact despite my clumsy ways, drink my own lemonade from a coffee mug, and stay my errant tongue until I knew how to talk right to company again.

So I sat meekly quiet while they discussed me. Mama told him

I was right smart and had worked in computers up north, and he said programming? Which she didn't know the answer to, so I had to chime in and say no, nothing so complex as that. And he waited for me to elaborate, so I said you know, just keeping up databases and correspondence, office stuff. Glorified typing.

He said he was a Luddite, hopelessly so, but the future would not be denied and a computer had already been donated to the church—how nice it would be for making the Sunday bulletins and so forth. But there was no money in the budget for training, and poor Mrs. Eberly, church secretary for some twenty years, had threatened quitting when he suggested she try it out.

And Mama jumped right in with, oh Avie needs to get out a little, maybe meet some young people like herself, the church has a lot of new members, young couples and such, so many new faces in town, getting to where you didn't know people anymore, an awful lot of Mexicans, though none had so far joined their congregation, perhaps because they were mostly Catholics— hard workers, though, on the whole. I felt myself scowling, and before I could reset my face into something pleasanter she had of- fered Regina Witness Baptist Church my services free of charge. "You know her father was a deacon," she added, as if further en- ticement.

"I understand Mr. Goss was among the original members," he said respectfully.

"I don't know about that," she said sharply. "I don't much as- sociate *that* church with this one."

Saul looked confused.

"She means," I interjected gleefully, "that the founding minis- ter started preaching desegregation, so they forced him out and basically started a new church under Pastor Joe." Pastor Joe had been the minister of Regina Witness for all of my life. He was a kind, well-liked man whose views, if he held any, were kept carefully to himself.

"Don't you put words in my mouth," Mama warned me. "You don't understand how it was." She turned back to Saul, whose mouth was slightly agape. "Anyway, her father was always very active, and he even had some aspiration to preach. He didn't have the calling for it, though. You didn't need the schooling for it then, just the calling. He was meant to serve in other ways."

"There are many ways to serve," he observed neutrally. After securing a reluctant agreement from me to at least stop by and examine the donated computer, he excused himself and said goodbye. Whatever his feelings were about the history of his new home church, he'd already learned Pastor Joe's discretion.

"I like that boy," Mama said after he left. "He has some sense."

As I'd watched him holding my mother's hand, the thought that had come to me unbidden was this: Saul was the type of person who could preside over her death. I feared I was not. I sometimes thought about fleeing the scene, as Dahlia had. The scene of her death. Not her illness or convalescence, polite and inaccurate names for what was going on here. She was my mother, yet sometimes I had to force myself to touch her in her frailty. Her phlegmy rattle could make me sick to my stomach, likewise the sticky-bland foods I had to prepare and the stale odors that rose from her body when I helped her wash. For all my smothering vigilance, I wondered if I'd have to shackle myself to her bedside when her time came or else she'd die alone. And I'd come here for redemption, to do the hard things and come clean. I just didn't have the calling for it.

mabry goss

I met Linwood when I was fifteen and him already a grown man renting his own patch. He didn't shirk from working hard, but on Sundays he laid it all aside. He invited me with my ma'am to church, which pleased her though she declined; we had too many little ones to keep quiet, she claimed, but to me she said it was that we had nothing fit to wear in the Lord's house. Linwood started coming around after Sunday services. He always brought something—half a bushel of sweet potatoes, a jug of milk or cider, sometimes even a chicken already killed and plucked—and my brothers and sisters would crowd around him to rifle through his coat pockets for the candies he hid for them there, Ma'am scolding while he laughed.

She served what he brought, rounding it out with the things

that we had, and we'd have us a good dinner. After, Ma'am would read from the Scriptures and sing, her voice first quavering, then true. *And am I born to die? To lay this body down? And must my trembling spirit fly into a world unknown? A land of deepest shade, unpierced by human thought; the dreary regions of the dead, where all things are forgot. Waked by the trumpet sound, I from my grave shall rise, and see the Judge with glory crowned, and see the flaming skies!* The world lay heavy on my sweet ma'am, but she always looked ahead to the Glory.

My daddy had been pulling up stakes on us every year or two. He'd see something better ahead and get to fussing with the landlord and changing farms, and once he gave up farming to follow the timber till it went bust. We trailed along behind him, my ma'am wearier with each step, babies pulling on her. She gave out, trying to make every place we landed into home. "It's not fit to keep a dog," she would declare at the threshold, then sweep and scrub through rotting floorboards. One time we had a pretty little house, clean and well kept, one room aside for us children to sleep in. Landlord let Ma'am put in a little garden plot and keep some chickens, and we ate so good! But Daddy got on with a bigger farm and that was that. Not many owners would spare even the littlest square of yard for your own doings. Forget having you a few rows of beans or tomatoes. Every inch was tilled for cotton, and later tobacco.

If I studied a map, I'd be sure we hadn't moved forty miles altogether, but so many of the miles was walked, pulling a cart. Ten miles would be too far away to go back and see friends made at the old place, not with all the work there was to do just to keep living. I know my ma'am was lonesome all the time with only us for company.

So many roving children then, changing schools every Christmas, when the crops were in and the tallying done. The schools had to line up their studies for us tenant children. Grammar in the fall, poems and stories in the spring was the rule everywhere, to keep us from repeating some lessons and missing others. I loved to go to school and could catch on right quick to whatever we were learning. I was smart with figures, and when Daddy saw that he put me to tracking our expenses. Every time the landlord or storekeeper made a mark in his book, I'd make a mark in ours. In the end those figures hardly ever matched up, and Daddy would try to judge from the difference just how bad we were being cheated. I never could be sure I was adding up our debts right, because that interest was a murky, shifting thing.

Nor were the deals he struck ever clear; was it thirds or half-shares we were working? Sometimes one and sometimes the other; sometimes we brought a few tools and furnishings to tip the balance in our favor, and sometimes we showed up empty-handed. More than once the landlord had to front us a sack of cornmeal and some salt first thing so we could at least line our stomachs with mush before setting out to the new fields. If the wife had Christian leanings she'd send over a little saltpork, or come herself to greet us, bringing castoff clothing and blankets. Ma'am never refused anything offered us children. When I turned up my nose at something dirty or full of holes, she promised to whip me for acting proud. "If we can't clean or mend it we can use it for rags," she'd say. "It's precious little enough, and we need it." Ma'am never did whip me, but I knew she'd been stretched thin by the time she threatened it, and I humbled myself.

My daddy disappeared into the fields when Linwood came calling, though later he'd eat from the cold plate Ma'am set aside for him. "It hurts your daddy he don't bring the little ones sweets himself," she confided to me. "And we never ate so fine before your beau came along; it shames a man." When she called Lin-

wood my beau it made my face go hot, and when next he came to
call she had to bid me three times, then threaten a whipping before I would meet him at the door. It wasn't from not liking him
I was scared to go.

Linwood brought a bolt of flowered dimity, saying it was
given him to pay a debt; he had no use for it but hoped I might. It
was sheer, but Ma'am cut me a dress overlay from it to pretty
up an old navy-blue frock and gave me the coins she'd saved. I
bought stockings, a hair ribbon, and a pair of hard leather shoes;
then I could go with him to the church. We walked there in silence and sat apart, him up front with the deacons. The prayers
uttered then were mournful, aimed at Him who bled the trees
dry of turpentine, who burnished the land with worthless tobacco as far as the eye could see. All of us were poor. I studied
Linwood's straight back and the loose cut of his jacket, the seams
squaring off just past his shoulders. I watched his wet-combed
hair spring into curl at the nape of his neck while I waited for the
slow hour to pass and our quiet walk to resume.

The preacher's words stirred in me a dread I could not name.
He sometimes read from lost books, not the King James Version
of events. *Before Eve, there was Lilith, but she was made of earth. She
would not be Adam's helpmeet. When he tried to make her his wife, he
pressed her beneath him. She whispered God's secret name and disappeared.* The preacher was a learned man, one that had given a portion of his own land over to the church. It was his timber, planed
by his hands, that made the building we gathered in. Heads
bowed, we let his words pass over us. *Adam was not lonely for God
was everywhere, if a cold comfort. God was creator, not mother. Eve was
plucked from Adam's side, but she had her own ideas. Beyond the Garden
were outcast animals and thorny brush. Adam dreamed of Lilith and
woke to Eve, who clung to him.*

I don't know what Linwood made of these strange stories. "If the Lord would have it in me to speak, I would," I heard him say to Ma'am once, and I wondered whether he meant to cross the preacher. Then I fancied he was wishing for courage to break the silence of our walks. I came to understand that he was waiting for the call to preach himself.

There was a weeknight service as well, and Linwood soon invited me. I left the field early that evening to get ready but was still washing the dirt from my legs when he came for me. It was just us two on the porch, and I didn't know what to do. I kept stomping in the shallow tub, then I upended it over my feet. He offered his handkerchief and knelt as if to dry them himself. It was a jest, but I thought of the woman rubbing Jesus' feet with her own hair, smearing ointment, and my face got so hot I couldn't see. I just shook my head no and hurried into the house to change into my dimity.

Still, it was me, shy and foolish girl, who suggested that we walk that night instead of pray, thinking to avoid the struggle of sitting quiet through a strange, tedious sermon while my limbs twitched and ached from the day's labors. Knowing, too, that he saved a square of foil-wrapped chocolate to offer me after the service, and I craved the melting sweetness. I thought to get at it sooner, greedy girl. I didn't consider what it would mean to have an hour free and unaccounted for with a grown man while the sun dipped down and offered shadowed places.

Linwood begged my pardon, but by then my dress was already crushed around my waist and I was holding him to me. He wept and moaned into my neck while we lay in the sedgegrass that banked my pap's field. "I'm sorry, Mabry," he kept saying, "I'm so sorry." I thought that was sweet, but we couldn't take it back.

"If we are promised," I told him, "it'll be all right," but Linwood didn't say anything to that. It got me a little angry, and I pushed him away. I said, "Let's just go along then."

I smoothed my clothes the best I could, but dimity crumples like paper. I knew I would have to clean and press it in secret, and I was grateful for the dark to hide me from my ma'am's eyes. I couldn't think what my daddy might do. When I rose up to walk it felt like my legs had come loose from the sockets.

We meant to do right after that, but Sunday found us in the same place as before. We started out praying forgiveness and ended with the same sin, and this time I knew for certain it was me started the whole thing, because Daddy was looking to move again and I was looking to stay put. I told Linwood, "Now you and me have got to be promised," and he turned away from me, crying like he'd been caught. But it was me who was caught, because the man can go on as before, not the woman.

avie goss

I was growing dangerously idle. When Mama had first come home from the hospital she was very sick and weak, which kept me plenty occupied. Then she rallied some, and that period held pockets of excitement as she began to walk and do for herself again. I needed to be on hand even more to see that she didn't push herself too far too fast. But as her condition stabilized, it meant that less of my time and attention was pulled into the vortex of her illness. She was still dying, I just didn't have to be there every minute of it.

Still, I put off going to the church. I resented the way I'd been conscripted, I worried that my computer abilities had been exaggerated, and I dreaded the mingling Mama was so keen on me doing with other "young people," a bunch of fresh-faced Baptists I had no use for.

There just wasn't enough to do at home anymore, no matter how indispensable I tried to be. First thing in the morning I was standing by to help Mama with the nebulizer so the medicine didn't pool uselessly in the wrong chamber. She could manage it herself most of the time, but in the groggy morning hours I thought it best to be on hand. For breakfast I'd just float a few cereal flakes in the milk to sweeten it and hope for the best, because the woman couldn't eat much in the morning, and worse, it sometimes came right back up. I kept the kidney pan nearby just in case. She could fix her own bowl of cereal, of course, but I was certain she wouldn't even attempt breakfast if I weren't there to enforce it, and she was still about eight pounds below her normal weight. The weight needed monitoring for other reasons, too; a sudden surge might mean her congestive heart was flooded, but without my standing sentry she couldn't be troubled to step onto the scales at approximately the same time every morning—the only way, we'd been told, to accurately gauge any changes.

Before lunch the yard needed watering, damn the utility bill and the county's conservation measures. "I've had enough of watching things turn brown when the rains don't come," Mama said. "Spray that patch good morning and evening, because if you wet it in the heat of the day you'll kill it quicker than drought." And there were the beds to be weeded and sprinkled with a half-dozen poisons from the shed.

Sample lunch: I'd dig through the snowy freezer, past the change purse stuffed with tens and twenties under the ground chuck (Mama's stash for emergencies), for a pack of chicken thighs. After thawing them in the sink, I'd practice frying them— each successive attempt leaving them less burned on the outside and less bloody on the inside, a measurable progress. The failures could be boiled for soup, which was all she wanted, anyway.

Still there were hours left to murder.

I tried experimenting with slow-cooking foods, grains simmering in pots I had to stand over and stir, a mindless hour of steam. Polenta, risotto—but Mama wouldn't abide such things. "Yellow grits and dirty rice," she called them, "only fouler." This from the woman whose kitchen still smelled faintly of collards cooked long before the house had caught fire, whose stovetop used to feature a coffee can of grease drippings collected from frying bacon and sausage. It had once been her joy to scramble eggs in that amber paste. Now she couldn't cook and barely ate, and it was futile for me to prepare anything but the blandest, simplest fare. Opening cans and rinsing bowls took up almost no time at all.

Sitting still for any duration was giving me a terrible restlessness. Television depressed me, and I couldn't seem to concentrate long enough to enjoy a book. I wished I'd learned to knit or throw pots or work in stained glass. Something worth converting that musty shed back into the workshop it had once been for my father. I had to find something else to do to turn the direction of my thoughts.

So one interminable Monday, even my makework complete by eleven-thirty and the rest of the day gaping before me, I gave in and went to Witness Baptist. The office was open but unoccupied—Mrs. Eberly, the longtime secretary, pretty much set her own hours, Mama had said with trace disapproval. Her desk was positioned by the room's only window, and the trailing pot of ivy set in the deep sill threatened to engulf her telephone, typewriter, and assortment of stuffed animals. A folding table was set up against the rear wall, next to the doorway leading to the minister's office. Beneath the table were two large cardboard boxes extruding bubble wrap. Taped to one, a note in neat block lettering, which read, "AVIE HERE IS THE COMPUTER THANK YOU VERY MUCH!! S.P."

The components were packed tightly, wrapped in layer upon layer of bubble wrap and wedged in with blocks of foam. I was struggling to pry them out of the packaging when Saul arrived, a greasy paper bag in one hand and a waxy soda cup in the other. He was dressed in jeans and a T-shirt. "You!" he cried, with accusing delight.

"Me," I admitted sheepishly. "I guess I'm a little overdue."

"Your mother said she's been keeping you pretty busy," he said, and I felt a little pulse of something—indignation? flattery?—that he'd checked up on me. And Mama had covered for me. "I knew you'd come when you had the time. Here, let me." He set down his lunch. He took a Swiss Army knife out of his pocket, scored the sides of the box I was struggling with, and tore it away from its contents, releasing a torrent of Styrofoam peanuts.

Extracted from their thick cocoons of foam and bubble wrap, the monitor, keyboard, and hard drive seemed almost puny. I began untangling cords. "Well, this is where I get off," Saul said.

"It's not so hard to learn," I assured him. "Nowhere near as hard as it was to unpack!"

"Maybe you can help me," he said. "I'm supposed to do the whole service Sunday after next, sermon and everything. Do you think I could put my notes on it?"

"Sure," I said, "if this thing comes with a word processor, but I'm not sure it does." I thumbed through the short stack of floppy disks that had been enclosed. "This just looks like system stuff."

"Oh, wait a minute." He ducked inside Pastor Joe's office, returned with a shoe box. "I didn't want to leave these sitting out," he explained. In a stage whisper: "I think they're illegal!"

The box was full of hand-labeled floppies. I sifted through and pulled out disks marked "Word," "Draw," "Paint," and "Page." "What, are these pirated?"

"No!" He looked around in mock terror. "Well, yes. A friend from seminary copied all his software for me when I told him we got this computer."

"Aren't you breaking a commandment? I'm pretty sure stealing is on the list."

"I employed situational ethics," he said. "The situation being, we don't have money budgeted for software now, but if it turns out we're really going to use this computer, we'll know exactly what we need to buy. Oh, and I think there's a bunch of games in there, too."

He offered to share his barbecue sandwich and fries, and I declined at the very same instant I could feel my stomach yearning, realizing that once again I'd fed Mama but neglected to feed myself. Luckily he pressed the matter, so I was able to give in. He hacked the sandwich in two with his Swiss Army knife and we ate it in Pastor Joe's office, sitting on either side of his desk, missionary newsletters in our laps to catch the grease and vinegar runoff.

"How'd you end up in Regina?" I asked. "You're not from around here, I don't think."

"I'm pretty close. I grew up about thirty miles east of here, in Laurel."

"Forgive me, but you don't sound like a Southerner."

"No?" he said. "Neither do you, much. You sort of slide in and out of it."

"My identity crisis, I guess. I must have stayed in Ohio too long.

Everybody thought I had an accent there. I got self-conscious. Now I don't know how to sound."

"Well, my parents were from Philadelphia, so we didn't speak Southern at home. Hey, maybe your accent will come back full-time once you've been here awhile," he mused.

"If I'm here much longer. I don't know what I'm doing yet. Depends on Mama, I guess."

He nodded solemnly, and we ate in silence for a few minutes.

Had I been baptized in this very church? he asked, I think to change the subject, and I said, "Yes, for all the good it did me."

"You don't think it took?"

"I'm not complaining. The water was warm and the pastor let me hold my nose while he dunked me, and then we had cake. But no, I don't think it took." At eleven, I'd been expecting the firmament to open up and angel choirs to descend, but all I'd come away with was an ear infection.

"My father," I found myself telling him. "I know my mother said he didn't have the calling. But he used to speak to me sometimes, not about God, exactly. More about the universe—how big it was and how small we were. But that's nothing to do with church."

"Oh, I disagree," Saul said.

"He'd usually had a little to drink before he got to talking like that," I said, to clarify.

"Still."

"Still. He would put on that chafing suit week after week and come here. He tithed ten percent of his earnings, to the penny. But I feel like it frustrated him, this place. It couldn't contain his thoughts. There was something—I don't know—humbling, in the way he forced himself to come. I can't shake the notion that they wouldn't let him speak his mind, and it makes me not like it here." Of course, he was also a suspected, or known, adulterer. Couldn't fault the church for that.

"Well, I sure hope that wasn't the case," Saul said. "Maybe you'll give us another chance? Perhaps *you* would like the opportunity to speak?" He gave me a teasing little grin with that.

"No, I would not. And don't try sticking me with a Sunday school class, either. I don't like children."

His grin widened.

"Especially *Christian* children." I added a mock shudder.

"You're funny," he said brightly.

"Yeah. I'm beautiful when I'm blaspheming." And I wondered: was I either of those things? It kind of mattered.

"I think laughter is pleasing to God."

"Oh, *Him* again," I scoffed. "You people are just obsessed! I'd come to church more often if you all would talk about something else."

"We can talk about something else," he offered. "Anything you'd like." And so we talked about toast. Dry versus buttered; lightly browned or charred, then scraped. The merits of white and wheat, respectively. It was an absurd exchange, but we kept it going for about five minutes.

He was such a good sport, so unflappable. I couldn't help liking him, though I suspected he was the shrewdest of converters. If he refused to let me offend him, I'd stick around, and he could sneak a little saving into our "secular" conversations.

But I'd already been baptized. That fact hadn't stopped me from just about ruining my life. I didn't blame church. I was just being a smart-ass; it gave me the only joy I'd had in weeks. I thought of claiming that double jeopardy barred me from being baptized again.

"Avie, I have to tell you something," he said, when the toast conversation had run its course. "No matter what we talk about, we're talking about God."

"Says you," I shot back. But I didn't mind him saying it.

I greeted Saul the following week in the most disgruntled tones I could muster: "I suppose I'm expected to attend next Sunday." Truth was, I was curious to see how he'd do up there behind the pulpit. Did he truly have "the calling," assuming there was such a thing? I wasn't sure I wanted him to. It was easier, more promising even, to flirt with a fraud.

"I don't know if *I'm* going," he lamented. He'd started up out of Pastor Joe's chair, disoriented, when I walked into the front office. There was a smear of ink on his cheek where he'd been dozing on a newspaper. "But I wouldn't mind you being there if I do."

"Aren't you afraid I'll heckle you?"

He laughed weakly, then covered his face with his hands. "Oh, I can't joke about this yet!"

"Is it that bad?"

"It's just all over the map." He brandished a yellow legal pad covered over in ballpoint. "I've got a lot of ideas, but nothing's panning out."

"Well," I said, warming to the occasion, "if I remember the protocol here, you need a topic. It should be simple and broad— how about Sin? Then you quote the Bible on it, starting with the applesnake and on through the Ark and Solomon Gomorrah and so on, till you end on Christ's blood. Or just pick a commandment. You could turn it into a series—that's ten sermons right there. Has your Bible got an index?"

He started toward me. "Avie? I'm going to close the door on you now." He strode over and pushed it gently shut. Then he opened it back up a crack and added, "I left everything by the computer for you. There's a lot of extra material this time. Pastor Joe's letter from Bolivia, for one thing, and I know it's way too long, but just see what you can do to fit it all in. Is that okay, Avie?" His voice was strained and shaky, as if he was on the verge of tears.

"Yes! I'm all set. Don't worry about me, just do your thing."

"I'm sorry," he said. "Thanks. I'm sorry." He pulled the door closed with a final, muffled, "Thanks."

The Page program fit on a single floppy disk, which had made it easy to learn, and I'd soon grasped the rudiments of a simple layout. Too many typefaces had made my first bulletin look like a ransom note; it was slightly disappointing to learn that limiting it to a couple of basic styles worked best. The others were mostly novelty fonts, anyway, letters shaped like neon tubing or gothic brushstrokes, lacking lowercase letters and essential punctuation marks. I was after something spare, simple, and clean, like the minimalist white walls of Mama's house—or rather, like how they would look if I'd done the finishing work and razored the dried paint splashes off the windowpanes.

I found myself fidgeting restlessly, in constant expectation of the door. It felt suddenly, and most unsettlingly, like my former job—the job I'd left and was expected to return to—the highly stressed but sympathetic boss sequestered in back while I picked at my makework up front, ever alert for his summons. I didn't need to help Saul so much as I needed him to call for me. It was a troubling nostalgia. Unable to concentrate on my own task, I left within the hour, the complicated bulletin barely started.

I came back that evening. I needed to finish, but I also knew he'd be there, and he was, slumped at the desk in a circle of lamplight. I rapped lightly at the doorframe to get his attention, and he cocked his head up and gave me a weary smile.

"I've got most of a pizza here if you're hungry," I said. "Mama ate about half a slice." I set the box in the extra chair and paced the small room. I felt a little giddy, circling him. "So why'd you go joining up with the Baptists, anyway? Why not Unitarian, say, or Methodist? Too easy on the women?"

"It's not——" he started, then waved it off. "I had my reasons."

"Such as?"

"I don't know, Avie; I don't think I should discuss them with you right now."

"Why not?"

He sighed. "I don't feel like having them ridiculed."

I stopped pacing and stood behind him. "Is that what I do?"

"I don't know. No. I'm sorry. I'm just too tired to play."

"Stop apologizing to me. You need to take a break, eat something." I began kneading his tired shoulders, sensing he'd be too logy and confused to resist. Whatever made me do it felt more predatory than tender.

He leaned back into the massage with a moan of abdication, but froze when his head glanced my breasts. Before he could retreat I swiveled his chair around so he was facing me and smashed my mouth into his, which had dropped half open from astonishment. At the first responding pressure I clambered onto his lap, straddling him, driven to greed by the tedium of weeks on end so lacking in this pleasure of snaking into someone's flesh and striking hard.

"Whoa, whoa, wait," he tried weakly, but when I ignored it and pressed in harder he gripped my shoulders firmly and lifted me away, unsealing our mouths.

"What is it?" I gasped, furious.

"You just caught me off guard a little," he said. "Let me catch my breath."

I slipped out of his lap onto the floor and crouched warily between his knees.

He took some deep breaths. "Okay," he said, "Okay. So I guess we like each other." I was silent, but tending toward derisive laughter. "Well, I like you," he slogged on. "And I think you must feel something for me."

"I felt something," I said wickedly, planting the heel of my palm in his thigh and plowing toward the center rise by way of explanation. He blocked me with his forearm.

"I like you," he persisted. "I think that's obvious enough. But this is pretty intense. We seem to be skipping a few steps."

I jerked my hand away and scooted back until my tailbone pressed the wall. "For God's sake, I just wanted to fuck," I snapped. "I'm not looking to *date* you."

He reared back slightly as if struck, blinking with surprise. When he recovered, he said evenly, "Whatever's going on with you, Avie, I'm your friend. I know you're not a hurtful person."

"You know nothing," I said, and got to my feet.

"Don't go," he urged.

"Don't worry; I'll still do the bulletin." How I hated his earnest face and his insinuation that I was a nice person.

"That's not what I mean and you know it. Stay and talk to me."

"Look, I'm sorry I bothered you," I said. "I just want to finish this and go, okay? I don't want to talk."

"All right," he said wearily, then lowered his forehead until it rested on the desk. As I slammed the door he called out with forced cheer, "Thank you for the pizza!" He left it shut, thinking I wanted it that way.

I slept the insipid sleep of the unsuccessfully wicked, dreams flecked with the dull flotsam of church news carefully retyped and set. Pastor Joe's letter from Bolivia kept veering off topic and I would attempt to excise the meandering passages, but the proper command eluded me. At the margins of the page, errata gathered in crackling heaps: An anonymous donor had contributed five hundred dollars, not fifty, to the baptismal font's recaulking; the covered-dish supper took place the first Wednesday of the month, not the second Tuesday; Alcoholics Anonymous meetings were held in the fellowship hall and not the basement, there being no basement at Witness Baptist; Interim Pastor Saul's sermon topic was neither Patience nor Temperance, but Temptation. In a rage I tried to sweep everything from the colt-kneed worktable to the floor and with the exertion felt my very center twist and seize. I woke to ink pulsing from the bottle, and the bottle was me.

My period had arrived, and it was a bad one. Not that there'd been many good ones, especially lately. It seemed like a good enough reason to duck the church service; it always had been before. I conjured age fourteen, languishing in my nightgown, a heating pad pressed to my belly, syrup-drenched breakfast in bed and the TV carted to my room, Daddy's bashful checking in before and after the service.

But Mama, already in her best slip, dearly lacked sympathy. Her crepe de chine blouse and jersey A-line skirt hung expectantly on the outside of the closet door, and she'd set out sensible navy pumps and a matching purse of the same genus she'd worn and carried for years, only over time the heels had dropped and thickened while the purses expanded. She'd been able to replace much of her lost clothing with near-exact replicas through weeks of poring over catalogues.

"You can make it," she said when I simpered my excuse. "Shoot, if you were to call in sick every month you'd soon find yourself out of a job."

My face must have broadcast rage, because she quickly changed tactics, adding, "If *I'm* able to go, I would think you'd be able to carry me."

"You're sure you're able to go?" I said, slow to acknowledge how successful she'd been at getting herself ready.

"I pulled these stockings on by myself." This was irrefutable evidence. The last attempt had taken both our efforts, left her in a wheezing heap, hosiery shredded, and the outing had to be postponed. We hadn't yet made a second attempt.

She loosed her hot rollers one by one, leaving sausage curls she would spray to a crisp finish. "That young man has treated me like a friend instead of a feeble child, and I aim to go and see him preach. I would like it if you took me, though I suppose that's not the only way to go." Some implicit threat there, but what? That she would call for a ride? Attempt to drive herself or walk? I'd never called her bluff, and I guessed I never would.

I knew I should get her out of the house while she was so willing and apparently able, but two possibilities awaited me at the church, both similarly appalling: that Saul would either direct the tone and message of his sermon to me, pinned and wriggling in the pew, or he would not. I clutched at my middle and sighed.

"Take you two more Tylenols and eat some protein, you'll be all right," she advised mercilessly, then added, "I think I could manage an egg myself, if you don't fry it too hard."

We agreed to slip in late, therefore last, and sit on the end of the back row in case we needed a quick exit. However vigorously Mama started out, her strength could drain suddenly and without warning, and she didn't want to attract attention getting out of there.

As we entered the chapel, the wheels of Mama's oxygen cart slowed and sank, mired in the faded eggplant carpeting, leaving furrows where I shoved it on through. People still called it the new chapel, though I'd been a baby when the original was not dismantled so much as folded into an all-inclusive brick compound more closely resembling an elementary school, which also housed the church office, a few classrooms for Sunday school, and a fellowship hall. Even near the door, the place felt hot and close as ever. The lone stained-glass window, a childish suncatcher depicting a milk-skinned Jesus, still striped the painted cinderblock walls with grimy light. Communion cubes of stale sandwich bread lay drying in stacked plates, with a few stingy drops of grape juice in medicine cups provided to moisten them. How I envied the Catholics their jeweled windows and their stamped wafers like crisp rice coins, their shared goblet of wine and sexy, black-garbed priests.

When I was little, Mama used to let me spend the service drawing on the bulletin with those bowling-score pencils provided to fill out tithe envelopes. Daddy may not have approved, but he'd always sat apart from us, with the other deacons. I'd thought of them as offstage, emerging only on cue to flank the pews and take up collection plates or usher a wobbly matron. But I was a grown-up now and could only fan myself with the bulletin I didn't care to examine too thoroughly. My frenzy had channeled itself into some bold design choices. A brief glance confirmed that my halftoned shadowboxes—and there were far too many— had been muddied by the photocopier.

I let my eyes rest uneasily on Saul instead, who approached the pulpit looking nervous if somewhat buoyed by the youth choir arrayed in a semicircle behind him. His robe was unbuttoned, worn like a jacket over the familiar maroon tie and pilled gray slacks. He wasn't wearing his glasses, and I hoped that meant he couldn't distinguish my face from the others. He managed a timid, just-audible prayer, then seemed to turn over the service to the choir, retiring to a side bench while they sang "Old Rugged Cross" (uptempo, with tambourine) and "How Great Thou Art" (extended dance remix). Mama had just murmured to me, "Are we having a concert instead?" when they launched into a rapid-fire doxology, during which Saul resumed his place at the pulpit.

Just to have it cited in the bulletin, I'd titled his sermon, "The Christian Journey," reasoning it would fit whatever he ultimately devised to talk about. I still had no idea what that would be, and remorseful for having hindered his efforts, I was hoping he did. I didn't believe he'd get fired if his sermon tanked, but I wondered if failing would cause him to doubt his vocation, even his faith. He may as well have slept with me, then, I concluded ruthlessly, stamping out compunction.

He began by invoking the metaphor that well-meaning Christians everywhere used to justify their meddling. If you were walking along, it went, and saw a house up in flames, heard the screams within, would you walk on past, finish your errands (he embellished nicely here with *buy your quart of milk, your day-old bread, your toilet paper, exchange pleasantries with the clerk*), and return home without another thought? No, of course you wouldn't. You would do everything you could to extricate that person from the fire. Well, the unsaved soul (he used *alienated from God*) is the same as that person trapped in flames. His danger, his suffering, is that great.

I couldn't decide whether he was talking about me or not. The burning house reference struck me as too close to our real-life burned-up house, so either he was being rudely pointed or grossly ignorant of the coincidence. Certainly it was insensitive to Mama, though I saw no indication that she thought so as she perched there, attentive and calm, fingering where the cannula joined at her neck as if it were her old string of pearls.

I grew increasingly flustered and indignant as my abdomen wrenched, the Tylenol's precarious hold broken. I felt myself leaking, envisioned the slow, spreading circle of crimson on the back of my skirt now seeping into the flat cushion. Oh, why couldn't we be among Satanists, gathered in a dark room swathed only in reds and blacks, where blood was prized? I got up quickly and backed out of the sanctuary, hand-signaling *okay* to Mama's fierce, divining gaze.

When I emerged from the bathroom, I was among the blessed again, having determined the trickling wetness to be sweat, no blood breach of the underpants. A red-haired woman in a floaty, sky-blue halter dress was loitering in the vestibule. She let out a jubilant little squeak and leapt over to greet me.

"I thought that was you, Avie Goss!"

"Hey, Minnie," I said shyly. She kissed me on each cheek, light European pecks. We'd known each other in high school. Not well, she'd been a couple of grades ahead of me, but we'd served on the yearbook committee together. Minnie Mangum had also been editor of our school paper, *Currents,* a subtle riff on the fact that we were the Black River High School Polliwogs. At sixteen she'd entered the local public domain for getting pregnant (mercy!), then married (phew!), but had dropped out of school before graduation (sigh). Then she'd dropped out of sight.

"Tell me what you're doing now, Avie. I hear your mother's been ill. Just down for a visit?"

I turned that one over in my mind. "Visiting, yeah. Maybe a little more long-term than that." Minnie nodded sympathetically.

"Did you used to go here?" I asked, to change the subject. "I don't remember us being in church together." What I remembered were girls, some from my Sunday school class, trumpeting the fall of Minnie Mangum, who thought she was so smart. It was the black girls who had taken up for her, I recalled, befriending her, even throwing her a baby shower when her own mother wouldn't, and this had tagged Minnie a "nigger lover" on top of everything else.

"We went to Methodist when we went at all," she said. "But in a small town, this is how you network."

"So you've moved back?" I asked.

"Terms of my probation," she said. To my quizzical look, she added, "That sounds like I'm being figurative, and maybe I am, but it's also true. Long story, not worth missing church over."

"Let me be the judge of that," I pleaded. "I do have to get back in there in a minute, though, or Mama'll come staggering after me. Can I call you?"

"I'd love to catch up," Minnie offered. "I'd say let's meet for coffee, but there's really nowhere around here to do that. Tell you what: come see me when you get a chance." She extracted a business card from her tiny snap purse and handed it to me. "You can find me here most days; I'm trying to jump-start the paper." The card read, "Minerva Mangum, Editor-Publisher, *The Regina Progress,*" and included a downtown address.

"Cool. I want to hear all about it." I pocketed the card. "Hey, did we 'network' just now?"

"Almost. It'd be the real thing if you provided a contact for me. Maybe if you introduced me to your new minister. He's pretty cute, don't you think?" She flashed a brilliant if slightly toothy grin as she said this and tossed her silky cap of hair, and her lacy silver jewelry tinkled like distant sleigh bells. She was horsey, but in the prettiest possible way.

Pretty cute, yes, I did think, but I tried to be noncommittal. "I guess. He's not really the minister; he's just subbing."

"Poor thing! I hope he didn't think we were walking out on him. I just recognized you, so I jumped right up and followed. Should we get back in there for moral support?" I nodded assent, and she pried open the heavy chapel door and waved me back through it.

I resumed my place beside Mama. Minnie had slipped back into her seat across the aisle before I thought of asking her to join us.

Saul seemed to have rallied during my absence, and his speech had grown in volume and confidence. His hands had ceased clenching either side of the lectern and instead made graceful gestures.

"But let's also be mindful of the rescuer," he was saying as I settled back in, "who in his arrogance would leap into the fire and make himself a hero. If he succeeds in bringing out the person trapped inside without succumbing to the flames himself, all right, what then? Does he carry ointment and bandages? Can he resuscitate the victim? And is it possible that he wants to find fire where there's only smoke, and so he barges in uninvited, waving his ax like a maniac?"

He had a soft boy's face, and when I'd hurt him he'd answered only in kindness. Even now he seemed to be reassuring me, *Don't worry, I won't save you.*

A lot of people had moved to Regina in recent years, lured by cheap acreage and a deluded sense of the town's proximity to Raleigh, but so far they hadn't revitalized its dying core. The downtown had definitely been declining as far back as I could remember, but a few stubborn business owners had stuck it out through the seventies. Growing up I could and often did walk downtown for what meager delights it still offered. At the full-service gas station on the corner I could buy a Tab and an ice cream sandwich and call it a good day. The dimestore was fine for foam curlers and nail polish, but the only sanitary products they carried were those horrible belted maxipads, because the lady who ran the store said that tampons would *compromise* a girl. (What she had against adhesive pads I never learned.)

Things were pretty quiet once the dimestore shut its doors, but the closing of the Main Street diner seemed to have finished off the downtown; now the old men gathered at the Hardee's on the bypass for their morning coffee.

Minnie's office was downtown, above the abandoned dimestore, between the empty barbershop and the failed dance studio. The whole area wore a gutted, forlorn look, with all the aging FOR SALE or LEASE signs flapping in empty store windows. But as Minnie pointed out, the rent was insanely cheap, and there was ample street parking.

The office was crowded with boxes and equipment in various stages of assembly. Scattered papers and file folders fanned out to nearly cover the flower-patterned rug, and a perilously low-hanging ceiling fan made swipes in the air to stir them slightly. A raw plywood counter that appeared newly added ran the length of the rear wall.

She gestured at the whole of it. "This mess is my dream!" she said, and she laughed grandly. After her recent "legal and spiritual troubles," she explained, she'd done a lot of soul-searching. How, she'd wondered, could her talents best be utilized to enrich the world? What Regina needed that she could provide, she'd concluded, was a local paper, something to remind people they were part of a community. Once upon a time people had conducted their business here and gathered in gossipy little knots on every corner. Surely things still did happen here, and if people knew about them and showed they would take part, there would be more. Of course it would be a very modest venture at first, and she'd have to enlist volunteers to dredge up stories to report, and there were production problems yet to tackle, but all in all she thought she'd hit upon a very good idea.

The problem was, the town still had a local paper, sort of. For years the *Regina Progress* had actually been produced in nearby Stoat, in tandem with the *Stoat Dispatch* and the *Bumgardner Expositor*. Essentially they were all the same paper printed with different mastheads, and due to some logistical complications, the *Progress* had not actually been distributed in Regina proper for nearly a year, though twenty-five hundred copies continued to be printed weekly. When Minnie tried drumming up advertisers for her new paper, though, people declined, saying they were already appearing in the *Progress*. "How would they even know?" she cried, incredulous. Nonetheless, they didn't wish to cause hard feelings by taking up with a competitor. There was nothing for it, Minnie concluded, but to acquire the *Progress* leg, so she did.

Now she had to get an issue out in four days or the advertisers she'd managed to re-sign would back out. If someone could type in and clean up some of the copy and cover the phone sometimes and maybe even devise a better look for the thing, she could drive all over town and drum up more ads and hopefully find a damned *story* or two to report on and this thing would be a go.

Maybe someone could, I ventured.

There were seven shopping centers in the area altogether, mostly pitiful, she swore, but three of them with grocers who could run their weekly specials, and there were several barbecue places way out in the country subsisting on word of mouth. New-comers didn't know where to find the good barbecue! Introductory ad rates were so low, she figured individual people could take out a full page wishing someone happy birthday, graduation, or anniversary, or get well soon. There were gala events by at least three community groups she knew of, constant church pot-lucks, blood drives, and two new realtors to hit.

"There's a lot to promote and I haven't yet sorted out what's story and what's advertisement," she gushed, "but you know the classified section could be the centerpiece, especially if we could get a kind of Lonely Hearts section going. You know, attractive widow looking for friendship, or single white male seeks same?"

Scattershot hours and pitiful pay were all she could offer, but I jumped at it. The only woman I'd ever worked for was Mama, and our enterprise was failing.

We hadn't gotten around to discussing those "spritual and legal troubles" yet, but Mama took it upon herself to fill me in on what she knew of Minnie's life: She'd divorced, and lost custody of the child—"That took some doing!" Mama said, shaking her head—but apparently Minnie was now reformed and had gotten more schooling and lately taken on this project.

"Lord knows how," Mama went on. "Her people must of helped her. I can't imagine her getting any payments off that hus-band if he's got the boy. I don't know what all went on there. She ran around, was part of it. I imagine she come off pretty bad to lose her child. They said she gave him up willingly. That's no kind of mother."

It troubled me to hear her sanctimonious talk—not that I hadn't been subjected to it all of my life, but learning Mama had her own past demons had made me hope she could be more generous about other people's errors. Her attitude toward Minnie let me know the things I'd held back from her needed to stay put. I knew she wouldn't talk about me to other people that way, but I couldn't stand to have her even *thinking* of me in those terrible, insinuating tones. Better for her to believe nobody ever even wanted her daughter than to know how badly I'd been . . . compromised.

All my life I'd done sham work. Daddy would have me scour the yard for impediments before he mowed it and pay me a nickel for every big stick, rock, or chunk of brick I removed. Mama would send me to the dimestore with a five-dollar bill for some trifle and in return I could spend the ample change as I wished. Zephra paid me in candy or quarters for every spider I squashed in her house. Later attempts to earn money independently by babysitting were diminished by the chaperoning presence of either Mama or Zephra; I'd grow afraid after dark once the children were in bed, and I would call and beg for company.

Even my work-study program in college, originally devised to foster a service ethic in the student body, offset tuition costs, and keep the institution self-supporting, had devolved to where most of us assisted professors who already had graduate assistants. This was where I developed the photocopying skills that helped me secure the summer internship where I further honed my duplication abilities to a razor-sharp edge.

So it was that by graduation, I'd been essentially useless for a smidge over two decades, and it was now time to parlay that into a suitable profession. When I was asked by my adviser and later in interviews about my career goals, my reply was, "I want to help people." I said I considered myself a "people person." That I kept mostly to myself and rarely managed more than one close friend at a time throughout college did not alter this claim. As for wanting to help people, I'd effectively avoided majoring in any of the helping professions. I was too skeptical for social work and too queasy for health care, and any inclinations I might have had to teach were hobbled by stage fright and an irrational dislike of children rooted in my failed babysitting venture.

I felt as though Daddy, had he not died my freshman year, would have sized me up when it came time to declare a major and told me in no uncertain terms what it was I was cut out for. His death had left me floating. Mama and Zephra seemed confident I would excel at whatever it was I set out to accomplish, but they must have assumed I had private aspirations I would reveal when ready. I couldn't bear to set them straight, so I was on my own. An English major sounded lofty and gave me permission to read, but fear of the foreign-language requirement caused me to veer into a bachelor of science degree in business administration.

With a little bit of ambition, that degree might have served me well. But I foundered, blowing one interview after another by wearing a gauzy dress more appropriate for a tea party and stammering my vague career goals without conviction. Faced with moving back home unless I secured a job soon, I leapt at the offer to join my roommate in moving back to *her* home instead.

Lydia was from Steerage, Pennsylvania, a small town that from her accounts seemed not unlike Regina, except for the exotic fact that it was states away to the north. Her father owned a good bit of property in the area, and we moved into an empty half of one of his duplexes with the agreement to pay rent when we started earning money. For three months it felt like college minus the studying and heaps of laundry; we had a washer and dryer and no big impetus to find work. We spent the summer tanning on the back deck that overlooked a dank canal, drinking light beer and casting a fishing line baited with wadded-up bread into the swill that flowed past. We mostly caught plastic grocery bags, limp and slimy as seaweed, but once I hooked a tennis ball and we were awestruck for the rest of the day. It flew in the face of physics, we thought. Some kind of portent. Then Lydia got back together with her high school sweetheart and suddenly I was alone in the Steerage duplex.

Soon even the neighbors vacated. The land was being sold to developers, and the eventual razing of the duplex was assured. I lingered into fall, jobless and without prospects, subsisting on a diet of popcorn and the care packages of Nabs and poundcake Mama sent. I was afraid at night and barricaded the door by pushing the sofa against it, reading by flashlight until sunrise. Then I slept on the sofa until afternoon, when I shoved it aside and ventured outdoors, sometimes only as far as the mailbox. Sometimes I went to visit Lydia at her boyfriend's house, but I didn't do it often because she kept asking what were my plans.

Lydia's father stood to make a fortune from the land sale that would render me homeless, and he took pity. He invited me to lunch, where he introduced me to Jack F———, the developer with his eye on the acreage containing my doomed duplex. The project was extensive, Jack explained (I was to call him Jack), a mall in the works, a couple of office buildings, and would require months of negotiations and his almost constant presence in Steerage until he'd completed his role in it.

I was bleary from lack of sleep and ravenous for protein by the time my tuna melt arrived—I thought I would chew a hole in my cheek before it did—but I'd had the wits to comb my hair and wear lipstick to this lunch, and I managed to act normal enough to get myself offered a temporary position as Jack's on-site administrative assistant.

"I like your accent," he said. "You'll be great over the phone."

He studied me intently, and I tried not to wriggle under his gaze. "Your attire will need a little more polish," he began with tact, and I must have turned bright crimson, because he stopped short and said, "No! You mustn't take offense. You're a lovely young lady, and there's been no reason for you to wear a suit. For the most part you won't need to. But every so often a client will come to the office or I'll have you with me at a meeting, and for that you need the uniform."

He pulled out a shiny, embossed black wallet—ostrich skin, I later learned—and extracted a credit card, which, to my astonishment, he handed me.

"Get something transitional for fall, medium-weight cloth, not too dark, and a wool blend for winter. Don't skimp, and have everything tailored so it fits." He brandished a perfect pin-striped sleeve that just skimmed his wrist. The chunky silver links of his watchband glinted, and I caught a glimpse of crisp white cuff.

Jack seemed too much older than me for romantic consideration, but from the first I was taken by his details. My own edges were blurry, but he was an indelible line. He gave me things to do, specific tasks, and when I executed them well, I got to bask in his approval. Never mind that the tasks were mostly simple ones, such as field his calls and divert those callers not on his "action list" to a purgatory of message-leaving. The greater challenge was pulling together a suit with accessories—shoes, belt, purse, jewelry— that would pass muster. I made endless returns to the only department store he deemed suitable, sixty-five miles away in Portage (hence his interest in developing Steerage, he explained), and he counted those hours as work and compensated my mileage.

My hair was a source of endless frustration and amusement to him. Its eccentric kink couldn't be tamed into a more professional coif, and I refused to cut it short, so we compromised on a gelled-back ponytail that would degenerate into spiking corkscrews by midafternoon. Once, before a meeting, he ran a damp hand across my scalp to smooth it back and I shuddered with pleasure, a dog stroked by its master.

I was permitted to stay in the duplex up until the bulldozers were summoned, then Jack put me up in a hotel suite for the final weeks of his portion of the project. Once construction was well under way, he would move on. Again I was sent to Portage, for there were only motor lodges in Steerage, another reason why development was so urgently needed, he explained. He told me that at this point it was unnecessary for me to make the lengthy commute into Steerage every day and gave me a beeper so I could be "on call," in case something came up for which I was needed. Meanwhile, I was to consider myself on the clock, but should come and go as I pleased, order room service when it suited me, and use the credit card for meals out as well as whatever else I required.

The suite was opulent in my estimation, with deep-pile carpeting, curtains and bedspread in a matching floral pattern, and a bathtub offering frothy jets of water. There was a channel playing movies at all hours on the big TV, and I could stay up all night to watch them, but I didn't need to because I wasn't afraid, snug in my little cell, aware of being both separated from and surrounded by others, which became the mode in which I was most comfortable.

I must have sensed this wasn't a real job, that I was being kept for some other purpose, but I blithely ordered room service, wandered the orderly streets and piers of Portage, and made weekly long-distance calls home to dissemble about my situation. Since I'd never truly worked a day in my life, it was all the easier to convince myself I'd landed a dream job. When Jack invited me to accompany him to Fortune, Ohio, for his next project, I played it off to Mama as a transfer—a promotion, even. And that was not entirely untrue, for within weeks of the switch I'd moved up to being Jack's mistress and began earning my keep for real.

He was married. A father. I kept myself out of eyesight and earshot of friends and kin to pursue this folly freely. It ate up two years of my life and made rubble of my health and good sense.

When we began keeping company he'd been the drinker, but I caught up quickly and passed him. He trained me to have expensive thirsts. Fine wines and port like dark clots of jelly in the glasses. Scotch older than me. I could—and at times still do—blame him for making me a drunk, but truth was I'd been tiptoeing around the edges of it for a while, waiting for something to flip the switch. An affair—an *affair* lent me permission to drink unabated, no more careful rationing. I needed to stun myself to sleep; then he could leave for his legal bed without my having to know it.

I kept a low-grade fever and would wake up parching in the middle of the night, my skull hot and plush. Unravel my limbs from the sheet and go stick my head under the tap, then perch on a kitchen stool until dawn, hands clasped around a mug of coffee—instant because the apartments he set up for me (for us! he said) lacked practical things that would ease our settling in: no can opener, no ice trays, no dustpan. If I attempted to introduce further housewares—a coffeepot, say—he'd accuse me of applying suffocating pressure. So much as a goddamn set of salad bowls could prompt a discussion on realistic expectations. So I drank my bitter instant brew and cooled my forehead periodically against the bare countertop.

On those mornings I felt the length of every mile that separated me from home. I couldn't keep my boiling mind out of the clutter of that long-ago kitchen where my mother and Zephra sat sentry. The percolator's sweet gurgle. Hot, sugary milk for my own china cup, just a drop of coffee, enough to turn it beige.

My daddy would have had to work up a nervy thirst to brave past those women if he wanted a cold bottle of beer to chase a flat pint of something stronger. "On his liquid diet today," one of them might quietly observe. They wouldn't outright confront or prevent him, but their presence had a tempering effect; he'd pace himself and not badly misbehave.

Remembering this would make me weep, because I was far from anyone who would get between me and the things I wanted that would harm me, and I could not stop myself.

Somehow Minnie sold enough ads to fund the first issue. She wasn't shy, didn't mind knocking on doors. I knew I couldn't, and at first I marveled that she could. She had a notoriety, after all. I told her she was brave.

But reputation was not something that concerned Minerva Mangum. She called it an outmoded concept.

"Reputation among whom? For every busybody in this so-called community, there's a dozen newcomers who never heard of me and couldn't care less. Anyway, do I look like a drug addict to you?"

Decidedly not, with her impeccable pantsuits and careful hair and obvious healthy glow. I shook my head no.

"How about an unfit mother?" Her voice more unsteady here.

"No, you don't." I tried to keep it light. "You look like a wonderful mom, fresh out of a PTA meeting. I wish you were *my* mother."

"Well, I'm a drug addict and an unfit mother, and I have the court documents to prove it. Doesn't mean I have to look the part or explain myself or apologize to anyone but those I hurt."

"People hurt you, too, I imagine," I said. I could see Jack's face. It floated before me at odd hours, once I was sure all thoughts of him were banished. But any little thing would conjure him. A wrist emerging from an oxford cuff. Tassel loafers. A Great Lakes neutral accent. Any talk of anything to do with missteps and mistakes.

"Can't help what they did. Can only help what I do," Minnie said.

Fleeing Jack, I'd loaded my little hatchback in secret. Not much to take with me. I'd been afraid of the drive back, afraid of checking into hotels, eating in restaurants. Afraid of all the things I'd never done alone.

Minnie was my rehab. To her alone I said I'd been a drinker, a bad one. I was trying to put it behind me, but I admitted to her that I thought of taking a drink at the least thing. The cup of swizzle sticks by the church kitchen coffeemaker, little squares of cocktail napkins, the clashing of ice or condensation on a glass made my throat ache. Condensation on a glass. And of course those things conjured Jack, too.

"Listen," Minnie told me. "It's that your body, your brain, needs a new set of rules. It takes time, because your ways were set. But they're not fixed, see? They were frozen, but they're fluid, too. The body is mostly fluid. And you know what it needs most? Air. That's the true thing it craves and can't get enough of. You give it enough air you won't want for the other things.

"I started practicing yoga when I was still smoking, still drinking, eating red meat and other crap, pretending I was clean because I only smoked pot and maybe did a little coke if it was around. I didn't go looking for it. So I started practicing, by my-self at first, with a cassette tape and some diagrams to go by. I'd heard somewhere it would help you relax, and I couldn't sleep for anything. All the custody stuff was going on; I was losing my kid. Then I found a teacher, Len, seventy-three and looked fifty, tops, had been in India for eighteen years to study with a master. It was Len got me breathing. Once I was breathing true, those shitty habits began to fall away."

"I don't have trouble breathing," I countered. "That's my mother's deal. But I've never even smoked! I jog a little. A very little, but I jog." I would jog in the roadside gravel to Dr. Black's pond, where I'd been told babies came from, and back. Babies brought on Jack. And passing cars. Sore muscles.

"You breathe too shallow, just little puffs to fill your chest. You need deep, full belly breaths to get the air in that cleanses you." She demonstrated. It seemed her entire trunk swelled, then receded with her exhalation, back to drum-tight. Her body was unnerv-ingly fit, her trunk like that of a young tree, narrow but strong. Mine felt more like the trunk of a car, hollow but cramped, a few frayed bungee cords worming around inside. No spare, no Jack.

The office cried out for order, Minnie declared, and we spent considerable time sifting papers and devising a workable filing system. We would need to keep track of our advertisers—there were now several! And several, according to Minnie, would be enough to print an issue with. I soon moved on to putting to-gether an actual workspace and surprised myself at the rightness and economy of what I devised, little stations along the high counters for scanning artwork, printing, waxing, and pasting up the oversized pages, work that was best done standing. Mean-while, Minnie decorated the walls with a mishmash of corporate inspirational posters (icy pinnacles and sunrises, all striving and goals) and Tibetan swag (prayer flags and handmade paper smashed through with flowers). We had only one desk for the time being, but it was big enough for me to set up the gigantic monitor; she'd financed a decent computer and laser printer for me to use, far nicer than the church's and with legally obtained software. There was even enough desk surface left for Minnie to pull up a chair and make phone calls or greet advertisers, should they ever come to us.

When we finished, she stood in the doorway and took it in. "Now this," she pronounced, "is an office!"

"No, it feels too good here," I retorted. She looked at me quizzically. Though she knew about my drinking and vaguely of my failed romance, I hadn't confided that I'd more or less worked for the man I was involved with. Had been involved with and was no longer involved with. It bore emphasizing, even if it was only to myself. "I don't know what I meant by that," I dissembled.

"I think I do," she said. "We've made work a drudgery in the West, something to be endured. But work should be your self-expression!"

"Okay, sure," I said. "That's what I meant."

"I thought so," Minnie shot back. "Now get back to work!"

With an old copy of the *Progress* spread out beside me, I tried to replicate the masthead and basic layout on screen. My fonts weren't an exact match, but they were pretty close. Building the front page was a lot more challenging than the dinky church bulletins. This layout required actual columns, and tinkering with leading and kerning. Columns and leading and kerning, oh my! Things must be made to fit. Everything was measured in tiny increments. Text had to flow around boxes, those boxes would have to contain photographs or ads, those photographs would need to be half-toned, the ads set. I was grateful we'd be limited to black-and-white for now. I wasn't ready to take on color.

Off and on as I worked, I tried to practice breathing. A series of deep inhalations made me dizzy; I was hyperventilating and still filling only my chest. I couldn't grasp what Minnie meant by belly breathing; my lungs were set in my damn rib cage. I found I couldn't really stay on task while I had to keep thinking about drawing the next breath. It was tedious. Then I'd get distracted and forget about breathing, but that meant reverting back to my shallow old way. Minnie said all that was normal; I needed to practice the breathing when I wasn't occupied with other tasks. It was something that needed your full attention.

"Yeah, and I can't walk and chew gum at the same time," I said. I can't give anything my full attention, I thought.

"Everyone does it wrong," she placated. "It's something that has to be relearned."

That's what it was to start again: everything needed relearning. I wanted to give it an honest try, but I couldn't help being dispirited. After all, even my breathing was wrong, something so fundamental as that.

Everything needed relearning. That implied I'd possessed some knowledge to begin with. I must have known how to make friends once, how to be a friend. You do things for friends, you help them out, you confide your innermost—

You do things. You help out.

I went to visit Saul. I tried to pretend nothing had happened, and so did he. He sprang from his chair to greet me and gave my shoulder a manly squeeze, like I was a golfing buddy.

"Hello, hello!" he chirped. "You're well? You look well."

"Me? Um, yes, I'm well enough."

"Well, you look it."

"And you?"

"Great." He smiled broadly, teeth glinting, evangelical. "Busy."

"Me too. I've been meaning to come by before now and tell you, your first sermon—"

"You were there? Thank you. I wasn't sure if—" he faltered.

I leapt in. "You were good."

"–if you'd come or not," he finished. "But I'm glad you did. I've had two more since, and they were much smoother. I'm getting the hang of it now." He went on to tell me he'd found a member of the youth choir to update the weekly bulletins using my templates, and he'd even learned how to type his notes into the word processor.

He didn't need me, I realized, and the knowledge made me sour.

"I've been thinking about you," he said abruptly, then amended it. "About something you said. About your father, wanting to speak, and not being able to. Do you think he wanted to speak out about what happened here?" Saul had been curious about the founding pastor ever since I'd mentioned him, he explained. And, of course, there were no details about his departure in the church records, only that he'd retired.

"I don't know any more about that than I told you," I said, flustered by my own disappointment. "I don't believe Daddy was in favor of forcing him out. Mama certainly seems to have been. But there's a lot about Daddy I don't know. I thought he hung the moon. Turns out he was just a man."

"That's all right, you know. For him to have been just a man."

"Of course it is!" I sputtered, though I wasn't sure. To change the subject, I started telling him about my new job helping with

the *Progress,* and in a nervous gush found myself going on about
Minnie, her ideas and ambitions, her thoughts about creating a
community and the paper's role in that. Her style, her sense of
humor, her sense of comfort in her own body and in the world. I
envied and admired her immensely.

When he said, "Red hair? I think I've seen her at the service,"
I fought to ignore the tiny caving in my chest. He hadn't known
whether I was there, but he'd certainly noticed her. Just another
little dip, I thought, just your own hard vanity dented.

"Yes, probably you did," I said. "She's really striking."

That flustered him. "I mean I noticed her because she was
new. I'm supposed to make an effort with newcomers? Not that
she isn't striking," he added shyly.

"She mentioned wanting to meet you." I studied his reaction
but couldn't read it. Startled interest? I pressed on. "She said you
were cute."

"Oh, is that what she said?" He looked at me sharply.

" '*Pretty* cute,' she said."

"What is this?" Saul demanded.

I put my hands up. "Hey, don't shoot the messenger."

We soon ran out of things to say. When I left, he told me,
"Don't be a stranger." I felt admonished.

When I next saw Minnie, I announced, "I think Preacher Boy's
unattached."

Minnie laughed at me. "Really? And?"

"Just thought you'd like to know. It appears that he *noticed* you
at the service."

"Noticed me. Well."

"Do you want me to give him your number? Or do you
want his?"

"He's a minister, Avie. Don't you think it would bother him that I'm divorced and have a son?"

I shrugged. "Everybody's divorced. And Saul's the *youth* minister; I assume he likes children."

"How about my criminal record? And the fact that I'm not a Christian?"

"What are you?" I wondered.

"I don't know. Not an atheist. I'm spiritual."

"Well, that should be all right. He's very hip and now. He's very *Today's Living Bible.*"

"Tell him the other stuff, Avie. Tell him I have a child and a bit of past. *Which I have bravely overcome.* If he doesn't make the squinchy face, I'll meet him."

"Squinchy face?"

"You know, like your mother made when she saw me again for the first time in five years."

"Like she smelled something foul but it pained her worse to have to acknowledge such unpleasantness?"

"Exactly."

"Well, Mama doesn't make that face at you anymore. Give Saul a chance. Anyway, I thought you didn't care what people thought."

"I don't," she said firmly. "I just don't know if I'm ready to date again. I don't know what I'm looking for. Avie, you're single, no encumbrances—why don't you go for it?"

"Oh, I've got encumbrances." I tried to make it sound like a joke. "I am so encumbered, you've no idea."

"You've got your mother, is all. You need to have a life outside of that. Besides, I'd think your mother would adore your going out with him."

"*She* would. He's not really my type."

"What makes you think he's mine?" she cried.

"You said he was cute!" I shot back.

"And so he is. What's your type? Homely?"

"Yes, and old." Married, I wanted to add. The sinning kind. "Look, I thought you wanted to meet him, and he seems to be available *and* interested, so quit acting like you're being forced to take some nasty medicine."

She laughed at that and finally agreed to let me give him her number. "But at least tell him I've got a kid. He can choose not to call me if that bothers him and save us both some time."

After arranging the thing with what I thought was great subtlety and tact—I left a note for Saul with Minnie's telephone number and a few details—my swelling sense of my own magnanimity suddenly punctured, and I grew morose. Everybody's divorced, I'd said with facile knowingness, and it kept echoing back to mock me. Except Daddy didn't divorce Mama, and Jack didn't divorce his wife. Daddy must have loved Mama too much: good for her. Jack must not have loved me enough: pity on me. Forget whatever Saul might have felt for me; I'd ruined that. And from my end I just felt humbled, all desire erased. I wasn't good for anyone except maybe as a friend, so that's what I would try to be.

I managed some happy noises when Saul called Minnie, but when she asked me to come to her house after work to help her get ready for the date, I said evenings could be difficult for Mama, and I needed to be home with her. It wasn't a complete lie.

"Can I come to your house, then? I'll bring my makeup and a couple of outfits, and you can help me choose. It'll be fun. Girl stuff." The look on my face must have stopped her short. "Avie? Are you sorry that you set this up? You did set this up, you know. You practically insisted."

"No!" I blurted. "Come over! Of course, come over. I was just wondering about Mama, but you know she'll love it. In fact, she'll help you more than I could."

By the evening of the date, I was nauseated with jealousy, struggling to be cordial. Mama, however, was gracious and charming, glad of the company. She declared the outfit Minnie was already dressed in to be "the smartest."

It wasn't her best pantsuit, a loose, slubbed fabric the color of weak broth, though the jacket darted in nicely at her waist. Minnie protested mildly, saying it was what she'd worn all day to work in. The dresses she'd brought to choose from were bright slashes of color with high hems and low necklines. Mama gave them a dismissive once-over, then replied, "All the more reason. You're comfortable in it. You can go all out when there's a second date."

"If there is," Minnie corrected.

"Be that as it may. You don't want to look like you're trying too hard."

Minnie nodded appreciatively, then turned to me. "Avie? What's your vote?"

I swallowed hard. "I never go on dates," I said bitterly. "Never. I never have to dress with that in mind. So I can't help you."

"Avie!" Mama barked. "What a thing to say!"

"And I'm sure it's not true," Minnie said. "What about—?" She stopped at my warning look, glanced quickly at Mama, and didn't finish. She shrugged, helplessly confused. So I'd had a boyfriend in Ohio and we'd broken up, so what?

"You always look nice, no matter what," I said, softening. "Mama's probably right about being comfortable. Wear what feels the best."

"I'm going to cancel," Minnie said. "This is just too weird."

"No!" I cried. "You can't cancel. It'll hurt his feelings."

"It's your feelings I'm worried about," Minnie said.

"I'm sorry," I pleaded. "I don't know why I'm acting so strange. Don't let me mess up your date because I'm feeling sorry for myself. I want you to have a good time, hit it off, kiss good night. It'll be fun. Just don't give me all the details later."

"I don't understand you!" Minnie nearly shouted in frustration. "You've practically bullied me into making a date with someone you really don't want me to go out with. Why?"

"I think she wants him for herself," Mama ventured. Minnie clapped a hand to her mouth, masking her amusement with a look of shock.

"That's not it at all," I insisted, glaring at Mama. "I *want* you to go out with him. I think you'd make a nice couple."

Minnie started to respond, but Mama intervened. "I'm crying mercy," she said. "You two are going to worry each other to death and take me with you. Minnie, go on home and finish getting ready for your date. Don't keep him waiting. Add a scarf to that pantsuit if you're feeling too plain, but you're very becoming just as you are. Avie, please fix us some supper. I want cream of chicken on toast. Say good night, girls. Be ladies."

"See you tomorrow?" I ventured meekly.

"Of course." Minnie grabbed my hand and held it a minute.

"I'm an idiot," I whispered.

"No," she said, and she smiled. "You're just a little bit crazy, like me. I'll see you tomorrow."

"You ought to be slapped," Mama said, once Minnie was safely out the door and beyond earshot.

"What? I was just trying to do something nice for the both of them."

"If you want him, you could find out whether he likes you back without sending her out to test him for you."

"I didn't—"

"Hush now and listen. Minnie's your friend; she's not to be played with like that. Saul neither. Now anything can happen, you see. You opened that door, but what comes next is not any of it at your bidding. Serves you right if they run off together."

"I don't care. I don't like him, Mama. I don't. Not like that." I meant it, too, but felt the tremors, the plates shifting in my face that prefaced sniveling, felt the hot tears squeezing out.

"None of that, now. We've had childish games enough today," she said, but her voice had grown gentle. "Go on and fix us a little supper now, baby. Whatever you want to make's fine."

In the kitchen I thought of something that made me laugh out loud. "Mama!" I called. "You sent her out in that terrible pantsuit. She brought two knockout dresses over, and you talked her into wearing what she had on."

"She asked my opinion, I gave it to her," Mama maintained. I stood in the doorway, arms crossed, and stared her down until she cocked her head slyly. "Well, if he likes her, he likes her," she said. "But we don't have to serve her to him on a platter!"

The next morning Minnie terrified me by showing up for work in the same broth-colored pantsuit. She laughed at my gaping expression and said, "Oh dear God no, no, nothing like that. I just felt like being invisible today, and apparently this outfit really does the trick. Do me a favor, would you, and never play matchmaker for me again?"

I swore I wouldn't.

"I think he thought I was looking for counseling. We spent most of dinner discussing how I might regain custody of my son."

She waited a beat, then grinned before adding, "We spent the rest of the time talking about you."

"You did not," I said, surprised by how light the knowledge made me.

I started helping Minnie distribute the paper around town, leaving stacks in every little shop, restaurant, and gas station in the vicinity. It wasn't long before distribution became my operation entirely. The leftover papers were always a scattered mess, so I played around with some cardboard and masking tape until I came up with a small display holder. It was simple, just a tray deep enough to hold ten or fifteen papers with a taller rear wall to display the paper's masthead. Elevated on cardboard panels and reinforced with duct tape, the tray became a wobbly stand. The bare cardboard and two kinds of tape looked shabby and patchwork, so I gave it a base coat of spray paint and found myself covering the whole thing over with bright, splotchy tempera-paint scenes of Regina as I'd dreamed it from Fortune, Ohio: the old depot/jailhouse, now Chamber of Commerce (I returned the bars to the windows); Dr. Black's pond full of babies floating on lily pads; the graffitied water tower overlooking endless tobacco rows dotted with stooped, sack-dragging bodies; the rusted gasoline pumps lined up behind the WELCOME TO REGINA sign.

My prototype garnered curiosity, admiration, and amusement in equal parts. "It's so queer-looking I expect people will have to stop and see what in the world it is," Mama predicted when I brought it home to show it off, "and then they might as well have a paper. It's smart business." Saul said it looked like folk art, and Minnie contended it *was* folk art, as I was entirely untrained. When it wasn't raining or too windy, I set up the display downstairs from the office, in front of the dance studio. From the window I could see people pause and then resume walking with papers under their arms.

I found out I really wasn't afraid to talk to people once I overcame my initial apprehension. Everyone was friendly enough, and few had objections to displaying a free local paper. Some people had known me since I was a child. They asked after my mother and wanted to know where was my boyfriend. Because they had a son, a nephew, a cousin. I deflected these offers but knew they were well meant. I was quickly warming to the small talk and pleasantries. I'd been so isolated—first with Jack, though I'd chosen that isolation, conveniently forgetting how to meet people or sustain connections with those I already knew. Then there were the weeks with Mama when we both were shut-ins. I could now count two friends, Minnie and Saul, and a widening circle of acquaintances. It felt as if I was entering the world again.

Several Mexican-owned businesses had opened in the area, and once I bit back my shyness and crossed their thresholds, I was made to feel welcome there, too. I spent much of an afternoon devouring powdery sweet yeast rolls with the owner of the bakery as we discussed adding a Spanish-language section to the paper. I floated home in a giddy carbohydrate haze, surprised and pleased with myself. I had ambitions, I thought, creative endeavors. I would paint as it suited me, and all the knowledge I'd ducked in school beckoned. I would really learn Spanish this time around. I would grow the paper.

I was still sounding out title ideas for the proposed Spanish section as I walked in the door, enjoying how the unaccustomed sounds tumbled like stones in my mouth. "Las Noticias. La Prenza. Las Páginas."

"Your boss called," Mama cut through my reverie.

"Minnie?" I said, holding fast. *"Mi jefa?"*

"Your whofa? No, baby, your *boss*-boss. He said you should call him back collect."

Elation and plain dread. Part of me thought, Took you long enough, goddamn you, Jack.

"He was real nice," Mama said. "He asked after me and all. Wonder does he want you to come back?"

I wondered that, too, of course, had been wondering it every minute I couldn't pave over with something else. Most shamefully, I'd used Mama's accident and illness as a means of escape that could brook no argument.

"I didn't tell him you were moonlighting," Mama said.

Maybe I'd hoped he'd take the hint when he noticed I'd removed every scrap of clothing from the apartment, and that never hearing from me again would confirm his suspicions.

"I don't mean to keep you forever," Mama said. "I know you've got a life of your own. There's no telling what all you left hanging to come here."

When I left Fortune, Ohio, there was twenty-five thousand dollars in my money-market account. It wasn't my money, though it was in my name. There'd been varying amounts in the account, sometimes less, sometimes much more. Jack had a number of strategies for keeping the government from knowing (and therefore taxing) his true earnings, and this was only one of them. The account served a dual purpose in that it also provided me with a living allowance, which we pretended was a salary. I was free to spend what I needed, as long as I didn't exceed what Jack considered reasonable, and since I was never sure what was reasonable, I was frugal.

Jack saw no need to dismantle the account just because I was leaving; it was too useful, and besides, I'd posed my departure as temporary. "You'll need a little fallback money," he said. "I'll feel better about you being there if I know you can get what you need." I didn't argue, though I had no intention of drawing from the account past what I thought I'd earned that month. I wouldn't need to, I thought; I would be staying with my mother.

In her damaged house. Which was no longer insured.

She'd let the policy lapse, the sort of oversight she'd begun to make over the last couple of years as her health declined. She still believed she was fully covered, and I wasn't sure how she'd handle learning otherwise, so I let her go on thinking it. I considered my options: I could fight the insurance company for months while she languished in a nursing home, or I could hire a contractor to start repairs immediately. Promise him extra if he hustled his guys to have it ready for her homecoming. My cause was just, the need was great, and the money was in my name. I opened up a new account in Regina and transferred twenty-three thousand dollars into it, leaving the minimum two thousand to keep the Fortune account open. When things got settled, I reasoned, I would try again with the insurance company. If I really pressed them on it, perhaps I could return much of what I had taken—no, borrowed.

As the money was siphoned into the house, though, I started adding up the ways it had been owed to me all along. Throw in some Christmas bonuses, the price of my silence, my honor, my body, the imposed neglect of my mother that had at best not prevented the insurance fiasco and at worst had led to her house catching fire. Tallied in that ledger, twenty-three thousand dollars seemed a reasonable sum.

To tell you the truth, I sometimes wished there had been more. Severance pay, call it.

"You shouldn't try to contact me here," I told Jack in low, furious tones from the back porch. I hoped that if Mama hadn't already dozed off in front of the TV, it would mask my voice, but I hated taking the chance.

"How else was I supposed to reach you?" he countered.

"We agreed you wouldn't call here."

"Oh yes, 'we' 'agreed,'" he mocked. "No. You told me not to call. You also said you would stay in touch with me."

"It's been pretty crazy here, Jack. I'm sort of overwhelmed."

"Your mother was so charming," he said, trying a different tack. "She must be feeling better."

"She's dying, Jack." Adding "eventually" lacked the moral weight, so I omitted it.

"Okay, Avie. But for all I knew, she was already dead. *Because I haven't heard anything from you.* Jesus, even Simone's been asking. "

I seized on the chance to get outraged. "You want me to call so she won't be suspicious?"

"I want you to call so I can hear your voice. I think I've been very patient."

Oh. Well. "You know I would have called you if anything happened."

"Perhaps if you ran out of money?" he said, a teasing edge to his voice.

"Now we're getting to it," I said. "Okay. I do want to explain that to you."

He chuckled lightly. "That was quite an advance on your salary."

"God, Jack, things were such a mess when I got here. The house—"

"You must have needed it," he broke in. "We don't have to discuss it all right now. This actually isn't a good time for me. But since I'm not supposed to call you, do you mind telling me how we're going to continue this conversation?"

"I'll call you back," I promised. "Just tell me when."

"Yes, you've said so before. So I guess I'll be leaving messages with your mother again soon."

"No. You don't need to do that. There's another place you can reach me." I gave him Minnie's office number.

"Okay," he said briskly. "Talk soon. Take care." Dial tone. This was familiar. He'd sever the line, all business, and I was to infer that Simone or one of the children had entered the room. I'd always hated that summary dismissal. I suspected he used it whenever it suited him to end a conversation. That was just another one of the indignities I signed on for when I agreed to be mistress. If I truly wanted to be through with all that, I shouldn't have taken the money. There was no such thing as severance pay. The debt hung there between us, the cord he could pull me back with.

It was Saul who called the office soon after that, and I was testy with him, unnerved by the male voice on the line that wasn't Jack's, which meant that Jack's call still loomed before me.

"I'm afraid you've just missed Minnie," I said brusquely.

"Hmm. Well, tell her I said hello."

"I'll give her the message," I said, all business.

"Um, actually, your mother said I might find *you* here. I was wondering if you were hungry."

"I can't really leave," I said. "I need to be here to answer the phone while Minnie's away."

"Well, you're doing a bang-up job. I don't think it finished the first ring before you snatched it up."

"But now the line is busy," I pointed out.

"Oh. Yeah. Okay. See you, then!" he said brightly, and he hung up.

I had about fifteen minutes to regret my rudeness. Then Saul made a live appearance, all smiles and entreaty.

"What are you doing?" I whined.

"What? I said I'd see you. Now we're not tying up the line, and you don't have to leave." He held out a paper sack. "Also, I brought you your very own sandwich. We don't have to split one this time."

"I'm not hungry," I said. "I suppose I should have emphasized that."

"It'll keep." He was scanning the office's eccentric decor with interest. He reached up and stirred a tiny set of brass chimes that dangled from the ceiling fan. "Nice place."

"I'm also busy," I added.

His face fell. He set the bag on the desk. "I'm sorry. I'll go."

"It's just that I'm having a real bad day," I hastened to add.

"You want to talk about it?"

"Not especially."

"*Minnie* thinks I'm a pretty good counselor," he tried playfully.

"I don't doubt it," I said.

"In addition to being cute."

"Yes, you're being extremely cute right now," I said, scowling.

"Avie, why did you want to set me up with her? I mean, after what happened."

"What happened?" I shot back angrily.

"Between us," he murmured, eyes cast shyly down.

"What happened between us? Nothing, that's what."

"Just because I wouldn't fly into bed with you doesn't mean nothing happened. Is happening."

I stood up. "Nothing is happening." My face was on fire.

"It doesn't mean I don't have feelings for you, or that I wouldn't want to—"

"Have you ever heard of a grudge fuck?" I enunciated, and relished the way it made him wince. "When you're mad with your lover, and looking to get your own back, you jump on the next warm body. That's what I was gunning for that night."

"Minnie said you'd ended a relationship. She had the impression it had gone badly."

"Well, Minnie doesn't know what the hell she's talking about. I'm in a relationship. *In* one. Things are complicated because I'm having to be here instead of with him. I guess I should be grateful you didn't want me; I could have really screwed things up there."

"My guess is things were plenty screwed up already, if you were wanting to have a grudge—if you were wanting to do that."

"Please," I tried. "I just can't be . . . available to you. Not in any way that would suit someone like you. My mother likes you too much, for one thing. And I'm still . . . *in* this." I sagged back into my chair, ground my fist against my forehead.

"It's all right. I get it." He paced the room restlessly, then circled back around to face me. "I have to be careful with you, anyway. You remind me of someone, and I know that's part of the pull."

"Who?" I couldn't help asking.

He sighed. "My fiancée."

"Oh. Yikes."

"I mean, not anymore, of course. A girl I got engaged to when we were seventeen. I didn't think it was ridiculous. I was deadly earnest."

"But you didn't end up married?"

"I intended to. I abandoned my dull, sort of Methodist roots and joined her church. That's how I became a Baptist."

"So what was the problem? Sounds like a match—"

"Made in Heaven, right. But I got saved. I mean *saved*. I got 'the calling,' just like your mother said, and I wanted to become a minister. It wasn't what my fiancée was expecting. She was jealous, I think. And scared of it, too."

"Well, I'm not her. For the record."

"I know! It's just that the way you tease and challenge me is kind of like her sometimes. Anyway, it's only part of the pull."

"It doesn't matter," I added uncharitably. I didn't like reminding him of anyone else.

I watched him take that in, struggle with it, and decide not to answer me in anger. "Do you know what I did," he asked instead, "after you stalked out that night so angry with me, and we were both so worked up?"

I shrugged.

"Ate every bit of that pizza you brought." He picked up the sack and dropped it back onto the desk, and it made a crumply *oomph*. "I came to have lunch. I will settle for lunch. Please have lunch with me. Let's be in lunch."

"Say 'lunch' some more," I said.

He lowered himself into Minnie's chair. "Say grace," he challenged.

"Blessthisfoodforthenourishmentofourbodiesforwhatweare abouttoreceiveletusbetrulythankful," I said.

"Lunch, lunch, lunch," he intoned. And for the moment, grace was granted.

For the moment. Like any craving, it sprang right back to form and made a slave of me again. The prospect of Jack's call had me dropping by the office at all hours. My halfhearted early-morning jogs became late-night walks that invariably placed me at the building, and while I was so close, why, I ought to just dash upstairs and check. No message, so I'd linger for an hour and proofread some pages or set an ad so I'd be there in case he did call.

It made me nervous, because even though Mama was doing well, nights were a fragile time. Even if she wasn't having breathing trouble, I thought it would frighten her to wake and find me gone, and then she would get breathing trouble. I wouldn't let myself stay more than an hour, and I'd run straight home, breaking into a panicky sprint.

By the end of the week, Mama was on to me. When I brought her evening meds, she had me stay while she swallowed each tablet with careful sips of milk. Then she handed me her cup and said, "That's it. That's the last thing I need for the night. I'm all set now, you're good to go." I must have looked confused, because she laughed and took my hand. "Honey, if you want to go off at night, you don't have to slip out when you think I'm asleep. Go out, stay out all night if you want to. You're a grown woman."

"It's just work stuff," I said, startled that she might be thinking I was up to worse. "I didn't want you to be scared at home by yourself at night."

"Well, I'm a grown woman, too," she said. "Even if I do wear diapers." She deemed the incontinence pads, a recent necessity, her worst indignity, trumping the oxygen tube or every one of her teeth falling out. They arrived through the mail in plain brown packages, like pornography. "If it's who I think it is," she went on, "I don't see why you feel like you have to slip around. I already knew you liked him."

"You think I'm 'slipping around' with the preacher boy?" I asked.

"Why not? It wouldn't be the first of such goings-on," she said, grinning.

"Wonder is it anyone looking in on her?" Mama ventured almost idly the next morning, catching me completely off guard. "You know she can't half drive anymore."

"Who?"

Silence.

"Zephra?"

Silence.

"Do you want to pay her a visit?"

"She can't half drive anymore."

"Do you think she needs help?"

Silence.

"Mama, do you want me to go?"

"Somebody ought to be looking in on her."

"I'll go. Is that what you want? I'll go today. All right?"

Silence.

"You want to come?"

"Me? No. I'm wore out. You go."

"Might do you good to get out."

"You go on ahead. I'm wore out."

I brought Zephra a sheet cake from the IGA. It said *Happy 37th Jean!* in pink cursive against white icing, rosebuds set all around. It was a kind of peace offering, this long-favored treat of ours. Unclaimed cakes went for half price at the IGA, always had. We'd eat the icing until we were sick and feed the mealy cake to the birds.

She smiled ruefully when I held it out to her. "Oh child. You know I can't with the diabetes. Got to test my blood sugar every week. If it's high, Dr. Wilson will be all over me."

"This is the first I've heard of you having diabetes," I said, alarmed.

"Well, I don't go around shouting it."

"Are you giving yourself shots?"

"Lord, no. I've got a lady comes by. I can't stand needles, but she does it quick." She set the cake on the counter, pried the plastic lid, and swiped at a rosebud. "Haven't seen you in a while," she said offhandedly. She licked the pink glob off her finger, gave me a wink. "Your mama doing all right?"

"Stable. She won't get any better, past a point. But she's pretty good."

"I was wondering when I'd see you again," she said. "Thought you might be going back soon."

I didn't know what to say. "Well, you know Mama," I offered lamely.

"She wouldn't keep you from coming to see me," Zephra admonished.

"No, of course not," I said.

"Nor make you stay and look after her."

"I didn't mean that. It's just that she kept me running for a while there, when she was really bad off. I can't see leaving her yet." I paused. "You could have come—or called, something."

"I'm not wanted," Zephra declared flatly.

"That's just not true!" I insisted. "She was looking for you all the time. It hurt her that you didn't come. And she's worried about you; she nagged at me to check on you."

"We fought before she got so sick with that fire. I bet she didn't tell you."

"No," I said. "Not in so many words. I got the idea you'd had some disagreement."

"It nearly came to blows," she said, and she laughed harshly. "Imagine two old women carrying on like that!"

"But why?"

"She meant to forget everything that's happened," Zephra said, "and I wouldn't go along with that. So I wasn't wanted. She was like to shut the door on me again. I wanted to know, Where does this go when we go, Mabry? Does it just die with us? How do I even know I've got it straight, with all these years gone by? I needed to talk it over. But she acted like I was asking her to live it all over again. She said she wouldn't go through it."

"She wouldn't with me, either," I said. "It made her ill for me to ask her anything."

"And here I am sick unto death from holding on to it so long. With Linwood gone, we're the only ones left who really know how things were. Dahlia knows some, I reckon, William some."

"Knows that you and Daddy were lovers?" I offered.

She shook her head ruefully. "Is that all you think bears knowing?"

zephra overby

Aspersions were cast long before me and Linwood had our—
what would you call it? "Love affair" sounds foolish. And it wasn't
true until Mabry made it true. She named it before it was so, and
then she left us alone for two long months to see to it.

Linwood worked on into the dark each night after she got
gone and no sign of her. He'd made the shaming visit to her
daddy, hoping for news, but there was no news. Long after sup-
pertime I'd find him on the front steps, staring dumbstruck into
the black. When I brought him a plate, he'd eat from it, but
otherwise he seemed to forget to look after himself.

He'd left off going to prayer meeting, and soon Preacher
came knocking. At the time Linwood was off helping in another
man's field. I was in the house weeping over a batch of scalded

preserves. The smell had about knocked me out; I'd put Dolly in the yard so as not to smother her. I had a length of ribbon, one end knotted to her waist and the other to my wrist, to keep track of her while I worked, for she was a scrambling-around thing by then, but the ribbon was too short for me to be inside with her outside, so I'd looped it to the pump handle and kept an eye out.

So that was the first thing Preacher saw, the baby tied up in the yard like a dog, dusted head to foot from wallowing in the dirt, fistfuls of wild onion, shrieking with joy. He called out, "Is there anyone looking after this child?"

I came out on the porch by way of reply. I didn't like that man after how he'd done Mabry. And it was clear he didn't care for me, the way he stood so stiff in his black suit clothes, hesitating before removing his hat. He didn't know the protocol for such as me—I was not the lady of the house, but I wasn't a colored girl, either. He made a show of brushing the dust off his hat, then tucked it under his arm, as if to suggest he'd keep it off now that he had it off, but I oughtn't think he doffed it for me. His graying hair was ropy with pomade, and his scalp shone through in places.

"Mr. Goss is helping the Pitchers today, two miles up the road," I said. "Was it something you needed?"

"It's you I come to see," he replied.

What in the world. Keep your head, I cautioned myself. Aloud, I said, "And here I am a sight. Please set right here." I motioned to the bench and went to untie Dolly. "I won't have you in to smother. I misjudged the stove and now there's tar for jelly and a good dress ruined." I tried to laugh, but he was silent. Dolly clambered at my legs until I caught her up in my arms and swung her around, then fitted her to my hip. I felt him appraising. Go on, get you an eyeful, I thought. I am good to this child, and she clings to me.

He swiped at the rough slats with his handkerchief before perching on the bench, then he got right to business. "Miss Zephra, where do you go for worship?" He looked about ready to spring.

"I've not settled anywhere steady," I said, to be slippery.

"Well, let me tell you Linwood Goss has been knit with us for some time now, and he brought his wife into the flock."

"That's the way he tells it, too," I sassed back, but I dared not look him in the eye meanwhile. I busied myself jostling the baby; she wanted constant motion, rocking and bouncing.

"I've not seen Linwood for three Sundays gone," Preacher went on.

"It's hard times," I said. "Surely you heard Mrs. Goss has gone off, the Lord knows where." Soon Dolly would break out of my arms and back to scrambling in the dirt. Things had got real busy now she was crawling. You had to be everywhere at the once, on full alert. That was how I'd backslid on the housekeeping in general and on that particular day ruined the preserves.

I watched his Adam's apple bob as he spoke. "Yes. I had heard. All the more reason he should be keeping company with us."

I kept my eyes on the satiny knot of his tie. "I reckon he's been praying quite a lot, just on his own."

"Ah, but he's not exactly on his own, is he?" I felt his gaze flicker over me.

"I'm needed here," I said.

"I'm sure you've been a great help to the Gosses," he allowed. "But you can see that this present arrangement is in no ways suitable. It's not fitting for you to be here with the wife gone." It galled me, but I couldn't argue. What could I be to him but a slattern who half-kept a grubby child? There was nothing he could see to refute it.

"I'm needed here," I repeated. Dolly started fighting her way out of my arms, and I lowered her to the ground for fear of dropping her.

"My wife has offered to take the child in." Dolly had scooted over to him and was tugging at his pant cuffs. He leaned over and slapped her dirty hands away. It startled her more than it hurt. She began to wail, and I scooped her up and took a couple steps back. I pictured making for those cornfields again.

"Linwood wouldn't have that," I said before I caught myself. Preacher's eyes lit up.

"Surely *Linwood* wants to do right by his child!" He had to nearly shout to be heard over Dolly's cries. "It's best for her to be in a house with a husband and a wife, not this bachelor arrangement." Those appraising eyes again. "And you nearly a grown woman. Don't you hope to marry?"

"Mabry's not gone for good," I said. Meanwhile the baby was fighting me with everything she had. Her britches were shitty, and I worried he could smell it. I set her down by the pump and handed her the dipper to play with. She hushed, distracted quick as that.

"So you've heard from Mrs. Goss."

"I've not heard from her directly, no. I just feel like she will." It seemed right as I said it. It would take both us women to run the place right and have a little something left for ourselves. One could take up where the other left off and beat back the chores, leaving us both a little room for dreaming.

"I fear she's lost to us forever," Preacher insisted, swatting at his pantsleg where Dolly had left her clay prints. "I don't know what demon seized her could drag a mother from her infant child."

No! I wanted to shout. No demon! She needed to tear loose. With me here she knew she could, and I'd meanwhile keep Dolly safe and Linwood consoled. She knew she could come back and

I'd ease the way. I couldn't say that, though. Alongside that feeling was pondering: What would happen if she never did come back? How would it go then? And which way did I want it to go? My addled thinking must have shown, for Preacher sighted an opening and pressed on.

"Linwood would want what's best for this child, don't you agree? And what of your folks? Don't you think Ida Snow has need of you?"

Her name, him calling them *my folks,* it was chills down my back. I hated Ida Snow, and I pitied her, and also I chastened myself daily for leaving her to go it alone. She was the closest I'd come to having a mother. More like a mother wolf with all those wild ones running loose and snarling about her. But for the littlest ones, who'd not got big enough to do harm, I hated them, and yet and still I felt beholden for the years I was fed, and I knew she'd held tender feelings for me, the only girl she would ever have. It was boychild after boychild she'd birthed, only for them to outgrow and lord over her.

"I'm hoping you'll make it easier on Linwood," Preacher went on. "He's not bound to put you out, but you peril both your souls by staying. If you want to help him, you'll relieve him of the burden of putting you out. *If* you want to help him."

I felt the man's true power then. It wasn't any healing touch or casting out of devils—those were bluff and bluster, working only if you already believed—but instead it was the way he recast the situation, made his way look reasonable and yours selfish and wrong. He weakened your opposing. And when he saw how soft and uncertain you'd become, he pressed your thinking into a new shape.

"It might be that Mrs. Goss is afraid to come back," he ventured. "After all, you've about taken her place now, haven't you? It might be that you run her out to begin with."

I flew mad at this, but he held up a patient hand. "Now, I'm not saying you intended it. But that's how sin creeps in, on stealthy feet. One thing happens, and then another, and then the way is cleared to sin and you've only one more step to take to pass over into it. I'm saying you're that close, little sister. And Linwood right behind you, bound to follow you in. That's why I've come. Let me pull you back from the brink. Will you pray with me?"

He bid me kneel before him in the dirt, and my legs gave in before I'd fully decided to mind. He bore his palm down on the top of my head, the fog of burnt fruit stinking like sulfur around us. The baby was gurgling behind me, her shit odor rising as she clambered closer and dug her little fingernails into my back. She clung to me, and his words floated over the top of us.

"Milk!" she chirped. "Milk!" That cleared us a path away from him. Preachers must be bid good day and hungry babies fed. But he'd soon be back, I knew.

I stirred the three of us a charm soup. In secret, for I knew Linwood wouldn't abide conjures. It wasn't a Christian practice, to be sure, but I didn't consider it devilment, either. Only a fancy, to bind us all together. It was a gift from my woman, Ida Snow.

I'd gone to her alone while Preacher had Linwood to dinner. He'd been entreated to bring Dolly with him; Preacher's wife said she'd made a frock for her and was longing to dandle a baby again. I knew Linwood in his right mind would never consent to their offer to keep the child, but he'd been overcome by rift and bafflement. I feared he'd give in to them and all would be broken.

Still, I bathed and powdered Dolly fresh and sweet, then dressed her in an eyelet gown, near like a christening gown it was so fancy—not that we held with christenings. Mabry had done most of the stitching, and I'd finished it out. I pincurled her one small tuft of hair like a Kewpie doll. I wanted it plain how well-cared-for this child was, so they'd know she wasn't generally hog-wallowing in the yard.

"Don't you come back here without that child," I warned Linwood.

He blinked in surprise, sputtered, "I'm not aiming to."

When they set off for the preacher's house, I paid a visit to Ida Snow.

I went so she could berate me and be done with it, then we could make our peace. Ida Snow had a wisdom, and sometimes she could alter the course of things in a small way, though she was fickle in her helping and seemed in no ways able to shift the sorry state of her own house. I kept a small blade in my pocket, not sure I could use it, but carrying it steadied me. I figured to stay clear of those men, anyhow: her husband and her eldest son. Sunday dinnertime meant they were sure to be laid up somewhere with a bottle.

Ida Snow seemed to me an old woman then, though she couldn't have been much more than forty. Her face was riddled with cracks, her hair steel-colored and patchy at the scalp from being pulled so tight in a topknot, and her skinny body was pure wore out, those stretched-out bosoms swinging loose inside her cotton shift. But her eyes shone like jet buttons. They didn't miss a trick.

"I knowed you wasn't coming back," she said to me by way of greeting. "But what have you gone and got yourself into? Is it true you keep house with that man and the wife gone?"

"I've already heard it from the preacher," I said flatly.

"You mark me; she'll come back. And you've no position in that house."

"I'm needed," I said, my refrain.

"Is your monthlies still regular?" she asked.

"Yes! If it's any of your business," I shot back. She'd been always so prying, and it still could shame me red. Used to if I'd slipped off to squat in the woods, she'd ask me the second I got back, in earshot of anyone, "Did you make a bad job?" She concerned herself with such as that.

"Used to be my business," she muttered.

"When was that *ever* your business?" I'd never got so bold with her and half-expected her to strike me. But she kept mild. Bid me come inside with her.

Filthy house, like no one had taken up a broom since I'd gone. She rooted around in the kitchen drawers until she found what she was looking for. Pulled out a paper packet of seeds. Ground them fine with a mortar and pestle, poured a mug of thick coffee, and shook a fat spoonful of the black powder into it. Then she sugared it well and handed me to drink, laughing when I balked.

"You've been drinking it five years gone," she said. "Ain't likely to poison you now."

"What is it?"

"To keep your monthlies regular," she answered, black eyes flashing.

"I told you they are."

"To *keep* them that way," she said. "If he's not been at you, he will."

I took a sip. It was the same strong brew I remembered, just a hint of bitter underneath the sugar. She'd fixed me a cup of that near every morning since she'd deemed me old enough to drink coffee.

"There's something takes hold of a man," she went on, "and if he's not learned to control it he's no more than an animal. I can't help it my husband's no account, but I did wrong by my boy. He was my firstborn, and I was so crazy for him I couldn't deny him a thing, and so he growed up caring only for himself and turned out no better than his daddy. Maybe worsen."

"Whyn't you give *them* something?" I demanded. "Keep them off of me to begin with?"

She shook her head sadly. "I done the best I could by you. I gave Ellis saltpeter the once and it like to have killed him. I didn't dare try it on my boy."

"I don't think much of your best," I said. "All the time you made out like I was the one causing trouble."

I hated her house where the wind blew right through the slats and you could see specks of sky through the roof unless it was drizzling rain right on top of your head and nobody swept the hearth so it was soot tracked everywhere. There was no rest to be had in that house. And in the hateful yard nothing but strown trash and crabgrass overrun with scrawny hens, their droppings everywhere you set your foot but seldom any eggs, and what few you could find had paper-thin shells and were like to smash in your palm.

"Well, I best be getting on now," I said, wearied.

"You'll want to finish your cup," Ida Snow insisted. "Then I'll show you how to do the seeds."

"I don't need any such seeds," I said, but she pressed the packet into my hand.

"Here's the rest of these," she said. "Lord knows I don't need them anymore. Come and let's walk. There's a few things I can tell you yet. You wouldn't know it to look at me, but I have managed to arrange *some* things to suit me in this world." And she walked me to a field of Queen Anne's Lace, where we picked the foamy blossoms clean. Sometimes she placed her arm about my waist as we walked along, and it helped to wipe clear thoughts of her flying at me. I understood, too, that when Linwood had come to fetch someone to sit with Mabry in her birthing time, it was Ida Snow he'd been seeking, and she'd sent me in her place, intending I should stay gone.

I told her about Dolly, how I loved her as my own and desired for us not to be parted. Of Linwood I said nothing, though my longing must have been plain. She described to me the binding soup in an idle, sidelong way, as if we were only speaking trifles. There was no other way for her to offer, nor for me to accept, such a gift.

Into the broth I dropped one of my eyelashes and a thread from my dress. Then I filched a hair from Linwood's comb and pared the tiniest sliver of Dolly's fingernail to add. Otherwise the soup was mostly barley and beef. The true receipt called also for binding herbs, nettle, boneset, a handful of grasses gathered during a waxing moon. My version was incomplete, for I feared to poison us. I knew it would do as she intended, but the result might be to bind us all together in death. Any power my soup held was in the stirring, the strength of my wanting spun thick. I filled two bowls, sopped a biscuit for the baby, and the three of us ate of it.

Of course it was with Mabry's ladle, her enameled stockpot, the well-blacked stove I boiled the soup on, her wedding gift from Linwood.

Linwood declined Preacher's offer to keep the child, though he did start back to Sunday services, even promoted my going. I begged off, saying Dolly was too fidgety yet to be held for a straight hour or more. He agreed, on the condition we study scripture together in the evenings, and I was glad to, for he left off his gloomy silences and joined us at the table for meals again.

I started taking my bath in the early morning while Linwood was still abed. Not so he could see—I kept behind the curtain—but he could hear the washcloth stropping at my skin, a scrap of cloth hung between us. I was doctoring my coffee with those seeds, but nights I kept Dolly curled up with me on the pallet. I didn't know what I wanted to have happen.

Then Dolly took ill, just milksick, but I was up with her two nights running, after long days of shoring up for winter, putting up new preserves, burying the cabbages and potatoes in straw pits, bleaching apples, picking the cotton rows clean of scatter in what was left of the daylight, set on gathering an extra bale. I was accounting for Mabry in our provisions, and the added work stamped out my sometimes wish that she'd stay gone.

At the first light frost, Linwood helped the landlord slaughter hogs, and I stood hard hours beside the wife, scraping hide, rendering lard. The wife was sharp and impatient, quick to scold me if I erred, but I knew this work well and gave her little to complain about.

Linwood was paid in hams that he salted down for later use. Snout, tongue and tail, paunch, heart, lights, and brains were offered me to clean and cook for my household, or dispose of as I would. Dead set against waste, I soaked and boiled and skinned those leavings, chopped and fried them, hid them in gravy, but after days of being elbow-deep in fresh meat and innards, I found I had little stomach for them. Only Linwood ate hearty, his appetite back.

Wore out, I took ill as I never had before, with wrenching aches and chills that set my teeth chattering. Then it was fever dreams: I dreamed of the Ellis Snows, Senior and Junior, running me down and grasping at me. Their hands were meat, leaking red on my dress. I dreamed I'd forgotten Dolly and left her tied at the pump for the sun to beat down upon, and she'd tangled in the cord and choked; Mabry was coming home and would not forgive my lapse. Jelly boiled over on the stove, hot black rivers of it that scalded the skin off me. Or else it was the soup in poison waves.

At the fever's peak I thought my head was busting open, but Linwood put me in his bed and doused me until it broke. I felt him praying over me; he'd pulled off my dress. When I came to again, my sweat had dried to salt and I was cool beneath the sheet. I was wearing a dimity gown, one of Mabry's.

I called out and Linwood appeared. He covered me with a quilt and asked was I hungry.

"Dolly?" I asked, still close to my dream.

"She's with Preacher," he said. I started up at this, and he bid me stay calm, explaining it was only until I got well. "If you can eat I'll fetch her back in the morning," he promised.

Landlord's wife had stewed a hen and she brought a great bowl of it to me, with orders that I eat every bite and have Linwood to scald the bowl before returning it. My illness had made her all the fiercer with me, but I understood it to be fondness and concern mixed up with not knowing what to make of Mabry's absence. I propped myself up in Linwood's bed and took slow sips of the broth. It was greasy and strong-smelling, and my stomach was shrunk to the size of a pecan.

Linwood sat by the bed, his own charity plate of greens and pork balanced on his lap. "You had me scared," he confessed.

"It was just an ague," I said. "Nothing for it but to sweat it on out."

"You cussed me when I made to get the doctor," he said, laughing a little.

"I did no such thing!" I had no recollection, anyway.

"You rose up out of that bed like a wraith and said you would be gone before I got back. And I believed you would, too, though I'd probably find you laid up in the ditch. You wouldn't have got far, sick as you were."

"I guess I didn't need no doctor," I said. It worried me to think I could say and do things and not remember.

"I guess you didn't." He grinned at me. "You're stubborn as somebody else I know." How is it you can love even a man's crooked teeth? I wanted to put my whole hand up in his mouth and count them, then rest there in the red roof of it, holding fast to his tongue.

With Linwood the joining was natural as breath. The one favor the Ellis Snows could be said to have done me was it didn't hurt. But they stayed far from my mind on that day. I reached for the man that I loved, and for a blessed span not another soul was on this earth.

The Baptists would not care for me saying so, but to my mind it was near like being saved. The feeling was not so different from that. Where you thought was solid brick and mortar, all of a sudden a door opens right smack in the center and you wonder why you never saw the light pouring in around the edges before, for the door was always there, it is your seeing has changed.

This was all stolen time; we didn't speak of Mabry, nor of judgment. If Linwood felt remorse, he hid it from me well. I thought like the child I still was, that here was the shape of the rest of my days rolling out before me.

But it was only days. Soon, a boy with Mabry's face brought me an envelope penned in her careful hand and postmarked Richmond. She'd sent the letter to her father, and he'd dispatched her brother to deliver it, still sealed, to her husband. Already our situation carried a stink. A wife run off, a girl with no people of her own still set up in the household with the husband. Mabry's father would not himself come, much less involve himself as far as reading the letter, and her brother couldn't linger, though I offered cake to tempt him into waiting until Dolly woke from her nap.

"Your niece!" I said.

"Daddy says I'm to come straight back," he explained. He looked to be no older than thirteen.

I said, "You're Wallace, aren't you? Mabry told me you were the dickens. You favor your sister."

He seemed to like that. He went with me to the back of the house and looked at Dahlia sleeping. He asked me shyly, "Is she good?"

I remembered he would have had a baby sister that size but that she died, and his mama had, too. It made me sorrowful for Mabry all over again, her grief pushing and pulling her every which way, sending her as far off as Richmond. And here I was, growing fat off her leavings.

Linwood was to town, and when the boy left I stood over the stove a long time holding the letter. It was not in me, finally, to destroy it, but I shut it in Mabry's old school primer the first day and slid it under a loose floorboard the next. It was a shameful thing to have hid it, but I did hold back from opening it. On the third day I carried it around in my pocket, hoping it would fall out and the wind would take it. When at dusk I patted for it and found it still there, I handed it over to Linwood.

I can't recall as we talked the matter over much, only that we were in accord: he must, of course, fetch her back, now that he knew where she was. There was precious little to talk about; she was his wife. We wouldn't have fine-combed the other matter, either. You just didn't work over every single thing like they do now, all your feelings and so forth, all your private business dragged into daylight. I mean sex. It would have mortified me to even bring it up. I'd done my leave-taking in the three days of holding that letter.

I did venture this: "She might not come back with you."

Linwood agreed. "She might not. And I can't force her to."

When he stayed gone three days, I knew he'd done his leave-taking of me. So I scrubbed that house from floor to ceiling. And boiled the linens.

With us women looking after the tobacco, Linwood could hire himself out more for carpentry. He was smart with that. That bit of extra helped us get ahead. And he had a good relationship with the landlord, who knew he didn't have to worry over us like he did over some. We took care of the property. As for what others might have said about our living situation, well, Landlord didn't traffic in gossip. He appreciated hardworking people, and the rest was between us and the Maker, he said. By the time he died he'd left instructions to sell Linwood the plot we were on. And by then Linwood could buy it, for there was cash money in the bank. Tenant farmers had only figures on paper for income, pluses and minuses and carryovers. But with Linwood working his trade, we had savings.

Once you've got to where you can buy some land, buying more isn't so hard. We took on more acreage and hired help to work it. Linwood bought an old Model T, a real rattletrap, held together with hairpins was how Mabry put it, but it served to take him each day to the center of town, where able men waited for work. He'd waited there himself many a morning, knew the eagerest were out before first light, so he came at dawn and many days loaded in as many bodies as the car would hold. I'd have them a batch of biscuits waiting and strong coffee to drink, for it was a sorry thing to set to work without something on your belly and dinner so far off. If we had a crowd it took me and Mabry both to ready the dinner, but oftener I went to the fields and came back early to help her finish and serve it.

Mabry kept the books. She learned to drive that hateful car, and she wore white gloves and nylon stockings to town to fight the bank for extensions, proud not to have to send her husband; they would deal with her direct. She put me in charge of the hired labor when Linwood started building houses, saying I'd be good at it because I made folks ashamed not to work as hard as me. I'm not sure she was praising me on that.

By the time William was born, we were doing all right. Since the government had stepped in on tobacco and set up the allotments permanent, the brightleaf wasn't growing just everywhere you looked; now you could hope to sell it for something. Linwood built three small houses on allotment acres, making us landlords. It took some adjusting to. Our own house was getting crowded, and the Delco lights strung overhead showed every dingy stain to full effect. Mabry wanted indoor plumbing and a sitting room. I started dreaming a bedroom. I was still sleeping behind a curtain and little Dahlia beside me, though we shared a bed by then and not a pallet. Linwood stayed so busy with the other houses it was hard to get him working on ours, but Mabry took a hammer to the walls to get him started.

He walled in the porch to make Mabry's sitting room and added on two small bedrooms. For a time I loved the room he made for me, with its smooth plaster walls, a window that looked out over the garden and the fields beyond it, and a door I could shut or leave open. The other room was for the children, who could be heaped together while they were little; I do believe he thought there would be a few more children yet.

We marveled at how quickly William started sleeping through

the night, but it turned out Dahlia was waking at his slightest sound and tending to him. She'd scooted his crib right up alongside her bed and would thread her arm through the bars to rest her hand on him while they slept. He was William, she insisted, never Willy or Bill, and if anyone tried to call him otherwise she was fierce in her objection. She'd long ago quit answering to Dolly.

When William started walking, I felt sure it was only so that he could follow Dahlia everywhere. The first time he trailed her to the road, she scooped him up and took him on to school with her. They were sent home early with a note, but you could tell the teacher was tickled because she wrote that he should be toilet-trained and know the alphabet when next he came to visit.

Linwood tacked that letter to the wall for the longest time and laughed every time he looked at it, but Mabry was furious and swore whippings if it happened again. She was ashamed, too, and I knew the true reason: I'd seen William follow Dahlia and watched her take him in her arms and head down the road. Something had held me back from saying anything to Mabry. I'd been waiting for her to ask where he was; I'd been waiting for her to notice he was gone. It wasn't fair of me to test her like that—it wasn't so out of line for her to assume he was being looked after, and it was only a couple of hours, after all. But that she could put him so far from her thoughts unsettled me.

William was stout, but Junior was poorly from the start. Doctor called it failure to thrive. That didn't tell us anything. A crop will sometimes founder, and you can't point to hail or drought or flooding rain to account for it. Such as that gave rise to folks planting by the signs or the bunkum of old wives' tales. Was the moon in the feet when Junior was born? A poor time for setting fenceposts or planting beans. What wrong threshold had been crossed, who missed the image in the well that foretold his death? Who swept under the bed or over someone's feet? We would have bathed him in three waters under a new moon to dodge his fate had we known. But we were modern folk now, buying mechanical cultivators and factory fertilizer in burlap sacks. Bottled formula for the sons, for nursing had passed out of fashion; it was too like an animal, and we were busy women, needing to pass babies back and forth.

Mabry told me Ida Snow came once the doctor said there was naught to do but pray. She dosed Junior with tonics, but he slipped away in his sleep as I held him. I don't recollect any of that, only that my hands shook as I sewed the satin liner for his box and the needle kept punching my fingers so that spots of blood marred the fabric and Mabry said it was all right, we could turn it the other way and it was altogether fitting that my blood should go in the box. I don't recollect his face, only that it turned up to mine as a flower drinking the light.

All of us sick over Junior, and then Dahlia was gone, never to return. There'd been trouble brewing with that girl, an early bloomer and stubborn, for a long time, but we hadn't heeded the signs there, either. William was a solace, but he came up in sadness and a silent house. Linwood grew to lean so hard on him. Put him to work soon as he could drive a nail. Mabry kept mostly to her side of the house and talked of bringing in a colored woman for the housework; the notion appealed to her vanity. Too, she was letting me know, and I heard: I was no longer needed. Not even for field work, as there were tenants on the land now, and they didn't welcome my visits. Thought I was spying. I hardly knew what else I could do, but I started casting about for other keep.

For near to a year I worked at the cotton mill over in Stoat and roomed with a widow lady who kept company with all sorts and drank herself to sleep every night. I was shut in all of the day breathing cotton dust and minding all my fingers stayed attached to me. I was shut in all of the night listening for the slap-together of bodies that told me the widow lady hadn't yet managed to kill herself, and the snores afterward that reassured me she hadn't gotten someone else to do it, either. It was miserable times, and I longed for William, who had to hide his soft nature or have it crushed. I worried he'd be taken out of school altogether and know nothing but labor and his father's grief hardened over.

I heard that one of the tenant families was moving on: a disappointing yield, some squabbling over numbers. Or maybe it was just that they were sorry at it. Some folks went into farming that had no business to. I don't like to think Linwood would have been less than square with them—he'd been dealt so fair by his own landlord—but I didn't feel like I knew him anymore. Nor my own self. I remember thinking I was owed something more than what I'd gotten, and on that belief I moved into the vacated house to work it on shares as any tenant would, only I didn't square it with the Gosses beforehand; I just moved on in and let them know my plans. I meant to lease it fair, but I wasn't asking permission.

I knew then as clearly as now: I'll live here until I'm buried, and that nearby, I hope. William stayed here with me often as he could, and when he grew into a man I hid my tears and pressed into his hands what little money I'd put by for him. I knew he'd go off, money or no, so I just as sooned he had some. By then he would have no more took from his father than his father would have offered. It tore Linwood up for William to leave, and though I knew he'd driven his son out of all our lives and had only himself to blame, I pitied him anyway. All of his children were gone.

I managed my plot pretty well with seasonal help and Linwood taking my leaf to market. When I was younger and still strong, sometimes I trucked cucumbers and melons for extra. One year I tried pumpkins and for a spell one small patch of Christmas trees. But always I grew the tobacco. Of course I can't grow anything anymore, can't half see, can't work for naught. The people who lease it now keep it all in tobacco. They own land all over this area, but most of theirs isn't allotment. They're mostly in soybeans, with some sweet potatoes and sod. That sod looks like rolls of carpet when they truck it off, and people pay all kinds of money to lay it out in their yards rather than to wait on some seed to sprout. I never thought I'd see such a thing as that.

They'd like to buy this little plot, I imagine, and once I'm gone they're welcome to it. Once I'm gone. I wouldn't mind at all a little family to put a trailer here and keep up that plot for themselves, but things don't work that way anymore.

avie goss

I still loved to go around barefoot in the yard, but the sensation seemed different than I remembered, and at first I couldn't figure out why. Where the grass left off, the ground stayed soft and mossy underfoot, spongy around the spots I'd watered recently. Then it came to me how it used to be with every step we were grinding pecan hulls beneath our feet, the cool dirt riddled with shards. There'd been two pecan trees then. The one that remained yielded nothing, just dropped a few indifferent leaves. I asked Mama what we might do about it, thinking some kind of fertilizer could set it right again.

"It won't produce anymore," she said. "Hurricane Edward took its mate tree. Probably too old, anyway."

I remembered that storm. It had struck three weeks into my

first semester of college, at that point the longest duration I'd been away from home. I'd enjoyed being on my own so much I'd been ashamed. I'd been glad about the storm's odd track across the middle of the state, hoping it would give me another weekend to myself—however much they wanted to see me, my parents wouldn't want me driving in that weather. I watched the winds lash trees through the rain-blurred windows of my dormitory room. Lydia, then my brand-new roommate, had a bottle of peppermint schnapps and we passed it back and forth. Until she slid open the window a crack and let the storm whistle in, I remember feeling safe, content. I don't recall wondering how Regina was faring.

But no. Mama had it wrong. It had to have been Hurricane Claudia that felled the pecan, just a couple of years ago. We hadn't lost any trees with Edward, though the storm slopped plenty of debris onto the lawn, which my father couldn't let lay. He raked and bagged sodden leaves and hauled off branches all the next day against the doctor's orders and my mother's wishes. "Go ahead, then," she must have said to him—it was the kind of thing she said when thwarted—"Go ahead on and kill yourself," and was more indignant than sorrowful when he collapsed and died.

When Claudia hit, I had just moved to Fortune, Ohio, with Jack—or, rather, *near* Jack, or *for* Jack—and my own storm clouds were gathering. I had been arguing with him and repeating my idle threat to leave. When I saw on the news how the hurricane had taken an unexpected turn inland and swept the North Carolina piedmont, I gleefully seized on it to prop up my case: I would have to go home to help my mother, and I would never come back. I had Jack scared, even offering to buy two plane tickets—round trip, of course—so he could come with me.

Then I got scared, too, when I couldn't reach Mama over the phone; the lines were down, and the television footage was of caved-in houses and sluiced-out fields—timely evidence that the world was bigger than me and largely indifferent, and a hurricane was not merely a force I could harness to add credibility to my bluffs. That this came as a revelation was only further proof of how small and closed my life had become since I'd put Jack at its petty center.

Mama got a call through to me a couple of days later, and she told me I didn't need to come; there was nothing I could do, anyway. Everyone was fine, she said. Nothing but a tree down and it frail to begin with. Neighbors were already slicing it into firewood. It had glanced off the roof as it came down, but the house remained sound.

That Mama could confuse two storms four years apart worried me a little, until I caught on to her track of reasoning. Hurricane Edward *had* taken her mate tree, my father.

With a switch Mama tapped out the rows she wanted for winter planting: peas, onions, turnips. The rest I was told to seed with rye grass to cover until spring. "Looks better that way, and it keeps the soil good," she explained. "We'll have the yard man to plow it all under when we're ready to plant there. That's if he's not too put out with us over the grass-cutting." She'd not even had to fire him herself; she'd only had to mention to her church ladies when they visited that I would be cutting the grass from now on. The news had made its way back to him, and he'd stopped coming.

"Never mind him," I told her. "If he doesn't want to do it, I'll rent a tiller and do it myself." I kind of relished the idea, though I had no clue how to work a tiller. I'd grown to like yard work on its own merits, not just as labor to distract and exhaust me so I'd fall dead asleep at night. It was still tiring, but it calmed me, too. In the evening that low dull ache in the small of my back was permission to sit and rest. I could let go of my mind for a little while without it veering into dangerous places.

There was a slight chill when the wind blew, enough for me to drape a thin cardigan over Mama's shoulders, but the air felt cleansed by it. Her breathing came unhindered that afternoon, and her color was good. Her still-smooth cheeks shone from the sunscreen she'd slathered on. She looked more vital than anyone in her condition should, trim but no longer scrawny, her once stick-straight posture now bowed only slightly at her shoulders. The walker and the wheeled canister of oxygen gave her away, but even these she bore regally as she carried out her inspection.

The maple trees were brilliant yellow, though shedding fast; I could clearly discern their skeletons of black branches. The scuppernong along the back fence was still lush and green but had recently been stripped of its plump gold grapes by birds, no doubt the same ones who'd fattened themselves on our cherries over the summer. There would be no jelly, Mama lamented, though she preferred Concord grapes for their color. "Can't seem to grow them no more," she said. "The vines were blighted." I thought of that spoiled batch of Zephra's jelly so long ago, the scalding dark rivers of juice she dreamed.

Mama still directed my every move in the yard, but I was slowly claiming some of it for myself, staking out spots for my own plantings. The border around the house seemed promising; it was mostly shrubbery, dull boxwoods alternating with maroon barberry bushes. There were two peonies flanking the front porch, but I counted those as bushes, too, clad in iridescent purple-gold leaves for fall; their anty, cabbage-sized blooms would only appear for a couple of weeks in spring before collapsing in the heat. In late summer, I'd clipped those sagging, rotten blooms, and the slumped-over branches had sprung back up, freed from the weight.

The rest of the bushes were gapped and uneven from my zealous but unskilled pruning efforts. "Cut to the quick," was how Mama described them. She hadn't minded much, saying they'd fill in again, but she still hadn't gotten over my pulling out the smilax vine that trellised the roof overhang. Early on I'd mistaken it for yet another of the wild vines that had tangled up her yard, binding tree branches to fencing and choking plants, the kind of weed that for days I'd ripped out with a vengeance, that had scored my palms like fishing line as I pulled. I'd only wanted the exertion then, the bliss of tearing out the roots, and was not yet up to making distinctions. Now that I knew one thing from another, I wanted to patch up all that wounded border with flowers.

"I didn't care a thing for outdoor work when I was younger," Mama mused, "and now I'm just crazy for a garden. Zephra used to live outside, but now she won't look after a houseplant. Her yard has pure wasted away since Linwood passed."

"It looked all right to me. Maybe she's hired someone," I said, and I saw my opening. "Though how she could afford it, I can't imagine," I ventured.

"Shoot," Mama said dismissively. "That woman has socked away and socked away. And she's worked all her life, at any little thing. I know she's got the money; I just can't believe she'd let go of any."

"Are you joking?" I said.

"For her own doings, I mean," she conceded quickly. "She'd give to anyone who needed, and she spoiled *you* rotten."

"I'd say she did pretty well by you, too," I said. "She never got married or had her own family. She just took care of yours."

"Well, that's just the way it turned out. By the time she might have started looking her a husband, most of the men had gone off to war. The good ones, anyhow."

"What about Daddy? He wasn't in the war."

She laughed. "Well, shug," she said, "your daddy was already married!"

"That's not what I meant," I said sharply, startled by how close she was skirting. "I meant Daddy wasn't in the war, and *he* was good." I was getting petulant and could hear the whine creeping into my voice. "You said all the good ones went to war." I didn't know how to feel about him and Zephra, but it seemed they'd all three agreed to it somehow, and it could even be said Mama's running off had started it. And anyway, my father was a good person. He just was.

Mama eased down the rungs of her walker, lowering herself gingerly to her knees. She began pinching the heads off browning mums. "You know I didn't mean your daddy wasn't a good man. He served his country," she assured me, deliberately casual, eyes to her task. "He built barracks for the German prisoners they shipped out here. He worked hard. We all did." She snapped a final blossom, then scooped them all up in her palm. "You can't think how it was then. Zephra had a better life with us than she could have managed by herself. We thought that Depression had settled here for good, even after the war. If you didn't own land, you were set to work on it till you fell over."

"Well, you and Daddy did all right," I said.

She rubbed her palms together to shred the flowerheads, scattered tiny yellow petals like confetti. "Linwood had seen a better life. He was born to it. His folks had land in Virginia and people to work it. He knew that to have anything, you had to have land."

I thought of the Gosses' grim portraits, blurred by smoke and time. They'd left him nothing, but he must have honored them to keep their pictures hanging. "Why did he break with his family?" I asked.

"Honey, I don't know much about that. There was something between him and his father that never was fixed. And then Mr. Goss was dead and it was too late for mending fences." She stared blankly for a moment, considering. "I tried to tell William about that, to warn him, but he was a stubborn boy grown up to be a stubborn man. You got to make it up with him, I told him. You got to make things right before he's gone. He wouldn't listen. Linwood neither." I must have made a noise in my throat, because she looked up at me then. "Don't you say a word," she warned.

"Say what? You ought to follow your own advice? Okay, I won't say it."

"Am I the one holding grudges? I credit her for the life we made. I give credit where credit is due."

"Okay, okay—"

"Course it worked both ways," Mama said, backpedaling. "She did for us and we did for her."

"Yeah," I shot back, "you got to have the land and she got to work it for you."

Mama said nothing. The crushed petals gave off a musky pollen scent as her hands sifted them. The yellow of the maples and the yellow of the chrysanthemums fused together with the sun behind them. A few stray leaves floated over us.

Then abruptly she clambered up her walker, struggling to pull herself to her feet. "Let me do it!" she snarled as I bent to help her. I backed away and waited, ready to lunge forward and catch her.

She was winded by the effort, too much so to speak, and she stood there hunched over her walker, hands gripping the rails as her breath came harsh and fast. I noticed her cannula dangling free, detached by her efforts, and as I moved in to replace it she waved me away and fit it to her nostrils, took a few labored sniffs, and began her shuffling journey back to the house.

In the evening I heard her switch off the TV. She called out to me, distress in her voice, but it rang out clear and strong. She'd been fuming all afternoon, framing her speech. Maybe if I riled her continuously, I thought, she'd have a full recovery, system purged by anger.

When I got to her bedside, she motioned me to sit. "I don't know what Zephra's been telling you," she said, "but Linwood wanted to put that property in her name when she first started living there, and she wouldn't have it. She insisted on working shares, said she didn't want special treatment. He banked all the money she paid him over the years and willed it back to her with the interest. *And* he deeded her the land."

I didn't know what to say.

"Your daddy was a good man," Mama said, "but that wasn't all he was."

Not quite winter, yet the seed catalogues now jamming our P.O. box admonished Mama and me to Make Ready for Spring! And we complied, dog-earing pages and dreaming of the months ahead. There was the lone hellebore's promise of khaki-pink flowers to get us through winter. It was an ailing shrub, so I staked and fertilized it and hoped for the best.

The catalogues, I couldn't help noticing, devoted whole sections to dahlias, their bright and showy blooms spread broad as dinner plates. Of the riot of flowers Mama raised, I wondered, why didn't she grow the one with my sister's name? Mama said she never could make them thrive in her carefully tended beds, black and fusty with peat, though they flourished in some other yards. Each season she tried to plant the costly tubers, she was disappointed.

She'd named her first daughter before she became a real gardener and knew her soil's limitations. The name seemed a little extravagant then, as the Depression still hung over everything. Yet the only luxury available to this child, she'd reasoned, might be her name, so let her have it—though Daddy quickly shortened Dahlia to Doll. She lent herself to it, being small for her woman's name and needing it clipped, like unruly hair or wings.

This was the sort of thing I knew about my sister. Though I'd heeded her demand to come home, and she'd been calling regularly and with all solicitousness since, we were practically strangers. After I answered her shy inquiries about Mama's progress, we struggled ineptly to fill in the years that lay between us. So many promising beginnings of conversations faltered on our reticence and careful dealings, if not outright halted by Mama's apparent terror that one of us should be bankrupted by the long-distance bill.

My notion of what had happened to Dahlia was therefore cobbled together by hints and details gathered over years, *a wild child, aimless, can't depend on her,* and colored over by my romantic notions, *the man she refused to name wouldn't have called her Doll, having known the full length of her.* I knew she'd gone away young, perhaps been sent away, hadn't returned as expected, and hadn't ever quite been forgiven. I concluded, naturally, she'd been "ruined." That old story.

It couldn't have been a local boy, I decided, or else a wedding would have been imposed. I imagined the man as a seller of notions, come to Regina to stake out new territory or just wandering on a lark and finding himself in the midst of a church social. He'd carry a false-bottomed valise, the thimbles and pocket combs and mother-of-pearl buttons displayed in the public top half, the compartment beneath concealing vile ointments and prophylactics.

Before him her suitors would have been mere boys, polite but furtive, glad enough to linger on the front porch under cover of twilight, pretending to play with her little brother while offering her soft words under breath, but none was ready to make a public bid on the boxed lunch of the girl with two mamas. It wasn't from virtue that she'd given nothing to these boys; she was curious and not unwilling. But she resented the secrecy. Her folks, after all, seemed to hold no secrets from anyone. "Blood will tell," I imagined the tight-faced ladies would cluck when Linwood ushered them into church each Sunday, but his family would witness with the righteous, he'd insist. Nobody whispered at *him* in the street. That was saved for the rest of them, who knew how to be ashamed.

The stranger fanned out crisp bills and held them aloft. Heads pivoted and necks craned so everyone could get a good gape at him. She was pretty, and it was generally thought she might do well for herself in some place where folks didn't know one another's histories quite so intimately. She was doomed as dirt in Regina. People stared, but no one spoke a word against her.

There were a few bewildered claps as the crowd cleaved open for him to claim his prize. He offered Dahlia his arm, and they joined the other couples on the riverbank. He made his money back, and then some, that afternoon, selling notions out of his case to curious parishioners. He might have fallen in love with her, in his fashion, he could see she was so new, so world-hungry.

She would have dived into his words so he would keep opening his pretty stranger's mouth to speak her.

He would have promised to take her places. He would have promised to buy her a dress of silky sapphire blue, cut to show off her collarbone. She could wear it when he took her to a cavernous hall where an orchestra played. She would marvel at the gleaming fiddles, how they swayed together as if in a great wind directed by the conductor's wand, sound pouring out and filling their ears— how they would dance as if borne along on that wind. Promises to tempt her into his car, down far-flung roads of rutted clay.

I clung to this pulpy narrative, though it hardly squared with the Dahlia I'd met. At Daddy's funeral, she'd given me a pen-and-pencil set by way of greeting, a belated high-school graduation gift almost studied in its neutrality. I hadn't seen her in years. I didn't think we were one bit alike. She was already middle-aged, heavily girdled and wedged into an old wool suit, her mudblond hair molded into a crunchy-looking cap. To me she was a sexless old nun, stoic and impervious to grief, and I disliked her immediately.

I was eighteen, skinny, and ocher-skinned from a fading summer tan. I wore my prom dress to the funeral, my only black garment, shimmery acetate with spaghetti straps, and I'd snipped the skirt short to flare above my knees. I was prone to flinging myself around in frenzied fits of sorrow and having to be led away and comforted. It was expected of me as the baby; moreover, my antics kept Mama busy looking after me until the last of the guests were gone. Then she put all the dirty dishes into the sink to soak and went to bed for eighteen hours straight, leaving me alone with my sister.

I let Dahlia clean up while I napped and made petulant phone calls and sulked in front of the television. I could smell lemon ammonia and bleach and hear her little grunts of exertion. When she was finished she came to sit beside me on the sofa, though she had to ask me to move my feet first. Her hands looked raw. She'd worked in cafeterias for years, so I figured her hands must look like that most of the time. My hands were soft, my feet soft, my hair gloss, my prom dress molded my breasts in silky little pockets. I was young and the whole house stank of sterile age, and as we sat there I schemed to go off with Harris Macon, my sometimes boyfriend from high school, that very night and let him do it to me.

Meanwhile Dahlia had been speaking to me, and I only caught on to the last bit of what she was saying: that I could do my part to help by returning the clean pans and casserole dishes to their owners.

"Maybe tomorrow," I intoned, staring into the television. I had no intention of doing anything at all to help. To my mind that was giving in to what had happened. She may have been able to clear away Daddy's death with a few soapy swipes, but I wasn't going to accept it without further railing.

"Suit yourself," she said. "If you do it now you won't be expected to stay and visit. It will take a lot longer tomorrow or the next day."

I turned to her to say something concentrated and hateful, maybe call her a lunch lady, *poor old lunch lady with your hairnet and varicose stockings, sneaking home gallon cans of succotash.* Then I noted the scaly red strip on her throat as she raked at it absently. Dahlia had dermatitis, same as me. Between news of Daddy's death and his funeral, mine had snaked behind both ears and scabbed up into my hairline, seriously jeopardizing my seduction plans for Harris. It was a small flash of recognition: Skin = kin.

Dahlia couldn't seem to cry over our father, but at least she'd had a flare-up. It made me relent on her a little, but very soon after the funeral I went back to school—fled, really—and left her to look after Mama.

Now it was my turn, fair was fair, and Dahlia would finally be making an appearance at Thanksgiving. I was a little resentful at the delay; I thought she'd been milking her sickbed aversion for all it was worth. But it wasn't all that easy for her to come, I realized. In her fifties, Dahlia seemed almost an old woman herself, with heart pills in a timed dispenser and arthritis eroding her knees. Her night vision was so poor she didn't drive after sunset. She at least *looked* more familiar to me now: myself plumper and steely-haired, load-bearing joints just starting to give way.

There'd be only three of us for dinner, because Zephra hadn't been invited. I knew Zephra had plans—Saul had organized a meal at the church and would pick her up and bring her home— but I didn't let on. I wanted Mama to think Zephra would be by herself and see if she could live with that, only it seemed like she was managing all too well. As for Zephra, I'd been surprised she'd agreed to attend what she called "the orphans' dinner," but Saul had a way of making people feel like they were doing him a service instead of the other way around.

"Nobody's spending Thanksgiving alone, so let's just leave it be," Dahlia said when I brought up Zephra and Mama's continued estrangement. She refused to get mixed up in it and said I shouldn't either. I agreed to stay out of it, at least for Thanksgiv- . ing. But what about Christmas? I might have to pull out the big guns for that, I warned her, with no idea what those big guns could be. Threaten to withhold Mama's oxygen? Lock the women in a room together for three days?

"They could both be dead by Christmas," Dahlia said. "And then maybe you'll be headed back to Ohio." She didn't mean that last part unkindly; for all she knew I still had a life there.

So it was just the three of us crowding the kitchen, bickering amiably. I was intent on making a Thanksgiving meal that at least attempted to observe Mama's dietary restrictions, but we were already at an impasse over the salt content of the dressing. The canned broth they wanted to moisten it with had too much sodium, I argued.

"I can't taste half of what I eat because of that no-salt business," Mama said. She was seated at the table, cubing slices of white bread with the outsized carving knife, her hands unsteady. I rummaged in the drawers for something smaller and handed her a serrated steak knife. She took it, experimented on a single slice, then took up the heavy carving knife again. "That just tears up the bread," she explained.

Dahlia deftly extracted a more suitable knife from the jumble of utensils. "We don't want any fingers with that dressing," she said lightly to Mama, and they swapped. There were lots of little things like that between them.

"Reducing your salt isn't something I try to do just to annoy you," I said to Mama, and went into my mini-lecture on fluids. People with congestive heart failure retained a dangerous amount of fluid as it was, I said. I reminded her of the edema that had swelled her feet so that they could barely fit into her shoes. Salt holds water. Less salt, less water. Even I was sick of hearing it. Nothing tasted good.

"Annoying you is just a fringe benefit," I added, tagging Mama gently on the shoulder. She reached up and patted my hand.

Dahlia smiled. "It seems like she doesn't eat enough to even worry about it," she said, "but we can stuff the turkey instead of making pan dressing. Then we won't need to add the broth."

"Great. Then we all die of food poisoning," I snapped. Dahlia's eyebrows raised slightly at this. "Well, we would if *I* made it," I amended. "You've probably cooked a thousand turkeys."

"Yes, I'm so old," she said dryly. "At least a thousand."

"I meant with your job."

"I worked the serving line until this business with my knees," she said. "I've maybe *carved* a thousand turkeys. But I can read a cookbook, same as you."

"Where's the cranberry dish?" Mama interjected.

"The turkey's probably too far along now to add stuffing, actually," Dahlia said.

"We should put out the cranberry sauce," Mama continued. "Not that anybody ever ate it but Linwood."

"It's okay," I said to Dahlia. "Let's just make the regular dressing. Maybe she'll enjoy her food for a change."

"I believe we can use the Goss china," Mama said. "Most of one setting is broke, but there's not but the three of us."

I must have overcompensated on the dressing, because in the end Mama declared it too salty and had me brown an extra batch of rolls. The turkey looked gilded, though, thanks to Dahlia's care, and we had last year's butter beans and corn from the deep freeze, a few token turnip greens from our struggling winter garden, and a dense, ginger-colored spice cake for dessert. I'd made the cake from Minnie's recipe the night before and was proud of my effort; my fingers were still stained orange from grating carrots. We ate on what was left of the fragile Goss china, still cherished in spite of its barely discernible pattern and flaking gold rims. It actually looked festive against the poinsettia tablecloth.

The cut-glass cranberry dish could not be located, so I upended a can of the crimson jelly onto a chipped saucer and left it to quiver decoratively, a food offering for my father. No one touched it, but Mama said it looked like Thanksgiving.

Mama ate slowly, with obvious pleasure. It was good to see. She hadn't seemed truly hungry since she was hospitalized, and she had always been a sparing eater, usually sitting back with her cigarette long before the rest of the table had finished. The food was better than our usual fare, but she'd said—and proven— many times that when you've got no appetite, it doesn't much matter what's put in front of you. It was a rare moment of contentment for her: both her girls with her and Zephra successfully out of sight, out of mind. Nothing to trouble her stomach.

The problem was, Zephra wasn't the only one who would bring up things Mama didn't like. Constrained by the phone until today, Dahlia and I didn't know what the boundaries were, and other than omitting Zephra, we spoke freely. Dahlia's upbringing was all privation, whereas mine was flush times—that truth was acceptable in the abstract. There were some entertaining contrasts to hold up, hookworm and polio fears versus the chicken pox, what the house had and didn't have, but college was a prickly item. Our parents had sent me, but not Dahlia or William. I wasn't comfortable with that either, especially when Dahlia made chastening comments about being able to read cookbooks, too.

To others Mama bragged unfettered about my meager accomplishment, but in front of Dahlia she must have felt she had to downplay it. When I referred to college in passing, Mama said to me pointedly, "All that schooling ever learned you was to *type*." That stung, and it wasn't even true. I was a lousy, three-fingered typist.

"It looks to me like Avie's done all right for herself." This from Dahlia. "At least she was smart enough to get to where she *could* go to college."

"You were certainly smart enough to go," Mama said. "If we'd had the means, you know we would have sent you."

Dahlia gave a derisive laugh. "Money was surely not the only thing keeping *me* out of college."

Mama was silent. Dahlia went on. "Don't you wish I would have 'kept smart' like you told me? 'Keep smart,' you said. Of course, I thought I was smart. I thought I knew everything. I didn't know enough to fill a jar lid."

"You had some troubles, yes, but let's not dwell on them today," Mama pleaded, casting nervous glances in my direction. *Not in front of the baby,* I inferred.

"Oh, Mama, it's all right," I said, exasperated. "I know about all that. I think I know all our dirty little secrets by now."

"Is that so?" Dahlia offered skeptically, but she seemed a little shaken.

Mama would barely look at either of us for the rest of the meal. Finally she offered, "This cake is queer-tasting. What'd you put in it?"

"You don't like it?" I sniped. "You don't have to eat it; you won't hurt my feelings." But my eyes welled up as I said it.

"I didn't say I didn't like it."

"It's not bad," said Dahlia, chewing thoughtfully. "But it's more like a bread. What kind of flour did you use?"

"I don't know. Wheat-wheat flour. It's supposed to be a whole-foods thing. Look, nobody has to eat it."

"It's not bad," Dahlia repeated. She took another bite and nodded encouragingly.

"The forks don't match," Mama announced. She'd pushed her plate aside.

"That's a *dessert* fork," I said. "It's supposed to be shorter."

"Don't you condescend," she shot back. "I meant the pattern is different."

Dahlia held two utensils up and studied them. "I can't see the difference."

"One is the sterling and the other is silver plate," said Mama, her voice torquing slightly, "only I can't recall which is what!" I knew what she was doing: She would either work up a froth over this, or she would seize on something else. She was good at creating diversions.

"They're pretty much the same, aren't they?" I said.

"One has a rose, a tiny little rose, down here at the tip of the handle. But is that one the sterling? Get me my reading glasses. Oh, why can't I remember?" she fretted. "Seems like it's the sterling with the extra rose. And no, they are not the same at all. Silver plate is cheaper."

"Maybe the sterling is shinier?" I ventured.

"If we'd polished it, maybe." This said bitterly; Dahlia and I had insisted it wasn't necessary.

"Oh, Mother, the sterling is stamped 'sterling'!" Dahlia said sharply. "We'll sort it out later. It's nothing to lose your mind over!"

Mama put down her fork and rubbed her temples. Her whole body seemed to slump with fatigue. She had been awake since dawn, after all, wanting fervently to help with the preparations and being doled out little pity tasks by her daughters. Cut up the bread. Put ice in the glasses. We'd behaved like spotters as she'd set the table, poised nearby at the ready in case she dropped something. We might have let her polish the silver, at least.

"You shouldn't mix them," Mama admonished me weakly.

"I'm sorry," I said.

"Will you quit picking at Avie?" Dahlia said, unrepentant. Mama started sniffling.

"What is it now?" Dahlia demanded.

"It's nothing," Mama said. "I'm being foolish. You girls made a nice dinner. It's just that I'm so tired now. I believe I better go lay down." She pushed against the armrests with a low moan of exertion, but couldn't quite lever herself up out of the chair. She let go and crumpled over, sobbing into her hands.

Though either of us could have managed her slight frame alone, Dahlia and I got on each side of her, linked arms, and whisked her to bed. Her feet barely skimmed the ground.

"So. Just what is it you think you know all about?" Dahlia asked me later, attempting lightness, though her face was tight with anxiety. I confided my speculations, minus some of the more fanciful flourishes, like the false-bottomed valise. Was I close? I wanted to know. She laughed. It was close enough, she said. She claimed she had nothing to add to it, but Mama was resting quietly, a third pot of coffee was brewing, and the evening lay before us. Years still wanted filling in.

The man took such audacious liberties Dahlia didn't know how to put him off. She'd only been instructed in how to rebuff a kiss, but when she turned her head so it would land on her cheek and not her chaste mouth, he nibbled her neck instead. His hands were frank and searching, and having found their way under her dress, soon made themselves at home. She'd let him do this before she had even the first drink, so she wouldn't blame the drink for that. He fed it to her from a slim flask of brushed silver metal etched with initials that didn't match the name he'd given. (It would be unclear to her later whether she would not or *could* not name him.) The liquor made her cough and sputter at first, but then a glow settled over her and soon it made sense to lie beneath his animal-warm body.

Dahlia understood what she was doing. She was cut from the family's cloth. Her blood told. Her hair was a flag; she sheared it to her chin. Linwood cried when he saw. Mabry admonished and Zephra clucked, but neither of them minded so much; hair is another burden to women, heavy and full of snarls.

She saw no reason to pretend. When the man's car came rumbling up the path, she would bid the family good night and run out to meet him. Her father wouldn't let what other people thought keep him out of church; she would likewise worship what she wished, as she wished.

It astonished her when they tried to make her stop. Then it enraged her, their punishments and prohibitions, when Dahlia had had only secret beaus and her brother for friends. If they didn't want her walking out that door, fine; she would step out a window. They'd block the window and she would smash it. She'd lived it their way and now she'd live it hers.

She knew there would be consequences, but she was thinking only of whispers and pointed fingers, pointed remarks, things she was used to. She laughed and kept going to church, all the while her dresses shrinking. The man stopped coming around. Dahlia's belly, now straining against the seams, roiled morning and night, and for a small satisfaction she would think of him sick in the ditches after too much love and drink. He'd not been much more than a boy himself, she knew that now.

Dahlia went to Zephra first, in private, hoping she'd give her something to drink, give her a little prod in the right spot. She'd already leaned herself nearly in two over the porch railing and waited for the gobbets of blood, but none came.

Zephra started basting smocks. Mabry went to bed for a week. Linwood made inquiries, first to find the man, and when that proved unsuccessful, to find a discreet place, a house for errant girls, until the matter was concluded. There were many such places then. A girl who found herself "in trouble" could wait it out among strangers, then come home and make a fresh start.

So Dahlia was to be sent away—for her own good, Linwood insisted, but by then he was barely able to look at her. She hoped her mother and Zephra might rally against him, but in the end they agreed it was best. Dahlia thought that their hearts were hardened to her, but saw later how they'd packed loving things in her satchel: cream-colored notepaper, a fountain pen, lemon cookies, and the softest flannel nightgown. Tucked deep in a book of verses a note from Zephra: *Mabry is your real mother but you are every bit as much mine.*

The note gave away no secrets; Dahlia had never doubted who it was that birthed her. She figured Zephra wanted to assure her that someone else could love her baby just as well. Dahlia only hoped whoever it was would do a better job, because she felt no love, no longing, no wistful regret for this child not yet born. She just felt fat and sick and cheated of pleasure.

You can put it all behind you now, everyone said. Dahlia took them at their word and didn't return to Regina. Some other girls from the home had found work and rooms for let, and Dahlia followed suit. Everywhere she inquired, they were seeking "girls of good character," and she decided that wasn't specific enough to exclude her from the running.

When she applied at the Sanitary Restaurant, the owner warned her there'd be lots of workingmen to lunch and supper, and some could be coarse. He didn't want a shrinking violet, but he didn't want a hussy, either. Dahlia began working there that same afternoon. She held little fear of men, but little interest in them, either. She felt that she'd experienced the extent of what they had to offer, and her curiosity was gone. The men were very interested in her, though. It was amusing.

Once, Dahlia accepted three dates for the same evening, and they all came to call. She ought to have expected it, but still she was surprised to see them waiting silently in what passed for a parlor in her rooming house: two rocking chairs and a bench on the neatly swept wooden slats of the front room, an oval rag rug the centerpiece. The landlady lingered disapprovingly in the kitchen, jumbling crockery in the sink. Her roommate had gone to the cinema.

"You're on your own," Alice had demurred, laughing when Dahlia had begged her to stay and help. Owen had a gold tooth Dahlia almost couldn't stand the sight of. She thought if she could get around that tooth, they'd have something to work with; he was quick and clever and worked steady at the railyards, but when he'd sought to press his face to hers she'd had to pull away. Paul had a lovely tenor voice but was too short and thick to suit her. His clothes ill-fit that blunt body, pants so tight at the thighs that the pleats flattened. He was the landlady's nephew and left sweet little notes for Dahlia in the stairwell, weighted by small parcels of fudge wrapped in foil. She would give the fudge to Alice, who held the notes aloft and sang them, reeling around their tiny room, Dahlia begging her to hush. It made Paul seem ridiculous, and she was afraid the landlady might put her out if she spurned him outright.

Harlan was the new one, the one she couldn't figure out. He was a distant cousin of Paul's and the two were companions, but the landlady held no affection for him. "His father and uncle are ministers," she'd whispered to Dahlia, "but no men of God. All dalliance." And Dahlia, whose father had inclinations to preach and also to sin, had noted Harlan's considerable height and fine dark features and even teeth and murmured *that would be fine* when he asked to pay a call.

Owen and Harlan sat stoic and furious, forced to share the bench. Only Paul tried to put a good face on it, handing out gum and crooning Sinatra tunes. A fine, rich voice he had, glossing over the silence and her cruel, hapless deed. Dahlia could only wait stricken, lips pursed to resemble a smile, not sure whether she wanted to cover her mortified face, burst out laughing, or weep. Why had she done it? She might have visited with each in turn and weighed their individual faults and strengths, let one emerge as best—or as least distasteful, as the best she might hope for in exile, her error laid aside. Her Fresh Start. She was demure in dress and speech and would surely have rebuffed a kiss even if Owen's gold tooth had not winked and flashed. It might have dazzled her, before.

The landlady ducked her head in the doorway to offer coffee, and Owen was the first to break. "I'll be on my way," he managed with the barest civility, and left. Paul seemed to believe Harlan had come to pass the time with him, not Dahlia, so he was jovial when Owen was gone. He'd brought Harlan around before, wanting him to see the girl he liked best. He thought Harlan had a steady girl and liked them more showy than this one, besides.

The remaining three were served coffee, and Dahlia stared desperately into the black depths of her mug.

"I see you don't take cream," Paul noted cheerfully.

"No, I . . . Helen doesn't normally keep it around. Now I'm used to it this way." She bit her lip. She'd as good as told Paul his aunt was stingy. Her offenses were piling up: Owen ridiculed and spurned, the landlady insulted by her remarks and common ways. She'd be turned out into the street. It was the old vanity made her assent to three callers.

"Helen's known for her thrift," Paul noted amicably, allowing the slight to pass. He turned to Harlan. "You want to go for some cards later?"

"Might be."

"I'll meet you there in a bit," Paul offered. Harlan stayed put.

In this way Harlan's will was accomplished, with silence, a refusal to budge or explain. He would wait, and there would be capitulation. That's the best she could come up with for why she married him: He wouldn't back down.

At the time she thought he must love her to want this so badly. But he wanted only what was withheld from him. She learned to comply quickly, not because she feared him, but because the pressure would cease, he would turn his attention elsewhere, and she could breathe again. She denied him nothing except children, but that was denying him everything. His drinking got bad, and when he was too laid up to go after another bottle, she brought him one. He liked her to drink with him, so she would. Then her drinking got bad, too.

She didn't think they could keep going like that. She thought she would get out once she'd had all she could stand. But you wouldn't believe, she said, what all you could stand.

Dahlia left off there and attempted safer topics, but that meant questioning me. What had I been doing? Was I seeing anyone? Surely I didn't plan to stay on here with Mama indefinitely. What were my plans? I didn't want to field any of those; moreover, her story was still unfurling in my mind. "What became of him?" I blurted.

"Harlan? Dead." Her voice was flat. "He promised me that's what would happen when I left, and he kept his promise."

"Oh my God," I said. "Oh God, I'm so sorry."

"Why be sorry?" she said sharply. "It's not *your* fault." It seemed an odd thing to say, but at the time I took it for the kind of sarcasm people lash out with when they can't bear your sympathy. Don't *you* be sorry; *you* have nothing to do with it.

For the rest of the evening, she held me more politely at arm's length, limiting our conversation to the care and feeding of Mama. She left earlier the next morning than expected, saying she'd like to spend a couple of hours with Zephra before heading home. Mama seemed relieved to see her go.

For days my thoughts darted in every direction, small, excitable fishes. Besides dermatitis, was that the only other thing Dahlia and I had in common, I wondered: a high threshold for difficult men? That was our inheritance, I decided for a few despairing moments—that and this shitty, madeover firetrap of a house. Abruptly I concluded that all I'd done with Jack was to blindly pattern my parents' relationship. Where else would I have learned to settle for such divided love?

Though if anything, my role had more in common with Zephra's, minus the cooperative understanding with the wife, the child-rearing and shared-labor aspects. Had Jack's wife known about and tolerated my relationship with her husband? It was possible, even likely. Ours was the flimsiest pretense. Why drag your young assistant from town to town? For her exceptional phone skills? Why would she always agree to go? Wouldn't she have her own life to consider, a boyfriend maybe? Jack's wife must have made a very concerted effort not to linger over these questions. Or maybe she considered me a silent partner in the care and feeding of her husband's enormous ego. Time he spent with me could have been respite for her. I didn't like to think I might have been causing her pain instead.

Maybe the thing my parents and Zephra did that weakened me to someone like Jack was to let me believe that no one who loved me could ever hurt me; they kept me too soft and trusting. Hard to fault them for that.

The unimaginable thing was that these were the same people who sent Dahlia away to have her baby. It seemed so cold and un-relenting. They must have thought it was for the best, to salvage her reputation, to keep her marriageable, but she was hardly more than a child when she was banished. All for the sake of some propriety that the rest of the household clearly had not ob-served. Was it their own reputations they were hoping to save? From what Dahlia said, people had known or at least suspected that Zephra shared more than Linwood Goss's house. The more I found out, the less I understood.

If legitimacy had been the issue, I wondered why Mabry and Linwood hadn't presented Dahlia's baby as their own, a common ruse. I doubted many people were truly taken in by it, having noted the daughter's confinement over the preceding months, having joked about the aging mother's sudden burst of fertility, her virtually symptom-free pregnancy, and how swiftly her figure was restored. But the claim would go unchallenged, and eventu-ally it would become the truth, and two futures saved. Widely spaced siblings trump ruined girl and bastard child.

Perhaps I would have been sent away, too, if I'd gotten preg-nant and there had still been maternity homes. When Minnie got pregnant, her parents tried to foist her off on family in Charlotte before the boyfriend caved in and married her. That was the cautionary summer Zephra took me to a clinic for birth control pills. I couldn't tell whether Mama knew about it, and I didn't dare ask. In some things they conspired and in others they acted alone. The pills helped my complexion but were otherwise unnecessary. I'd always been the pal-around girl in high school; my deepest crushes had treated me like a kid sister. I remained a virgin by default until college.

My first time was nothing special when it did happen, a sloppy bounce on a dorm bunk. I was drunk and a little high after a party—it took nothing at all to get me that way, alcohol fumes and secondhand smoke—and the guy got ahead of me and it hurt for a jackhammer minute before he let out a strangled cry and slumped against me. I got a little more practice in before graduation. But it wasn't my dubious sexual talent that eventually attracted Jack's attention.

I think he viewed me as another project, an overlooked property with potential. Certainly I didn't think myself incapable of all-consuming passions or above treacly melodramatics—I was just untested. I'd never even had a serious breakup. My few actual boyfriends and I had amicably drifted apart. I'd been incubating in that Portage duplex, waiting for someone to tell me what to do next. If my mother had had any idea how I was living then, she would have summoned me home, and I probably would have obeyed. But Jack found me first, and, I thought, saved me from that disgrace.

As a developer Jack could spy promise where others saw only floodplains or formidable zoning restrictions; that was what had made him successful. It must take a supreme confidence to change the very landscape, and Jack had that. He could make the most unnatural things seem necessary, even beautiful. Pave over all those goddamn stagnant fields! Give the people a place to buy a latte, or a fat velvet pillow, or fifty spiral-bound color copies of something. Nothing wrong with blacktop, its diamond glitter in the moonlight, hurling off heat like the desert floor. A place to linger by our cars until chat turned furtive. A place to leave my car, or his, for a few hours.

No one had ever behaved so rashly over me before. It gave me the illusion of having power, though I was more suggestible than ever. Very quickly he needed only to observe, *my wife does that;* behavior eliminated. Or better: *my wife* won't *do that;* I'd become an expert. I thought to define myself against her, figuring he must be unhappy or else he wouldn't rove, and by offering things she wouldn't or couldn't, I'd be the viable alternative. He wasn't going to leave her to marry me, and he never suggested he would. Still, it took me much too long to understand that by "we," he would never mean us. "We" denoted only "me and my wife." The "we" that was him and me had never haggled for automobiles or spent a week in the Catskills or chiseled up the bathroom tiles. I became a pinched grammarian, spurned by usage.

I learned things about her I couldn't bear knowing: that she was stylish, kind, thin, and resourceful. That her children were her life. That she would forgive if asked. When she showed up on my doorstep one afternoon, I hid like a thief. Jack wasn't there, but his scent was in all the cushions, the carpet, the wallpaper, and I was terrified of letting her in.

Two days later, I called her up, nervously intending to confess and renounce Jack, but she disarmed me by being glad to hear from me and prevented my disclosure with friendly chatter. Soon

we were talking on the phone regularly, and she—Simone—
began *confiding* in me. Her nine-year-old wetting the bed. The
unprecedented hair sprouting from her chin. Things about Jack
he'd never disclosed to me. He was Catholic, I learned from her.
I remember thinking perversely that if Mama could get over his
being married, she'd never get over that. The Catholics *idolatried*
the Virgin Mary, she'd told me once.

Sometimes I was convinced Simone was toying with me,
inviting me to disclose in turn what she already knew quite well.
Other times I was shocked and shamed by her innocence, and I
would want to do something kind for her, like maybe offer to
babysit so she could have a romantic evening alone with her husband. It was madness to ever pick up the phone.

"I want a baby," Jack said. We were in bed. He was inside of me.
Simone had had her tubes tied after their second child. She wondered sometimes if she'd made the right decision. I guessed she
hadn't. I knew such terrible, intimate things, it was intolerable. I
swore at Jack and pushed him away. "We can talk about it later,"
he said. He pulled me closer and tried to resume, hips rocking
gently against mine, but I started crying and he let go.

In a few days he started in again. "I mean it," he said. "I want
this to happen. I can make it work." To afford such a secret, to ab-
sorb it all with wealth, or to pay off the consequences—I think he
viewed how he'd meet the challenge as another measure of his
success. His mingled terror and longing for it would keep him
working late hours and hoarding cash.

I knew he felt himself entirely capable, but I'd seen him con-
duct a lot of business by then. I knew his method was to set a
thing in motion, then move on to the next project and forget

there was something rising up in his wake. It was no longer his concern. I was afraid of what he'd do (or worse, fail to do), and I was even more afraid of myself. I knew I needed to stop drinking, but I didn't want to. I didn't want to lose Jack, either. I had no idea whether I wanted a baby or not.

"You don't want a baby with me?" he demanded, incredulous. "You don't love me? Or you don't trust me, is that it?" To prove I did both love and trust him, he wanted me to throw away my birth control pills. I had three months' worth on hand, and he watched me punch each tablet through the foil backing and drop it into the garbage disposal. Then he brought champagne and waxy florist tulips, the petals thick and bright as marzipan. I got so stupid drunk I don't remember eating the tulips or getting sick after. Jack said the bathroom looked like somebody bombed Holland.

I threw away my birth control pills, but then I got an IUD, which I decided was none of his business. Slippery, slippery girl, wriggling like a trout out of his grasp. No courage but plenty of guile.

Let the buyer beware: An IUD is not recommended for women who have (a) never had children or (b) still want children. The first two doctors I went to refused to fit me. You're young, they said. You don't know what you'll want. In all good conscience, blah blah blah. By the third appointment, I dug my heels in. I said I knew what I didn't want. I didn't want to get pregnant and I didn't want to keep taking the pill. I said I had my reasons, I knew the risks, and I'd sign anything to that effect. I got the IUD and a pile of cautionary pamphlets.

It was cheap and effective, no telltale pink plastic compacts to hide from Jack, and technically I was holding up my end of the agreement. It also made for a bloodletting every month, to help remind me this union was either death or a kind of medieval barbering.

Snow started falling and gray skies descended, a smothering blanket I couldn't burrow out of. I didn't go to Regina over Christmas. I told Mama I couldn't get enough time off and that anyway the flights were tricky because of the weather. I couldn't stand for her to see me. My last visit had required a constant stream of lies, inventing friends and colleagues and activities, and I wasn't up for it. Not in a dry county.

There was a brutal ice storm in January, during which Jack stayed at home, at his home. Lots of roads were closed, downed power lines snaking and sparking everywhere. Simone called to see if I was all right; did I need anything? She told me that a child had been killed on his sled; the metal runners had sliced through a power line and conducted enough voltage to stop his heart. "I can't stop thinking about it," she said. "Promise you'll stay indoors."

I didn't leave the apartment for a week and quickly reverted to my Steerage routine of staying up all night and sleeping late into the day. I was anxious about my dwindling alcohol supply. I could feel the cold shimmering in through the walls. I longed to go fishtailing down the street, find an open grocery, but not even the locals were trying it. Outside there was only wind cracking branches. From my window I could see the parked cars mantled in a cloudy glaze of ice, unmovable, and I thought of something I'd read in a magazine, about cattle caught out on the prairie when the weather turned. As they grazed, the vapor from their breath froze, suffocating them where they stood, fixed as statues. When I ran through the brandy and wine, I drank cough syrup, then mouthwash.

When the mouthwash was gone I set out on foot for the liquor store, impossibly far away, and fell twice before I ever reached the main road. The first fall was no more than an icy slap; it cleared my head. The second time I came down so hard I heard my tailbone crack.

Impossible, the doctor would say. It was only a hairline fracture, the X-ray showed, painful and for a time debilitating, but no permanent damage. I couldn't have actually heard it crack. But as I lay pressed against the ice, my ears rang as if a thunderbolt had hacked right through me, and I knew I was broken.

"I think I'd like to get out of here a little bit tomorrow," Mama announced.

"I can drive you wherever you want to go," I said.

"I don't want to go anywhere in particular," she said, "I just want to do some riding around. If that doesn't wear me out entirely, we'll go visiting next time."

"Sure," I said. "Sort of a dry run." I hoped this meant we'd soon be headed to Zephra's house. One of them had to give in. I'd been to see Zephra once since Thanksgiving, and she'd sworn she'd not go to another orphans' dinner, she didn't care how young and good-looking a man came to pick her up.

I was still trying to understand Mama's anger. Not that there wasn't plenty to be angry about; Zephra had been her husband's lover, after all. But they'd lived with that arrangement for years, so presumably she'd accepted, even sanctioned it.

Zephra had her own grievances, and predictably, I found myself somewhat more aligned with her. Mabry could be said to have won, after all, if they'd actually been competing for Linwood. It was Mabry he'd married and stayed married to. She held on to the official title. What did Zephra have? Zephra just wanted to talk it over—not to broadcast it, but to get some acknowledgment from the only other living person who knew the whole story. And Mabry refused.

She might have refused all those years ago, when she came back from Richmond to find her place usurped (and why come back at all?); she could have thrown Zephra out and no one would have blamed her. But she hadn't. She must have needed her too badly. I imagined Mabry as Zephra had described her after giving birth, and I could see it in myself just as clearly, laid up with my cracked tailbone, how listless and spread to nothing you could get. To have someone step in meanwhile and run your world with tireless cheer and efficiency, mopping your brow until the cloud passed, asking nothing but scraps in return—that might be harder to forgive. "I'm beholden to her," is how Mama would have put it, and she'd have wanted to leave it at that.

We set out after lunch the next day, and I drove us as Mama directed, tracing the miles she used to walk, arms swinging, when her lungs were still pink. I'd rolled the car windows up tight to keep out the dust and chill, and Mama balanced the mini-tank petlike on her lap, where it sighed at regular intervals. We cruised out to the more prosperous edge of the county, where between pine thickets and stony fields whole neighborhoods of mansions were rising out of the clay. Could there be this many rich, we both wondered, and the bulldozers still gouging?

"Your daddy never built such as these," she observed, "but he'd build to suit the people who wanted to live in it. These are all pretty, but not one is special. Just big."

"I'd like to take a look at his houses," I said eagerly. I had a vague recollection of accompanying Daddy while he visited his tenants, collecting the rents or performing small repairs. Most of those arrangements had ended while I was still a small child.

"Well, you know he helped with the church, though they did over a lot of that when they added on. Other than that, not much is left, I don't think. Of course, you've spent right much time in the one," she added, referring to Zephra's house.

"Let's take a tour anyway, see what all of his is still standing." I turned the car back in the direction of town.

"Yes, get us out of Beverly Hills," she joked. "I'd hate to have to clean such a big house. Now, you want to see a real mansion, look at the governor's house."

"I've seen it. School took me and you took me." I couldn't remember it, though. "You need to tell me when to turn."

"Now, that was something. Gables and turrets and whatnot. And nothing else like it. The man who came up with that? He married a woman for love, but she was Indian, so by law she couldn't be his wife at all."

Fields of blackened cotton, a brick ranch house with a swimming pool. "Hmm," I said. A crossroads grocery, windows boarded over. A tobacco barn crosshatched by dried vines and filled with glinting metal scraps. "Tell me when," I reminded her.

"She was considered colored," she continued, "and with him white never the twain shall meet—except of course it did all the time. That was right after the Civil War, so there were hard feelings concerning the colored. It didn't matter she was educated. You should have turned back there," she added.

I pulled over to the side, counted to ten, then carefully got the car reversed without putting us in a ditch. "Don't say colored," I reminded her.

"All the society people would throw their parties and invite him to come, but not her. He'd broke the law, too, but he was still invited."

"Did he go without her?"

"I don't know. I reckon he would have had to go to some things if he wanted any more business to come his way. He started building her a house, way far off. Away from the prying eyes." She straightened suddenly and pointed. "Yonder's it."

I hit the brakes.

"One of Linwood's, I mean," she added. "Not that architect's."

"Yes, I figured that," I said.

Stranded in the middle of a weed-choked lot sat a simple A-frame, its buckling porch shot through with saplings. The rounded doorway was its most distinguishing feature, set in field-stone and mortar like the arch of a bridge. Otherwise it looked like Zephra's house, slightly larger, but with the same disarming symmetry that formed a face with blank window eyes. If the lay-out was the same, and I felt sure it was, the entrance, smack-dab in the center, would open up into the sitting room, which would back directly into the kitchen. There'd be a bedroom on either side of the sitting room, a bathroom off of the kitchen. Daddy must have been drawn to such a constrained, orderly design. Our own house seemed so eccentric in contrast, with all its add-ons and modifications and chockablock furnishings. I marveled that he'd kept on living in it, knowing himself capable of building something so much more suited to his nature.

I searched for a place to turn in, get closer, but there was no sign of a driveway or even any furrows in the dirt to give a car access. Just tall, forbidding weeds.

"It's all snakes and brambles now," Mama said. "Let's just look at it from here." She snorted with disgust. "I don't understand it. One part of the county is all up in gaudy mansions and another corner's left to rot."

The arbitrary eye of the developer, I thought. If you weren't looking to plant crops, it was all the same, trash trees and barren

field. But no, there were still factors in choosing one site over another. Availability was one. Ease of negotiations another. Lack of
restrictions. Dirt-cheapness.

"Who used to live here?" I asked.

"The Pitchers had Linwood to build it. Their son and his wife
lived in it a long time. It was their wedding present. Linwood did
all the masonry himself, learned it as he went. That was a job. He
swore he'd never do it again."

"That's too bad," I said. "It's pretty."

"Oh, he kept doing it." A sharp laugh. "He swore against a lot
of things he kept doing." She ignored my look. "Everybody wanted
that stonework. Get us back to the crossroads and I'll show you
another one out this way. Seems like somebody was even living in
it not too far back.

"He was always going to build us one from scratch," she
added. "He bought a plot way out in the countryside where he
was going to build us that dream house. But I guess he did good
to keep up the house we have as well as he did. He was working
all the time." She watched the scenery in silence for a while,
breathing in tandem with the sighing tank.

"You all right, Mama?" I asked. She was turned to the window,
so I could only see the back of her head, the hair thinned and
wispy from constant leaning against the pillows, tender scalp
showing through in places.

"I'm fine." She settled back in her seat. "I just needed to hush
for a minute. Do you know I believe the woman who rents that
plot now is growing gourds on it. The little ones you varnish and
put on the Thanksgiving table. Wish I'd remembered that before—we could have gotten our centerpiece from her."

We headed in the general direction of the gourd patch, not

so much from a need to see it as to have a sort of destination in mind. Along the meandering way we found:

A listing, weatherbeaten shack, its red tin roof just visible through the trees. *Used to be a little store my daddy bought from on credit, had run up a great big bill that Linwood paid off when my ma'am died. I don't think Daddy ever got over that. Linwood taking his debt, I mean. He got over Ma'am dying.*

An obviously inhabited (motorcycles in shed, trampoline in side yard) two-story A-frame with familiar-looking stonework. *What did I tell you? Linwood couldn't say no to anybody, and then the man who hired him to build that was so hateful he wouldn't hardly pay what they'd agreed. I had to haul that fool to court.*

An aluminum-sided bunker with no windows, a row of screen doors along the front flapping open or hanging off the hinges. *The first and last one of those he ever built. He said the rooms were like jail cells and each one to house a whole family of migrant workers. That really shook him. He said people ought not to live like that, and I said, Shoot, my family near about lived like that. Those were hard times, he said, nobody should have to live like that in this day and age. I said there's hippies living in tents and they like it; maybe the Mexicans like it, too. Anyway, Linwood was getting too old to keep up the carpentry work.*

A trailer ringed with yellow and purple pansies, *right pretty and they'll take the frost, snapdragons, too,* next to the sunken remnants of a house foundation, *doesn't surprise me one bit nothing left, filthy house should have been burned to the ground. Poor Ida Snow was pure useless as an herb doctor and had a mess of children she couldn't keep fed or out of trouble. All because her sorry husband was a seventh son. She wanted a seventh son of a seventh son, thinking he'd have powers. There's no telling what would have come of Zephra if she'd stayed among those people. Wonder are there Snows living in that trailer now? Looks too well kept.*

The gourd patch, once we reached it, was a bit of a letdown. Just a few cracked and overgrown crooknecks left among the vines. "Nothing that wants varnishing," Mama said. Subdued, we headed back toward town. I thought of how little remained of the work my father had done. And those self-righteous words of Mama's: *There's no telling what would have come of Zephra if she'd stayed among those people.* Had she fared any better with Mabry and Linwood? How could Mama just cut her off like that? It was like denying she'd ever had a life. I felt that we had to go to her.

"You missed the turn," Mama noted uneasily as we passed our driveway.

I took a deep breath. "I know you don't like for me to even bring it up," I began, "but I've got to get on you again about Zephra." I waited for the silencing glare, the admonishing struggle for breath, but she only shifted in her seat, slid the mini-tank out of her lap, and propped it carefully by her feet.

"I just had to move this thing," she said mildly. "It was putting my legs to sleep. Go ahead on."

"Don't you think it's time to make peace? Way past time? I don't care who started it. You need to put out the olive branch."

"You sound like that preacher boy. Neither one of you seems to understand that she doesn't care to see me."

"Was she supposed to invite herself to Thanksgiving? She thinks you don't want her to come. I'm thinking of putting you out here, just to get this over with." As we approached Zephra's yard I slowed the car, easing it toward the grass. Her house seemed barely to regard us, a sliver splitting the drapes.

"Don't you do it!" Mama shrieked, and half in anger, half jest, I jerked the car back onto the road and accelerated past the house. She grabbed hold of her shoulder belt and gasped as the mini-tank tumbled onto its side, narrowly missing her stocking feet, then rolled under the seat and wedged itself there.

"You need to mind your business is what you need to do," she said, but then she laughed a little and shook her head. "Tearing out of there like a fool," she muttered.

"You think she saw us?" I asked.

"Might have seen a blur as you went shooting by," she said.

I took us downtown. The sun was setting and I thought Mama would enjoy seeing the recently installed Christmas lights come on. We parked at the post office, but I kept the car idling so the heater would run. I pointed out the *Progress* office above the dance studio and described its powder-pink walls, the massive desk I shared with Minnie, the pristine almond cases of the new computer and printer, the lightboard and wax roller I used to piece together the tabloid pages—Mama was not likely to ever climb that many stairs again. Minnie had put up window decals of both a Christmas tree and a menorah, clearly visible from the street, and the combination amused Mama.

"She must be hedging her bets," she said.

I was glad my display stand was safely indoors, because the wind gusted suddenly and worked loose a snippet of garland from its lamppost. Half feather boa, half tumbleweed, we watched it writhe down the deserted thoroughfare as the sky deepened and the lights winked on. The mini-tank sighed. It was unbearably melancholy.

"You know she died before he could finish the house," Mama said abruptly.

"Who died?"

"That Indian woman. It must have been lonesome with her architect husband at his society parties and nothing for her to look forward to but a house set way off by itself. She didn't have a friend in the world. Not even any children to cart her around." She patted my leg and smiled.

"I've been stubborn, I know," she said. "Just let me be stubborn another day. I look a fright and I'm wore out. If she sees me like this, she'll think I'm like to die in her house. We ought to call first, anyway."

If she could face Zephra, I thought, surely I could talk to Jack. The familiar state of being hostage to the phone, needing to hover nearby, available, made me feel close to him all over again, as if we were constantly on the verge of meeting. I needed to get that conversation behind me.

And after I did, after I called him with such resolve and crawled back home with his terrible assurances still corrupting my ears, I shut myself in my room without looking in on Mama and, with the aid of two expired Seconals exhumed from the depths of the medicine cabinet and dry-swallowed, escaped into staticky sleep.

I didn't heed the phone ringing late in the night, or Mama struggling out of bed to answer it.

On the other end was silence—or, rather, there was no speech. Mama thought she could hear breathing.

(You came by the house today.)

(Yes. Avie carried me, and I was ashamed to knock. I'm sorry.)

(I'm the fool in this. I might have come to you instead, sick as you've been.)

(We both are fools.)

(I reckon so. Well, it's come my time, Mabry. I've got to set this burden down.)

(I wish you'd let me go first. I didn't want to be the last one.)

(It's not for us to choose.)

(Go ahead on, then. I'll not be long behind you.)

(This weight is heavy, Mabry, it pulls on me.)

(I'm carrying it now. It's mine and always was. Now fly. There's nothing here to hold you.)

Just breathing, Mama said, then the line went dead. But a weight, hot and dense and needful as an infant, had been passed to her.

OVERBY

Zephra Abigail age 75, December 12, in her home, of complications from stroke. Visitation Griffin-Mosier Funeral Home Monday 6–9 p.m. Memorial Service Regina Witness Baptist Church, Tuesday 11 a.m. Daughter of Strom and Nicey Overby. Orphaned at an early age, she was informally adopted by Ellis and Ida Snow. She worked as a domestic helper and field hand, eventually managing a small farm of her own, where she chiefly grew tobacco. She was a member in good standing of Regina Witness Baptist Church. She is survived by . . .

When Saul came to the house the next morning, his expression was so grim I thought for a moment he could tell I'd taken those tranquilizers. I still felt spacey and faint, and no doubt looked it. But he had other business.

Mama knew full well why he'd come. She was already up and dressed, waiting for the official news. She didn't blink when he told us. I didn't either at first; the message took time to penetrate the gauzy layers of my understanding.

"Miss Overby dialed the rescue squad," he explained, "but

apparently she wasn't able to speak because of the stroke. The dispatcher sent someone out to check on her, but she was already gone."

Which was more politely euphemistic, I wondered inanely, "gone" or "passed"? "Your father has passed" is how Mama had put it when she called me home from college. He'd passed, and now he was gone. Then I got hold of it: Zephra, gone. "Oh," I said. "No."

Mama just nodded. Saul had tissues at the ready, but she appeared too composed to have any use for them. He inclined the box toward me, and I clutched several in my fist, wadded them into a blossom I pressed to my face, inhaling the dusty perfume.

"Mama," I choked. "We could have been with her yesterday." I hadn't considered Zephra dying first. "I should have insisted on it." I didn't yet know about any peacemaking calls, real or imagined, and the shock of the news was rippling through me. "Now it's too late."

"Hush, now," she said gently. She leaned her head back into the cushions, pressed her cheek into the headrest, closed her eyes.

"But she was all alone!" I wailed.

"I don't think she experienced any pain." Saul directed his consoling words to me now. "I don't think you do with a stroke." He leaned across the coffee table and patted my shoulder. I flinched.

"You don't understand," I snapped. He couldn't know how the prospect sickened me. *Beloved wife of——? Beloved mother of——?* Her choices had robbed her of that. And when my time came, where would my beloved be? Dead himself, or caught up with his "real" family. I loved Zephra, but I didn't want her life.

"She wasn't alone," he said and put his hand back on my shoulder, more firmly this time. I lifted my head to dispute this, met his unwavering gaze, and for a moment he held me there, regarding everything mean and weak in me alongside my better self, assenting to it all.

"I can't—" I started to say, but I didn't know what I was refusing, so I stopped.

"I know it's sudden," Saul pressed on, turning back to Mama, "but do you have any sense of what she would want? When there's no family, the church will take care of the arrangements, of course," he continued. "There's some funds set aside, and for the rest I think we just pass the hat."

"Avie and I are looking after the arrangements," she corrected him in a mildly admonishing tone, as if he'd forgotten a plan they'd already discussed and agreed upon.

He glanced back at me, and I shrugged helplessly. "Well, it's a lovely gesture, and it seems very fitting," he allowed. "Are you sure you're up for it?"

"I wouldn't take it on if I wasn't," she said.

He nodded. "All right, then. Would you like me to pray with you now?"

"I've been praying all of the night, honey," she answered. "But I wish you would sit with me a little."

Of course he would. I thanked Saul weakly, went back to my room, and stripped off the fetid clothes I'd slept and sweated in. I got in the shower, soaped my hair, breasts, between my legs, letting the water scald uselessly down my back. I couldn't boil or scrub away the night before. It rose up stinking through my pores and clouded any proper thoughts of grief or respect for a woman who'd been infinitely kind to me.

Easy as a phone call, I could be driven to drink—or to grab whatever was at hand to blunt my senses. *It's your mother that's the issue, not my wife. She probably needs to be in a home.* (Her home!) *She could go on like this for years.* (Yes! I want years from her yet!) *She's not the only one who needs you.* (I cannot be in two places at once. From this place, you cannot put me in my place.) *And then there's the other matter.* (Yes, the precious goddamn money and your insinuations about how I might repay it, but you won't say, you won't dirty yourself by saying.) *You've put me in a very difficult position.* (I can recall many positions you've put me in, each more difficult than the last.) *It's obvious we won't resolve this now; I'll talk to you again soon.* (I cannot talk to you again soon, I thought with grim triumph; I've had a death.) In all ways I was failing where I might have succeeded if I'd fought harder against my own weak and lapsing nature. And now I'd had a death. I lay on the bottom of the tub and wept into the stream until it ran cold.

I had to put my mind right. Clean body, clean clothes, a cup of strong coffee, and gradually I began to feel as if I could perform. By the time I rejoined Mama and Saul I was still a little ragged, but airier than with a regular hangover, slightly foggy but free of the pulsing headache. I could drive, shop for coffins, do simple math.

"Can you think of anyone else I should notify?" Saul asked as he was leaving.

"No, they're all gone." Mama's voice quavered. "She's got no people." Then, "We're her people."

Visitation: My brother William moved like Daddy. Same graceful lumbering. Same simmering discomfort in a suit, as if the simple jacket buttons might not contain his dense energy. His same humbled shoulder slump, head lowered as Mama's former yardman recognized and closed in on him. *Well, I'll be dog. Is it? As I live and breathe.* Same shy smile in response. When he shed his jacket, I could see that his dress shirt still bore the cardboard creases. His silver-blond hair, damp with grooming ointment, was combed neatly off his ruddy face, watery blue eyes so light against that skin—I couldn't stop staring at him. He'd seem to catch me at it, and I'd look away, not wanting to embarrass him, but my gaze could only skitter briefly about the room before veering back to rest on him.

"You'll burn a hole in him staring," Dahlia murmured from behind. We'd been lingering uncertainly by the guest book. She gave me a little shove in his direction. "I've seen him plenty," she said in response to my pleading look. "Plus Mother's probably fallen in by now." She ducked into the restroom.

I stumbled toward William, terrified, as he searched my face. I saw the little glint of recognition before he stepped forward and shook my hand with formal politeness. "Well, hey there, Avalon. I think I expected a little girl."

"No one ever calls me that," I murmured shyly, and I forgot to turn loose his hand.

He tugged it gently out of my grip, a discomfited smile spreading across his face.

"Calls you Little Girl?"

"Well, that either. I usually go by Avie." Or Princess, Tender-foot, Butter Bean, or Peanut, if you were my daddy, I thought. But you are just his younger twin, and a stranger to me. My face burned from swoony, adolescent crush, or possibly it was my dermatitis starting to act up. Too soon to be sure.

"Well, then, Avie. Have you had a look at her yet?" he asked.

"No, Mama wanted to see her in private first, so I didn't go in earlier. She says they did a good job on her."

"Would they do all that much? I thought she wanted to be cremated," he said.

That rattled me. Mama hadn't mentioned the possibility. "This is the first I've heard of it," I said.

"I only just now remembered. Something she said to me a long time ago."

"It can still be done, I guess. We'll just have to talk to the director and get it sorted out." Mama will have a fit, I thought.

"I don't know how important it was," he said mildly. Daddy's easygoing backpedaling to forestall trouble—of course he had that, too. "I doubt it would matter much to her now. We might as well have a look."

I turned and led him to the viewing room, matching his heavy footfalls behind me to our father's cadence. I half expected him to place a guiding hand lightly in the center of my back. *This way, Princess. Step lively now.*

The casket we'd settled on was almost unspeakably girly, with a mineral-flecked gray-pink shell and pinker satin lining all ruched and quilted, a ruffle encircling the flat pillow. I'd wanted to choose something plainer, thinking Zephra would prefer it, but Mama had said no, the plainer was the bargain-basement model, and that wouldn't suit. "Nor the fanciest, either. She'd want something right down the middle, and she'd want me to pick her out something prettier than she would for herself." She'd sounded so certain of Zephra's wishes, as if the months of estrangement hadn't applied, yet cremation had not even been considered.

The temperature felt several degrees cooler in the dimly lit viewing room—to keep the meat from going rancid too quickly, I thought. I didn't know why such care had to be taken to dress and display the body for our gather and gawp. It had been drummed into me from childhood that the body was just a house you blithely vacated once the roof caved in and the plumbing was shot, or anytime God saw fit to revoke your lease, and if you'd been a decent tenant and neighbor, you'd get invited to stay forever in His House of Many Mansions. I could dismiss it all but the soul pulling free from the body, which was perhaps just as unreasonable as the rest, but for all I needled Saul, I remained unable to accept that dead meant the tomb and putrefaction and nothing more. I was just another chickenshit agnostic with a foot in each world.

We peered over the edge of the girly casket at the thing that was both Zephra and Not-Zephra. Her body did not look utterly abandoned, but neither did she appear to be merely sleeping, as people sometimes say. She never would have slept through what had been done to her. She wasn't completely averse to cosmetics—I'd known her to apply cold cream and a dusting of *rachel* powder, even to sketch in the suggestion of eyebrows with a dark-blond pencil. But now face, neck, and hands were coated thickly with opaque beige makeup, and a waxy coral lipstick rimmed her peeling mouth. *Baby, run go get me my Vaseline jar.* Working in the sun all her life had left Zephra's skin textured like a Jackson Pollock canvas, layered with irregular pigments and shot through with broken capillaries. It sounds ugly, but that was her patina; *she* wasn't ugly, she didn't need painting over. Even her hair, normally lank as floss, had been backcombed to the consistency of cotton candy and haloed out around her skull.

"She looks like a goddamned powder puff," William murmured solemnly. I twisted my head to glance at him, and he flashed me a wink without seeming to break his countenance. My brain flooded with woozy chemicals. "I can't tell the undertaker how to do his job," he continued. "I imagine we couldn't stand to see her without some of this. People don't look so good when they die. Still——" He pulled a handkerchief from the pocket of his slacks, and thinking he was suddenly overcome with emotion, I felt my own hollow chest and the tears worming out. But he only inspected the cloth, and finding it clean, offered it to me.

"Could you . . . wipe her off a little?"

I took it uncertainly and began dusting her hands, afraid to press, afraid of feeling the chill of the body through the sheer cotton. I knew I couldn't bear to touch her face, even if I was sure it wasn't her face anymore. My hand trembled, and finally William covered it with his own.

"Here," he said, reclaiming the handkerchief. He leaned in with it and stroked her cheek with such deliberate tenderness, this man who moved so like my daddy, who bore his affect and aped his expressions, the scrim that hid the past from me fell away for an instant. Now the satin was flannel, the casket featherbedding, Zephra's face was upturned to my father's and very much alive. I was the eldest child, Dahlia, seeing what I shouldn't, and feeling a girl's pure fury rise, thinking our house had been rebuilt for this alone; all the clamor and upheaval just so that there would be a room set off for them, and now I could no longer sleep in Zephra's bed.

A sort of skip, a needle jumping the groove, and I was seeing through my own eyes again. William straightened and turned to me. His eyes were wet. "That's a little more like her," he said of the dead, dear face. Then, "She looked after me. Tried to, anyway. She did the best she could." He folded the cloth with the makeup stain inside and touched it carefully to his own face before returning it to his pocket.

"She looks good," Mama prompted as we emerged. She'd been stationed to greet visitors from a wing chair set midway between the front door and the entrance to the viewing room. The funeral director swung the accordion doors wide and bolted them open as more people began arriving.

"Good as dead. Maybe better," William said under his breath to me. Then he squared his shoulders and strode toward her. He bent to embrace her and she patted the back of his neck as if discouraging mosquitoes. When he straightened, I noticed her cannula had been removed.

"It's good you could come," she said crisply. I opened my mouth to admonish her about the oxygen, then glimpsed the small tank tucked discreetly beneath the chair. I could see the clear tubing just under her collar and understood she could slip it back on in an instant if necessary. Her walker was nowhere in sight, but as she would remain seated for the duration of the evening, I decided not to say anything about that, either; probably the director had hidden it in his office at her request. Most of the people attending had visited Mama in the hospital or at home, had seen the oxygen and the walker, so I knew this artifice wasn't for them, as she would later claim. It was for William, the son she had summoned so she could feign indifference at his arrival. She must have wanted his first glimpse of her in years to be uncluttered by appliances. As for her first glimpse of him, if she'd felt the shock of his resemblance to Linwood that I had, she was covering it nicely.

"Well, I heard you needed a pallbearer," William said.

"We needed one the last time, too," Dahlia added dryly as she joined us.

"Sister!" Mama snapped, but she was miffed, I think, not so much at the indecorousness of the remark as the way it stole her thunder. Now Mama couldn't pretend to step delicately around the matter and ribbon him slowly on the edges of her remarks. *It's good you could come (since you couldn't be bothered when your father died).*

"Oh, I always give him a hard time," Dahlia said.

"I depend on it," confirmed William with a barely discernible wink for her, and I found myself a little jealous. Mama was shut out of it, too, for their friendship seemed to be one that had flourished outside of the family. Evidently he'd thought enough of Dahlia to lengthen his already interminable drive from east Texas by veering off course to pick her up in Cobb, Virginia.

"You'll come to the house after?" Mama asked William, all business. "Have supper? If the girls don't mind sharing, you'll have your own room."

"She's kept it just the way it was the day you died," Dahlia said, and he grimaced.

"What's gotten into you?" Mama demanded.

Dahlia shrugged. "I guess I don't know how to act at funerals," she said. "I keep waiting for this one here," she gestured at me, "to show herself." I stuck my tongue out at her. "Has she thrown herself over the coffin yet?" she asked William, who canted his eyebrows—huh?—in reply.

"I never did that!" I cried, slandered.

"This isn't a funeral, it's a viewing," Mama shot back. "And I expect you to act right. All of you," this last bit directed to me.

The four of us formed an enigmatic receiving line for the guests that drifted through. We'd have to kind of pull them aside and say, "Thank you for coming," so they'd know whose loss to say they were sorry for.

Not even the church ladies, those masters of ritual and right behaviors, were sure of the protocol at first—who's to get the food?—so the usual onslaught of funereal casseroles hadn't yet appeared at our house. Saul, mingling, quietly spread it around that the Gosses should be considered "next of kin," and at some point I was presented with a bucket of chicken. It left a dark circle on my skirt where I held it in my lap.

After the viewing Minnie stopped by the house to drop off a plate of pimiento cheese sandwiches and ogle William. "You're so near like Mr. Goss it's scary!" she burst out at the sight of him.

He reddened at that, but smiled politely and allowed, "So I've been told."

"I don't see it," said Dahlia, so deadpan I couldn't make out if she was kidding. Mama didn't offer an opinion.

Neither Mama nor I had had much appetite over the past couple of days—she'd complained her mouth tasted of dirty coins and blamed the funeral parlor, while my nervous belly had been full of tacks from talking to Jack and the prospect of William's arrival. But the sandwiches were arrayed enticingly, glistening orange cheese spilling out of soft crusts, and the bucket of fast-food chicken promised savory grease if not much else. William and Dahlia were surely hungry, too, from their long drive. Seconds after Minnie declined coffee and said good night, we fell upon the food.

"Fried chicken, sandwiches . . . ," mused Dahlia when she'd gotten her fill, ". . . can the layer cakes be far behind?"

"We'll have more food than we'll know what to do with," Mama said. "I don't know as I can eat another casserole after they buried us in them last spring. Not that I'm ungrateful, but Saul needn't have bothered to get after folks."

"We'll be glad enough to have something for people to eat to-morrow after the service," Dahlia countered. "Or else we'd have to fix. Avie'd have to fix, anyway," she said to tease me.

"I don't reckon we'll have many to the house," Mama said hopefully.

William spoke very little. He made his way through two sandwiches and three pieces of chicken, dark meat. I gladly gave over my drumstick to the cause. I noticed he'd been pretty quiet since the end of the viewing, when Mabry's oxygen and walker had materialized. "I must have my toys," she'd said lightly, in response to his stricken look, but she'd grown somber, too.

"Aren't you tired?" I asked him, still eager to be of service. "I'll bet you are. There's clean sheets on the bed; if you want you can go ahead and get settled."

"No, that's all right." He gnawed thoughtfully on the soft remains of a wing, fidgeted a bit, and finally mused, "I hadn't ought to smoke in here, I don't guess."

"The porch is safe, but the yard is better," Dahlia said. "She doesn't need to smell it."

"Oh, it don't bother me," Mama said. "I'd have one too if I could, but I can't, so what's the difference if I smell it?"

"I should be heading on, anyway." He stood up.

"You're not staying?" I whined, crestfallen.

"You're not coming to the funeral?" Mama said sharply. "Or you got somewhere else to stay."

William, mildly: "I've got to put her house in order, I might as well get on in there."

Was this why Mama had summoned him? I wondered. To put him to work? I'd assumed Dahlia and I would sort through Zephra's things at some point, then put the house up for auction. Of course, I hadn't really thought through the legal aspects of it yet. Had Zephra made out a will? Who among us was even permitted to deal with her things?

"You'll need the key," Mama said, as if she might dangle it before him and snatch it right back.

"You know she didn't ever lock the house."

"You've been gone a long time. People bar their doors around here now. Anyhow, the ambulance people probably locked up behind themselves."

"I'm not worried about getting in, so don't you be." He spoke gently, but I could feel the steel that girded him, and I was certain then that no imperious summons from Mama could have brought him back to Regina had he not been willing. He wanted to pay his respects to Zephra, so he came; he'd apparently felt no like compulsion to visit when Daddy died, nor during any of the weeks Mama spent in the hospital. I didn't know what to make of that. He may have been "estranged" from us, but he was not unfeeling. The sight of Mama so aged and frail had clearly affected him, and toward myself I sensed his curiosity and even fondness. Of course, I mused, that could have come from my mooning over him so baldly; he probably thought I was an idiot child and felt sorry for me.

"Avie, at least give him some linens."

I knew there'd be a clean set on the guest bed at Zephra's; I'd washed and replaced them myself. I didn't have to say so, because William insisted he wouldn't need any of that.

"You don't know what she's got over there," Mama tried as a parting shot. "She wasn't used to overnight visitors anymore."

"She'll have something I can sleep on. She always did." Carefully, he dumped his crumbs in the wastebasket, rinsed his plate clean, set it on the drying rack, and blotted his hands with a paper towel. There was no real hurrying in him, I felt, neither eagerness to go nor willingness to stay. I think he just wanted a cigarette. He hesitated at Mama's chair, then knelt and gave her a dry peck on her dry cheek.

I followed him outside, brimming with things to say, but they all got tangled up in my throat. Can you really be my brother? Am I anywhere near as strange and familiar to you as you are to me? Who are you what do you do have you any children? Will I come to know you, and you me?

He offered me a cigarette from his pack and I took it without a thought. He struck a match and touched it to mine, then his, and we stood there companionably, looking over the spent garden lit dimly silver by the December moon and the meager rays cast by the porch bulb. I took an experimental drag, managing not to cough, though I did get light-headed. I liked it, and I thought I might throw up also. It was the ghost of being drunk.

"The house looks good, by the way, Avie. You did a real good job on it."

"I didn't do anything but make calls and write checks. Well, yes I did, too. I painted. You should have seen the place. The water damage from putting it out was worse than the fire. And the way the smoke hung all in everything, the smell."

"Dahlia told me it was a real mess. It's a wonder it didn't kill her."

"Mama? It may well yet." Again that stricken look, just a fast, nicking glance. "Actually these were doing the job well enough on their own." I brandished my cigarette, took a last regretful tug, and ground it out.

"It's a nasty habit, I know," he said. "I keep it down to five a day now. Ten if there's a funeral." He lit a new one on the end of the burning one. "Zephra used to let me dip when I was a boy," he said. "They say that's worse."

"Gross!" I squealed, delighted.

"She said since I was doing it anyway, no need of me hiding it from her. Linwood would tear me up if he caught me. Got on her, too, for letting me, but she said if he was so set against it, he should find another living."

"It might seem strange over there tonight," I said. "Spooky. I wish you would stay with us. Mama may not act it, but she's glad you're here."

"It's hard to see her like this. She's so fragile now, the wind could snap her. I guess I hadn't expected she'd ever get that way. But I didn't come for her sake. I came to pay my respects and put Zephra's house in order."

"Why is that *your* job?" I had to ask. "I've been thinking we should talk to a lawyer first about how to deal with her things, since there's no real next of kin. I don't know if we really have the right to go meddling in there."

He gave a harsh laugh. "I believe I have the right to go onto my own property."

I quickened to this. "What, she left it to you? How do you know? Was there a will?"

"I haven't seen any will. But she's always been going to leave me the house. I'm sure she's got it written up somewhere. Not that I deserve a thing from her, but I'm not here to collect. I feel like it's my place to settle her affairs. There's no one else."

I took exception to this. "Well, just Mama and Dahlia and me!"

"And here Mabry's going to put her in the ground," he said.

"You said you didn't think it was all that important!" I half shouted. "If she wanted to be cremated, okay let's do it, but we've got to get up with the director right away. Tonight."

He waved away the entire notion. "It's not worth changing now," he said. "She wouldn't have wanted all the fuss of that. She'd have said just go ahead on now that you've stuffed and dressed me like a goddamn turkey."

"If Mama had known," I insisted, "she would have followed Zephra's wishes. I know it."

"Mabry has her own ideas about what's right and proper," William replied. "And what she thinks will always override what others believe. Their truth don't apply."

This was veering elsewhere. "I don't understand," I said.

"The thing I can't let go of is how she had me to *pretend* I believed. Let me think I was humoring the poor woman. Let me feel sorry for her."

"For who?" I asked. "Zephra?"

"Poor thing thinks she's your mother, what's the harm? Might be like waking up a sleepwalker if you try to shake her out of it, might really put her over the edge. So play along, be good to her. But no need of you to spread it around. "

"That Zephra was your mother?" I said, amazed, but knowing at the same time it must be so; once I could see past the heavy stamp of our father's features on William, it was clear enough that the rest came from Zephra, her reserve and the quiet force of her will. "Did you think it might be true?"

"I felt like it was," he said. "But it didn't make sense. Why couldn't I just go live with her? So I asked them point-blank: is it so? And you know what Mabry did? Do you know what she did?" As his emotions built, his voice got quieter, more controlled. It seemed worse, somehow, than if he'd been all fists and railing.

"What, for God's sake? Please."

"She showed me my birth certificate. Mabry Goss listed as mother."

Confusion was blooming up in my throat, thick, bitter petals. I had my own vague recollection to match, of being shown my birth certificate. But what did it mean? I'd never questioned who I belonged to. Still didn't, though the ground beneath my feet had turned to water.

"Proof, right?" William went on. "Zephra was just telling me a story. And Linwood right there all the time saying nothing. Not a goddamn thing."

I tried to stay afloat. "You didn't believe the certificate."

"I *did* believe. That's the crime of it. I took that over Zephra's word. Mabry's piece of paper and Linwood's silence over Zephra's word, when the woman had never lied to me, never. First I thought maybe she was just trying to please me. See, I'd said to her so many times, I wish *you* were my mother. And finally one day she said, Sugar I am. You are blood of my blood. Later I got to thinking: Woman lives all by herself, works her own fields, feeds every stray thing that wanders by. She was so lonesome, she had to make up a family. I decided she was just pitiful, like they said."

"Well, maybe she was," I ventured. "I don't mean pitiful, never, but maybe she did just love you so much she wished she was your mother until she believed it."

"Unh-unh. No. I'd seen them together. Linwood was a dog, couldn't stop sniffing around her. It's a wonder he didn't sire more bastards than he did."

"Stop it!" I cried.

He startled at my outburst, and so did I, my shrill volume splitting the quiet pitch of his evidence. "Avie, I'm sorry," he offered. "You don't need to hear any of that. That was all a long time ago. It doesn't have anything to do with you."

"Why shouldn't this concern me?" I demanded. "It has everything to do with me. It's my family, too, and this, this *mess,* is why you and I don't even know each other."

"No," William said. "That was my own doing. I cut myself off, and I wouldn't give them another chance. Especially him." He astonished me then by thumbing an angry tear off my cheek, printing me with that one swipe of callus. Every splinter, every scraped knee, every hurtful name or thwarted desire called for such rough thumbing away. How I longed for my father, no-good dog that he may have been. The tears he'd wipe from me were banished, never to return.

William said, "I see you now, apple of Linwood's eye, gone to college and everything, back here looking after Mabry—I can believe they changed. It happens. Not so long ago, you couldn't have stood to be around me. I've got two ex-wives who thought so, anyway. Now I'm almost tolerable." He smiled, a plea. "They did better by you, I don't know why."

"Doesn't seem fair," I said.

"Old people want to get into heaven, I guess. And to get handed a baby girl so late in life, I don't know. Maybe they were getting another chance after all."

mabry goss

Zephra carried William, that's so. And when you look him in the face, is it any doubt who sired him? The facts were not for me to rail against or ignore. When she came wringing her hands, I said only, and not in anger, that the thing could be undone.

We'll give you butter and eggs and what little money we can scrape, I told Ida Snow. Not by my hand, she said, but she would risk life and limb to steal a quart of lightning from her husband, and he woke to blame the son and beat him senseless. The son soon returned the favor, but Ida said never mind, we'd neither added to nor diminished the disorder of her house. You can do the rest, she said, and we dug the fleshy roots that she described and gathered the leaves as she instructed. One of the leaves was rue, another had sawteeth and left a rash on my hands.

The draught we steeped was tea-colored and bitter, the ruin of good lightning, to be forced back by the tablespoon, before each meal and at bedtime. I tasted it first, to give Zephra courage. When fever came upon her I tended her just as she'd done me in my birthing time, mopped her head, rubbed the ache from her limbs, while we waited for the blood to come.

Is this what you wanted to know? That she was William's mother and tried to stop him with my help? Linwood wouldn't have let us, had he known what we were about. And William so angry with his father he wouldn't see him buried. He doesn't know who to be angry with.

The blood didn't come and it didn't come, and Zephra thrashed with nightmares. When she woke the second morning, she turned her head away from the spoon and spat and swore she'd had enough. I held her by the hair and tried to put more down her throat. You must be strong, I said, and she was—strong enough to put me on the floor.

We'll have this one, she said. Now I see what's right. We'll have this one. You'll have a son. Linwood wants a boy. What's the difference if I bear it or you?

We feared what the draught might have done to him, but the baby was sound, born hollering. Linwood took them to the hospital in Raleigh, and Zephra gave my name for the certificate. You have that paper, people can say what they want, and so they did, but we had that paper. I'd gone around in loose dresses the months before, Zephra hadn't gone around at all, and then we had that paper saying William was mine. Named for my father; now how's that for gall?

We agreed there'd be no more children for a time. I went to the Sanger clinic, but Zephra swore by her seeds, saying William was proof of their worth; she'd conceived only when she'd stopped taking them daily. No more putting it to the test, she promised—

—and yes, I might have demanded she not lie down with my husband. Or demanded Linwood not lie down with her. I knew what were my rights. How to explain this? Sometimes I burned from the jealousy, and still it suited me to be half a wife. My own ma'am had been consumed with the full task, and it had killed her.

I was heavy and poison as lead when Ma'am died. Not even the sky looked right to me. Sometimes I saw my baby girl through dread eyes and feared to touch her. I could barely dress myself, but I could harm her without thinking, and I knew it. What if Zephra hadn't been by me then, to wrap her in safe arms?

I didn't leave Zephra my husband to clear a debt. I just fled and later conjured reasons to stay gone. Let them love each other if they would, I thought. Richmond changed me. I was not so wet and stupid when I left there, if you think I came home a timid wife. That's all I have to say about that.

Zephra didn't keep her promise after William. She only admitted she was carrying again when I confronted her. She said the seeds must have failed, but she wouldn't meet my eyes. Linwood already knew and was going around whistling. He would be mantled with sons. He now believed that even with two women, he was living in grace. The preacher, once sternly disapproving, had of late concluded this: Linwood was progressed in his relationship with God to the point that he could no longer sin. He said it was my duty to shield us from the scrutiny and judgment of others, but the Lord was not displeased.

Wasn't he something, that preacher? I pitied his wife's niece, come to live with them as cook and housekeeper, because if Linwood had such an understanding with the Lord, think what a preacher could get by with! The preacher didn't broadcast his philosophy, mind you, but it was no secret. No more than our situation was hid from anybody who cared to peer in. What galls is how the congregation put up with his dalliance for years—until he said something they didn't like. He didn't even use the word "integration." Just put it out there that we ought to consider whether heaven observed separate facilities for the colored. And suddenly he was on the outs for being a fornicator. And Linwood, he wanted to speak in his favor, but the deacons took him aside and said, "Glass houses, Brother Goss." But I'm getting ahead of myself.

A month before Zephra was due, she came in from the garden cramping and wanting to bear down. She said we should go straight to the hospital in case the baby was coming; she wanted to be sure he'd get that piece of paper. Linwood was off all day on a carpentry job, and I'd have to get hold of a car. What would I tell people? If I said I was sick, they'd want to drive me themselves, and Zephra couldn't pretend anything to anybody, bad off as she was. I resented the fix we were in. She'd put us in.

Let's wait on it, I said.

Linwood wasn't home until evening. By then Zephra was panting and grunting, passing some blood. He bundled her into the car and drove pell-mell to Raleigh. Better to have stayed home and let it happen sooner rather than later. But no, they had to put the baby in the light box, had to grant him months instead of days.

I've gone over it time and again, my part in it. Not that I think the delay caused it. Zephra had been sickly the whole time; something had already gone wrong. I mean another kind of fault, for the anger I nursed. I'd accepted the boy William, even loved him, but with this one I felt gone against and hard done by. Zephra meant to outdo me, I thought, by giving Linwood sons, plural. So I was some to blame for the new one's frailty, for stunting him with my meanness of spirit. Zephra blamed herself for having tried to end the first one—and so by association blamed me, too. Linwood was for a time struck dumb. A dead son did not square with being in God's favor. He'd been a good father once and would be again, but in grief and hardness over the lost child Linwood failed his living daughter and son, and would lose them as well.

I wanted Zephra out, yes. And Linwood turned away from her. He meant to keep our marriage bed sacred, he said, now and forever. It didn't make me glad. Oh, now he was all for rules and discipline, when it meant damping down an innocent boy, when it was too late to save our girl. I kept to my corner of the bed, my body cold as the ground, offering only stones and choking dust. To empty a house won't render it clean.

avie goss

Irregular as hail and twice as violent, my period arrived, aggravating all hell out of Christmas. On the eve, William brought us a small evergreen tree, which he set up before loading Dahlia's suitcase in his truck. Mama was so put out with them for not staying one more night, thereby spending the holidays, she dared me to decorate it.

Over the next several days Jack sent a succession of opulent things, starting with a tumble of orchids large enough to cover Zephra's grave, and that was the use I put it to. I'd been drinking a little (such a relative term) since the day of the funeral. It had begun as a family thing, William nipping discreetly from an amber flask, covertly passing it off to Dahlia. I'd intercepted, and by dusk he'd had to cross the county line for more. I didn't drink with them again after that night. Things had been said.

I now kept a small bottle of wine in the refrigerator, in plain sight, and two more in my room of jug variety, concealed in the closet under a heap of bedding, guest sheets I'd stripped the instant of Dahlia's departure.

A smart alligator belt arrived. A trench coat lined with red silk. Artisan earrings, heavy as doorknobs. I didn't bite, so Jack got out the big domestic guns: a matching towel set, dishcloths, a coffeepot. That last one, a stovetop percolator lifted from my own private memory, got to me a little, but I was too stunned to blink when the little booties arrived.

I was slowly bleeding out, sometimes not so slowly. Cramping and excessive bleeding, confusingly enough, are described both as side effects and warning signals associated with IUD use. I chose to view them as side effects. I considered them part of my penance, and if they seemed to be getting worse, well, everything hurt more lately. I waddled around in Mama's incontinence pads—they had greater absorption and were delivered to the house, which I rarely stepped out of in the days following Christmas. Why should I? I wondered. Minnie wouldn't need me for several more days. We had plenty of canned milk and tuna, and at the rate things were coming to the house—I'd just signed for a crate of grapefruit and clementines, apology for the booties— we'd soon want for nothing.

Knowledge seeped from me like blood; it stained everything and left me weak. William had been reckless in his talk. He'd been *in his cups, on his liquid diet,* and was surely not to be taken seriously. What he'd suggested had to be impossible; even if it made a slantwise kind of sense, the years simply did not add up.

Dahlia, dismissively: "I'm not your mother. I'm barely your sister."

I let that settle in awhile before I ventured to Mama, "I heard something I need to ask you about."

Mama, aggrieved: "Oh Lord, what is it now?"

She gave off the faint odor of rising yeast under gardenia perfume. I noted her hair, unwashed for days and forming limp dreadlocks, saw the crumbs cascading down her nightgown, which she hadn't bothered to change out of since the night before. Why hadn't she asked for help in the bath? I'd done it plenty of times before, though she preferred to go it alone if she was feeling strong enough, and apparently she wasn't. I'd been falling down on the job. Maybe that was literally what she feared, that I'd pull her down with me, crack both our skulls on the porcelain tub. I reminded myself she'd just lost her best friend and backed off.

"Nothing. Forget it. Something William said."

Mama: "I wouldn't take heed of much he had to say after the funeral." Suggesting he'd been drunk. I'd pegged him for a slow sipper, someone who knew from practice how to take the edge off and say when. Perhaps it loosened his tongue, but I'd been the one who hogged the rest of the whiskey and clamored for more. I'd made an issue out of idle words.

New Year's Day ushered in a freak heat spell, and the temperature shot up nearly to eighty. The ground extruded crocus, spear tips of tulip and daffodil. The cherry tree was fooled into blossom. "It's too soon," Mama mourned. "Frost'll come back, kill it all. We'll lose everything."

I was hot, too, simmering inside my clothes, a shut-in blaming the weather. I ate only the citrus, and my mouth was acid and ridged with soreness.

I called Jack at home late at night, not caring whether Simone answered or what she would think. I thanked him for the gifts, chided him about the booties, cried, all the while swirling my jug wine in the cup like brandy. He began outlining my "exit strategy" from Regina, and while I didn't say yes, I didn't argue with him, either, and for Jack that constituted agreement.

He allowed for one month, during which the "alternate arrangements" for Mama could be put into place: a woman in for day, a woman in for night, a woman in to clean, possibly cook. Perhaps the day woman could handle that as well, in which case we'd put her on salary. "We can get that done inside of a week," Jack said, "but I know you'll want to do the choosing, check references and all that. There's no need to rush if it will make you feel more comfortable."

We can get that done.

It was preposterous. Mama wouldn't have it. It would be me or no one at all. She was not about to give strangers the run of the house, and I'd be a fool to try to foist it on her. But the offer had its allure for me. To be freed of the constant responsibility, just swooping in monthly, laden with gifts like a hero. I listened.

"You'd still be in charge of her care," Jack shrewdly pointed out. "And anyway, don't you think this would be better than what you're capable of on your own? This would be around the clock." The crumby gown, the dirty hair—just about anyone could look after her better than I had lately. She was giving herself what she called "spit baths" at the sink, swiping armpits and private creases with a damp washcloth. She was sprinkling baby powder in her hair.

"And how would 'we' afford this?" I asked.

"I'm a rich man, Avie. Soon to be stinking. Life has been very good to me lately—with one exception."

"And what's that?" I was supposed to say.

So he could say, "I don't have you."

The next morning my bleeding seemed to have stopped. I put Mama in the shower and got in with her. It felt safer somehow. With me crowding the tub, I told her, how could she fall? No room to land. She laughed at my foolishness. It was less humiliating this way for both of us, I think. The way we'd done it before had her crouched and cringing in the bath, arms crossed over her breasts, me cringing on the other side of the half-drawn curtain, ready to blot out the sight with a towel when she emerged.

"This is how we used to do when you were little; do you remember?" she said, shivering and blinking in the steam.

"Really?" I remembered the frosted sliding doors we used to have for the shower and the harsh blocks of tallow soap Zephra made. Yes: Mama would undress me, then herself, and tie a rain bonnet over her hairdo. How awed, how cowed I'd been in the presence of her grown woman's body, the nests and swells and indentations, the slabs of muscle and the puckery fat, the polished juttings of bone.

"You always wanted to take a big-girl shower," she said. "I was afraid of you getting water up your nose and drowning if I wasn't right there."

She gripped the towel bar with both hands for support while I sponged her down. How the years had softened and collapsed her. The skin on her body hung looser but was still fairly smooth; only her hands, face, and neck bore the textures of age. I was a head taller than her now, at least twenty pounds heavier.

"You weren't no more than three. You'd say, 'Mama, let's us get in the rain!'"

I shampooed the gluey mass of her hair twice, and she purred,

"Oh, it was itching me so," as I scrubbed her scalp. I shaved her underarms, but left the sparse, downy hair on her legs alone. I washed under the flap of her breasts, swabbed her threadbare pubis.

"Now I'm the baby," she stated soberly.

I wrapped her in the inch-thick towels Jack sent. I dried her hair and set it with the hot curlers while she did a breathing treatment. She put on a cotton housedress still warm from the dryer and settled on the couch with her coffee and the holiday edition of the *Progress,* sighing in sleepy contentment.

I could take care of Mama. It was myself I didn't look after. I was still half-dirty and had soap in my hair. I'd rallied for her shower, but now I just wanted to go back to bed.

"Draw back the curtains," Mama said. "Let's see this pretty day. The Lord knows what we'll have come spring."

The day warmed on, the sun a pitiless convection lamp, and the sky lost its wintry pallor. It went hostile blue, spun great puffy clouds.

"Look at that sky," Mama said. "You could just wash your hands in those clouds. Eat them with a spoon. Such *unnatural* weather."

A soft riot in my guts, cotton tumbling in the gin.

"It's funny," she observed, "I hadn't seen Zephra in months, but the feeling is different now. I guess before she was gone I knew I could always still see her."

I murmured sympathy. I sweated. My blood was molten, thrumming in my ears, thrumming as it coursed out of me. The brief cease-fire had ended. Some deranged farmer was milking my womb.

"Something's ailing you," Mama said, catching on to it.

"Spring fever," I offered, and she let it stand.

Minnie returned from her holiday cruise, booked to stave despair when she'd been denied visitation—unjustly, again—with

her son. She stopped by the house the next morning, scanned
wordlessly the denuded tree in its base of shed brown needles,
the heaps of citrus peel, then turned her attention to me.
"Twelve days you've been bleeding? Go to the damn doctor."
She felt my forehead. "You've a fever as well. Tell her, Mrs. Goss."
"Listen to your friend," Mama said.

"From here on out, let's everybody take care of their own children." William had said it not cryptically, but as a sort of joke.
He'd been talking about his stepdaughters, lamenting the gifts he
had yet to buy for them, complaining that he'd somehow remained in charge of their Christmases, though the stepdaughters
were from one wife ago and nearly grown. But I'd watched him
cut his eyes at Dahlia, and seen her bristling response. It could
have just as easily been a jab at Mama, referring to his own confused upbringing. I should have left it alone.

"I think we should admit you," the doctor was saying. They'd
looked at my blood and pee, and they didn't like it. They were all
about white count. "Can someone drive you to the hospital?"
"I drove myself here," I said.
"You're not driving to Raleigh like this."
I felt as though I'd flunked my midterms and had my license
revoked as punishment. Okay, I'd call Minnie. No, I needed her
to be with Mama right now, and maybe to spend the night. Not
Saul; what would I say? The doctor threatened an ambulance. I
ticked down a list of friendly *Progress* advertisers, none of whom
I could bear to know my personal business, and suggested a taxi-
cab (Regina didn't have one). Have Saul to sit with Mama while
Minnie took me? Hardly any different, privacy-wise, from having
him drive me, just more choreography involved. I considered the

ambulance—I'd go in grand style!—and called Saul. Of course he came at once, solicitous but no questions asked.

I dozed feverishly in the car, then on a vinyl bench in the waiting area, jerking awake when my head lolled too far off its stem. I could feel Saul close by; it seemed my cheek had drifted over to rest against his cool shoulder. "Go home," I said irritably, and he laughed.

Then I was summoned to the exam room, where a gynecologist plucked out my IUD with angry efficiency. "You're how old?" she demanded.

"Twenty-four," I answered meekly.

"And who on earth agreed to fit you with this?" she fumed, and as I still hung in the stirrups, she told me my ability to get pregnant may have been seriously jeopardized. "That's why we don't give them to young women." She stuck a tube in my arm and told me to stay the night.

I called Mama.

"Tell me what's really ailing you," she pleaded. "They don't hold you overnight for some blame infection unless you're like I am."

I was tired and touchy. "You really want to know? I was using a device, an IUD?"

"I know what it is."

"Well, I'm all inflamed. I have a fever and they want to keep me until it goes back down."

"I thought you were on that pill," she said.

That threw me. "You just know all my business, don't you?"

"Evidently not."

Then there were hours in holding-room limbo until they could find me a more permanent spot. I closed my eyes and drifted into the familiar sound collage of scratchy intercom vocals, squeaky cartwheels, and bleeps and blips of equipment. For a span I thought I was there visiting Mama all over again. Only where were her dear nurses, so quick with a kind word or a single-serving tub of applesauce?

Saul had not gone home, but neither had he languished patiently in the emergency waiting room all afternoon, perusing old issues of *McCall's* until they found me a bed. Instead, clad in jogging shorts and nylon windbreaker, he'd relieved the chaplain and gone on his rounds. By the time he found my room, he'd comforted dozens; his face had that do-gooder's glow. He clutched some wilted tulips in his fist.

I eyed them with alarm. "For me?"

"I know, I know," he said, "but the gallbladder lady made me take them. They just need some water." He put them in a plastic pitcher and set them on the sill, where they listed colorfully. "So," brightly, "are you going to live?"

"I guess so. I'm too mean to die."

"Can I get anything for you? What about your mother? Is she by herself?"

"No, Minnie's with her. Look," I added irritably, peeved at his respectful discretion, "don't you even want to know what's wrong with me?"

"I got the impression it was some kind of 'female trouble.'" He actually made curly quotes with his fingers when he said this. "I didn't want to pry." His face turned grim. "Were you pregnant or something?"

"*Hell* no!" I blurted. "God!"

"Sorry. I overheard 'hemorrhage.'"

"I'm the opposite of pregnant."

"Oh . . . kay. Well, that's good, right?"

I didn't know how to answer him. The question of fertility would come to dog my waking hours. Much troubling review of

the time spent scoring up my insides, imagining the sinister etch-
ings and furtive scrollwork. What had been inscribed there? Was
it permanent?

The next morning, Minnie came to pick me up. My fever
gone, I was prescribed two kinds of antibiotic, given a pamphlet
about pelvic inflammatory disease (a.k.a. PID—mostly about pre-
vention; I tossed it), denied muscle relaxants (my eager lobbying
made the doctor wary), and discharged.

No refuge to be had in wine, either. As she drove me back to
Regina, Minnie confessed she'd found my hidden stash.

"I wasn't snooping; I needed sheets," she explained gingerly.
"And I didn't pour them out. They're in my refrigerator, and I'll
return them, if you want."

I considered what I could say that would bring them back
without tacitly admitting I wanted them. "Whatever," I tried.

"I didn't know you were drinking again."

"I'm not, really." I could just go get more, I thought. I was
supposed to stay at home and rest, but it would be a quick er-
rand. Maybe not so quick, since I'd have to drive outside the
county for alcohol. It would be simpler just to have her return
what she took. What she stole!

"My brother was going to stay over the holidays," I began.
"Dahlia, too. We were planning a big family get-together, a fancy
dinner with wine and everything, and it was going to be a surprise for Mama, so I . . ." Minnie was wincing with such discomfort, I didn't finish. We rode on in silence, over roads slick with
warm drizzle.

New grass fluttered like cilia around the stark trees, a bald-
faced lie that it was spring. Let frost come and knock you all to
hell, I thought. I stared into the sun until color globules blocked

my vision. "I'm probably going back to Ohio soon," I announced. "I thought I didn't like the winters there, but this crazy heat wave in the middle of January is really getting to me."

"Is that a decision you need to make right now?"

"I think I'm getting back together with Jack."

She kept her expression neutral. "Oh. Why? If I may ask."

Why. "I love him. I guess I owe it to him."

"That's the stupidest thing I ever heard. You don't *owe* any man anything."

"Just twenty-three thousand dollars."

She veered to the muddy shoulder, yanked the brake. "I'm listening."

I told her. Even the married part. I tried not to varnish it. She sat very straight in her seat, eyes focused on the dashboard, her hands clasped gently in her lap. I found it easier to confide to her profile than to be fixed in her intense gaze. She was breathing deeply, in through the nose, out through the mouth. Her pale lips seemed naked without their usual red gloss, and her blouse, though crisp and shot through with funky brooches, was untucked. For Minnie, that was unkempt to the point of neglect. I realized I'd upset her terribly over the past twenty-four hours, and she was making no small effort to stay supportive.

When I finished, she took a final controlled breath and sighed it all back out. "Okay," she began, "his marriage aside—for now"— she shot me a glance—"you realize you have to pay that money back. *Then* see how you feel about getting back together."

"That's just it," I countered eagerly. "He says he doesn't care about the money, he doesn't want me to pay him back. And Mama—he's talking about providing around-the-clock care for her."

"Nevertheless, this is the kind of debt you will have to settle. Unless twenty-three thousand is your going rate?"

"Look at me when you say that," I seethed, "so I can slap your face."

She twisted in her seat to face me. "I'm sorry. Plus eldercare," she enunciated. "He will own you."

"You don't understand the way it is with us."

"No? I got under a dealer who tried to moonlight as my pimp. My terms were much cheaper: Sex for drugs. I'm lucky I got arrested."

"God! Okay, it's wrong, he's married. But he does love me. You can't equate this with your sordid drug shit, Miss Born-Again!"

"Hunh. You're going to wish your arrangement was straightforward as mine."

"Just take me home, please? Mama's waiting on me."

The afternoon brought a fresh onslaught of orchids. They carried a funeral stink; I planned to freshen Zephra's grave with them.

"Somebody sure thinks a lot of you," Mama observed, her mild refrain with each new delivery. But this time she shook me up by adding, "Don't you think you better tell him if you're coming back to work or not? I've been wondering myself."

"I-I don't know," I stammered. "I was really starting to like what I'm doing here."

"Lord knows I love you here by me, but you oughtn't to think you're to stay right on."

"Mama, you can't live by yourself anymore." This assertion came off a little weak just then. Galvanized by my illness, perhaps frightened into action, she'd tidied the house quite admirably, insisted I remain in bed or at least swathed in blankets on the couch, and had been plying me with ginger ale and saltine crackers all afternoon.

"That's not for you to decide. Anyhow, I believe I could manage it with some side help."

I felt a prickle of alarm. "You sound like you want me to go back."

"I want you to do what's best for you."

That made me really anxious. "Mama, has Jack been calling here? Has he been talking to you?"

Her face darkened. "I can worry about your future all on my own; it doesn't take somebody *talking* to me."

"But he talked to you."

"I told him he ought to be talking to you, not me."

"Damn it! When? What else did you say?"

"Mind your swearing," she said firmly. "The man wants to give me advice, all right, but then fair's fair, I gave him some of my own. I said it didn't make good business sense to wait on you all this time. If he's gotten by without you this long, that ought to tell him something."

"Mama!" I was aiming for outrage, but nearly had to fight back laughter. That would teach him to fool with my mother.

"Shoot, babygirl. There's nothing *I* could say to him that'd make any difference. You've got to deal with him direct."

I fumed and I thirsted, even gagged a little; the cork-sized antibiotics weren't the only hard pills to swallow.

At my three-day follow-up, the doctor said, "You need to inform your partner or partners."

"Partner!" I protested. "Singular."

"He'll need treatment, too. As will any other partners he may have." I said nothing to that. I wondered whether Jack would tell

Simone she needed treatment (and precisely why). I wondered whether he'd need to tell anyone else. I wondered how my own stock would plummet if I turned out to be sterile.

I called Minnie. "I was a shit and I'm sorry and you were right and thank you. Now, how am I supposed to pay back the money?"

Minnie dove right in. "I've been thinking about that. I say let's wrangle with your mother's insurance company and see if we can't get some of that repair work reimbursed."

"They won't do a thing. She wasn't covered when the house caught fire. End of story."

"They did her a raw deal, I think. You don't just let a policy of some fifty years lapse without any follow-up. If she didn't cancel, but just stopped sending checks? They should have sent her a notice or something."

"Maybe they did," I ventured.

"Nonsense. Mrs. Goss isn't senile; she just forgot. She hadn't been feeling well. If they had sent her a reminder, she'd have sent payment. I'll make some calls, but meanwhile you're going to write them an officious letter. The phrase 'exploiting the elderly' ought to get their attention."

The possibility was wearying. "I don't know if I'm up for all this."

"Everything doesn't have to happen today. You need to rest and get well. Hey, I'm giving you the week off. How about that?"

"Can you spare me? I'd like to feel as if I couldn't be spared."

"Okay," Minnie complied. "This issue's going to *suck* without you. But I can't pay you for at least a week, anyway; that stupid cruise really set me back. Now, what should I do with these bottles? I have to confess I'm starting to feel anxious about them being here. I'm not made of stone, you know."

I pulled deeply through my nostrils, felt my belly expand and the oxygen-plump cells go tearing through my blood. Then I pushed all the air back out and let go of wanting for a few perfect beats. "Pour them out, I guess. If I change my mind I can always get more."

My first true breath.

I stayed serene until I ran across those fucking booties again. Why hadn't I thrown them away? Had I planned to hang them from my rearview mirror or have them bronzed? Made for sweet newborn feet, both of them fit the palm of my hand. Leather soles thin as cardstock, satiny baby-blue uppers—of course Jack wanted a boy.

If it turned out I couldn't have babies, I wanted to know who could. If I couldn't have babies, how was it that a forty-nine-year-old woman was supposed to have managed it? If it was so easy to not be able to, if one stupid decision could render you barren. If the body was so tender as that.

Which raised the question of Dahlia again. Yet it couldn't have been me she left home to have. *Who said it was?* It didn't fit; when she left home to have that baby she couldn't have been more than fifteen or sixteen. *Yes and . . . ?* She would have been closer to thirty when I was born. So it didn't fit. *It fit a pattern of behavior.* No. Why would a grown and married woman give up her baby? *She told you that herself. She denied him nothing but children.*

mabry goss

I've told you many times about Sarah, wife of Abraham, how she was too old for childbearing when God promised her a baby, and she got so tickled at the idea. God was a little put out by that and said, "What are you laughing for? You think there's anything I can't do?" And he showed her, too. She got that baby.

There's more to it, of course. Sarah hadn't done much to deserve such a miracle as that. She had her a maid, Hagar, who she sent unto her husband. Then she didn't like how raised-up Hagar was acting, and she run her off. Now why should Sarah get blessed after she's shown herself like that? And Abraham, he'd as good as handed Sarah over to Pharaoh, saying, "She's just my sister," and Pharaoh had gone right unto her, too, until God set him straight.

And yet these two sorry old fools get told their issue shall be kings.

You came to us when we thought the time for children was long past us. It was my change of life, and Linwood, well, he hadn't seen the soft side of me in an age, my forgiveness was so grudging slow. It seemed like a jest for us to be parents again. But here you come fat and sassy, eyes full of wonder at the world. You had us laughing for joy. I'm not saying we deserved it, but I feel like we rose to the occasion.

That's still your story, and none of it's a lie. It's just there's more to it.

I'll leave it to you whether to take this up with Dahlia. I'm not sure she could stand you knowing. She hardly knows how to act around you as it is. Credit her this: she knew her limitations. She knew she couldn't raise a child, but neither could she stand to sign another one away and never know its fortune.

We didn't force her to give that baby up. We sent her off, yes, but nothing was decided. Young as she was then, we believed it would go better for her away from the prying eyes, better for her, and yes, maybe better for us, but we weren't determined she should give that baby up. Linwood had come down hard at the first, no telling what he'd signed when he took her to that home, but he was softening as her time grew nearer, starting to say why shouldn't we bring that baby home and raise it? After all, wasn't that old hat for us? There was some overlap with the birth of Junior that might complicate the tale, but we could brazen that on out.

Meanwhile there's our girl off in Raleigh, surrounded by social workers who have as their job to get your baby adopted out. Just about the worst thing you could ever do then was have a baby out of wedlock. To their way of thinking there's just the one solution, and that is let some deserving couple give the child a better life than what you could ever manage with your sinning ways. (The child's not mixed, right? Why then, any proper folk would have it!)

There's one who really takes to Dahlia, says call her Jill, says she's her friend, heady stuff when you find yourself friendless. I see now how she did think that. Soon they're trading confidences the way young women will do. This Jill tells about fussing with her beau and makes fun of her boss, acting as if she's not like the others who work there, she can be trusted. Then it's Dahlia's turn, and she tells I don't know what all about the boy who wronged her, but she doesn't stop there, oh no, she's on the outs with me and her daddy. And the way we're living—well, it can't sound decent to any social worker in 1954.

So then they're pushing papers at her, saying sign here, you've got to save this child from such as that, and she signs. She goes into labor weeks earlier than expected, so by the time Linwood and I catch on, Baby Girl Goss is already gone.

A thing like that will grow you up. Dahlia wouldn't come back home, but made her own way the best that she could after that. Before I broke with Zephra, we went into Raleigh a few times to eat at the Sanitary, and Dahlia would wait on us and take her break with us. Linwood wouldn't come, but he'd say invite her back to supper. Dahlia wouldn't come. She'd say bring him next time. One day we came she showed us a ring, said she got married. Just like that. Never even mentioned a beau. When do we get to meet him? Oh, sometime, she said.

The years got away from us. William left home at seventeen, the day he graduated high school, and I think he stayed a little while with Dahlia and her husband, name of Harlan Franks and that's about all I ever did know of him. William joined the military as soon as he turned eighteen and went all over everywhere—including

Vietnam, I heard, though never from him—before settling down in Texas, where we'd sometimes get a card from. Where he called me out of the blue from and said Dahlia is in Regina, go and help her.

I found her at the Montclair Motel. It was falling to pieces even then, and all manner of rough people lurking about. She was a mess, stringy hair all loose and dirty jeans. She fell on me and we both wept. She said she was separating from Harlan. Things were out of hand and she needed to think.

"Does he know you're pregnant?" I asked. This time I could tell it just by looking at her, though she was early on. Skinny as a pole but for the little pooch hid under a man's shirt.

No, and he wasn't going to know. She needed to be where he couldn't find her.

"Well," I said, "Lord knows he's never been to our house." And she was so tired and lost she didn't need more convincing than that.

Oh how Linwood waited on her! Hand and foot. She wasn't a child anymore, but she needed the loving care. And it did him a lot of good, too. She wanted nothing to do with a baby doctor since the one at the home, and I wouldn't press her on it. I remembered what it was like to be no better than a breeding animal in the doctor's eyes just because you'd had a slip. Still, we intended her to deliver in a hospital when the time came, in case of trouble.

We did our best to keep her eating good and tiptoed around in the mornings so she could sleep in. I'm shamed to say, though, that I didn't put down the cigarettes, not knowing of the harm I might do. And I didn't grudge Dahlia one of her own now and again. It was companionable to sit at the table with my grown girl and smoke a little, talk a little, drink a little coffee. But God was good and didn't stunt you for it.

Harlan didn't ever come for her, like me and Linwood kept thinking he might. And Dahlia seemed in no ways inclined to return to him. As her time drew closer, we pulled out the old crib and started making her bedroom over into a nursery. Everything in yellow, as we were hedging our bets, though Linwood felt strongly you would be a girl.

Along around her seventh month, Dahlia started asking after Zephra. I told her we weren't in regular touch now but for the end-of-year accounting. "Will you mind if I go and see her?" she asked, and I couldn't say I minded, though I did feel the littlest bit of jealousy.

I thought I'd better get past it, so when Dahlia left for her visit, I had a poundcake baked for her to carry over. Not a word of thanks, but next visit, Dahlia came home with the cake platter covered over in brownies. "She says to tell you they're from mix," Dahlia reported, "but that they're mighty good," and it was so. When she went again, I sent two jars of blackberry preserves, and she came home with a macramé plant hanger. "She says to tell you she made herself one just like it, and it can hold a heavy plant." So I got a good hen and stewed it till it came apart in strings, and with the broth I rolled out my pastry so thin you could read the newspaper through it before I dropped it in the simmering pot. I poured it all into my biggest serving dish, covered it over in foil, and wrapped it up in towels so it would still be warm when I sent it over with Dahlia, but Dahlia had done slipped off on her visit while I was fixing it, and what she came back with this time was Zephra.

When Zephra took up her spot at my table again, any hard thoughts I still carried dropped clean away. And later, when Dahlia did what she couldn't help doing, I had my heart's friend by me, and I knew we could manage.

You ought never to think Dahlia held no love for you. In the days after you were born she sat rocking you, tears just pouring out of her. I thought it was the regular run of feelings after giving birth, feelings so strong they can knock you down. But she told me how they'd talked her out of ever holding the first one—or not so much talked her out of it as just refused, saying that was best. Holding you made joy and sorrow feel like the same killing thing.

I think she knew all along she wouldn't keep you. Before the week was out she allowed she might get back with Harlan, and added it wasn't a life she would bring a dog into, much less a child.

"Is that how bad we done you?" Linwood cried. "You think you're no better than a dog?"

"There's a piece of paper out there that says I abandoned my baby," she said, "and I put my name to it."

"If anyone's to answer for that, it should be me. I did wrong sending you off like I did. It's no reason to go back to this man." His words didn't seem to reach her, but they cut to my quick in a way that none of his remorses had before.

"There's another piece of paper out there binding me to him," she pointed out. "Everybody said get on with your life. That's the life I got on with."

"This is your life now, this little baby right here!"

"I can't look at her," she said simply, "without seeing the other one."

So we lost her the second time, though she couldn't reconcile with Harlan. He'd made a widow of her, whether by accident or spite it barely matters; fall or jump it broke his neck the same. When I learned it I had hopes she'd come back, but it only drove her further on.

I'm sorry I can't give you more about who sired you. I didn't know him to properly grieve, though I prayed God would take him in. I don't know what you'll get from her about it. She's shut that door.

Strange and merciful to say, there were no shadows over you, just three fools, Linwood, Zephra, and me. I mended with them both over your raising. Life seemed sweet with a little girl to tend. None of us had to work so hard anymore, and we had some money to spend on you, and time, though I don't think we spoiled you much.

I don't guess knowing these things can harm you after all this time and you grown, though I wouldn't have volunteered it. My ma'am used to say don't stir up more snakes than you can kill. I've made my final peace with Zephra by running my mouth like I have, though I've surely broke the peace with Dahlia. But maybe she'll be glad the snakes are loose.

I know these questions aren't all that's been troubling you. Even now you're afraid of what I'll think if I learn the whole of it, when there's not a thing in this world that would stop my loving you. Still, I've learned to put up with the coddling, even enjoy it some. I don't need my nerves ruined. I don't need all the details of what you got into. All I need to know is that you come out the other end of it. I see you are a kind person, not afraid to do a little work, and my heart is well satisfied at how you turned out.

avie goss

It was another kind of homecoming, this knowledge. I can see now how I'm part of my family's story, no longer cut off from them by time. There's a shadow man now, this Harlan who sired me, but in dreams when I strain to see his features, it's Linwood's face that comes into focus. I only lost Dahlia as a sister, and there remains a sister out there, that other change baby on whom the family fortunes turned. Perhaps she wants to be found.

Mama would always be Mama, and we went on much as before, me tending her, and her returning the favor a thousand times over. She came to speak more freely to me, referring to distant events as if I had been there, and I responded in kind. Linwood and Zephra seemed to come alive again, she talked about them so often and so urgently, in equal parts bitter and fond. She hunkered that past around her like a blanket as she grew weaker.

Despite all that she disclosed, however, Mama never permitted me a glimpse of those two months she'd spent in Richmond, when she'd left her young husband and baby and stepped into another existence, a startling act no less remarkable for its brevity. Two months is ample time to starve to death, to fall in love, or to decide there's no going back. Perhaps that was partly why she didn't want my full confession; she didn't want to owe me Richmond in return. And some grudging respect for her last shred of privacy keeps it just beyond my imagining. She'd had to share everything else in her life. It was the one thing that was hers alone.

She lived on another year after Zephra's passing. On her vital days she expressed hope of seeing the next century, still an ambitious six years ahead, but as her final months worked their slow murder, she began to say she'd have to make do with what she'd seen of this one. It became a race between heart and lungs, and I was rooting for the heart to finish first, for that fist in her chest to clench and fall open and her soul slip deftly free. If the lungs prevailed, it would be a slow, panicky drowning, the death she feared most. In the end it was too close to call.

I couldn't choreograph it at all the way I'd hoped, at home under soft lights and softer blankets, her people all encircling her. We were back in the noisy hospital under protest, because the doctor wouldn't agree to continue medicating her back pain, worsening from a series of falls followed by long strandings in bed, until she came in for an X-ray. I promised her this would be the last time, that after this we'd go home and numb up and nothing more would budge us unless it was the Social Event of the Season, which made her laugh, which made her gasp and weep.

On the table, still in her lead apron, she slipped from writhing pain into a state of semiconsciousness, and I got her admitted to ensure a steady stream of morphine. I hope it was the morphine that won. I hope she didn't register the high state of agitation her body broadcast as the death roamed through it like a petty vandal, slashing tires and flipping breaker switches, punching holes through walls. In the last hideous hours she was gargling bloody fluid, and I made myself believe she was sleeping through it, that the hand squeezing mine white was involuntary reflex. That hand was the only thing that held me there, but I was grateful it did, because when at last it came, the moment of her passing was swift and tender. Her hand released me just as the terrible rattle of her breath ceased, but she pushed air soundlessly in and out three times more, as if savoring the final, silent ease of it, the body's parting gift.

Dahlia arrived too late to say goodbye, but it was her final dodge where Mama and I were concerned. She dealt with the funeral home and had the hospital bed, spare oxygen tanks, and concentrator removed from the house. She made calls, booked airline tickets for William (on the phone with him: "It's not a question of whether you're coming, it's how soon and for how long"), and worked with Minnie on an obituary for the *Progress*.

I wondered how she'd designate the family relationships; would she list the three of us as Mabry's children, or would she go public with the labels daughter, stepson, and granddaughter? But she simply named us in order of appearance: *survived by Dahlia Goss Franks of Cobb, Virginia, William Goss of Hilary, Texas, and Avalon Goss of Regina*. That would have been Mama's preference—not telling an outright lie, but not broadcasting all our private business, either. She'd never been for full disclosure, and it didn't seem right to foist it on her now.

Dahlia's preference was harder to discern. Beyond that first angry renunciation ("I'm barely your sister"), she'd quickly resigned to being "outed" as my birth mother, and her stoical takeover in the wake of Mabry's death seemed driven by some sense of what duty that would now entail. But our essential relationship changed very little. She'd become a somewhat less reluctant ally in Mama's care, and she'd been tolerant of my questions about Harlan, if sparing in her answers. Mama's death didn't end Dahlia's cautious remove in all our dealings; if anything, she grew more formal with me.

It was William who let it slip about her breast cancer. At first I was angrier than worried, and I complained bitterly to Minnie, expecting some consoling outrage from a mother who was fighting so hard to reconnect with her son. But she chastised me instead: "Quit waiting for her to take the initiative! She doesn't know how to be a mother; she hasn't had any practice. But you're like a *professional* daughter now."

I've made a lot of trips to Cobb, Virginia, since then. I took some initiative for my half-sister, too, and quietly posted some ads on Internet adoption sites seeking her out. I'm not sure how Dahlia will react if we ever hear from her, but I decided I'd rather ask forgiveness than permission. And there's still time for that to happen. When Dahlia's five-year mark passed with no recurrence of her cancer, she teased, "I hope you don't think this lets you out of coming to see me."

By the time Mama died, her recalcitrant property insurance company had come through—sort of. They reimbursed for about three-quarters of the repair work, though the legal fees and deductible knocked it down to half. I deposited it all in the pillaged account Jack had kept in my name, and to cover the rest I signed over to him a small corner of the acreage I inherited, where Daddy was always intending to build his dream house.

Jack wasn't happy with the notion of a payoff (I thought of it more as a buyout), but my insistence clarified things for both of us. Once my vision was unblinkered by debt and dependence, I knew I couldn't stay with him. Even with Mama gone, I knew I was making my life in Regina.

Which is not to say I needed to go on living in her house forever. She was never sentimental about me doing that. The new owners, New Jersey transplants, have remodeled it completely. It doesn't look like the same house at all, inside or out, but the couple are avid gardeners and have kept Mama's best perennials and restored Daddy's lush green lawn.

I put my profit from the sale into Minnie's paper, making it my paper, too. We manage an occasional part-time staff of interested students from Black River High School, and when Minnie's son comes to stay for the summer, he delivers door-to-door on his bike, though we're not otherwise a home-delivered paper. There has never been enough local news to make the *Progress* a daily, and we hope it stays that way.

There aren't many businesses in the area that I haven't done some design work for by now, and four times a year the Chamber of Commerce hires me to paint seasonal designs on the store windows downtown. I'll never grow rich off the paper or my artwork, but between my earnings and Saul's, we could eventually build something to suit us. We've talked about reclaiming the whole of Daddy's acreage, but something in me hesitates to buy back the scrap of land that zeroed my debt to Jack. He wouldn't try to develop it anytime soon, if ever, though it would be his right. I have found it a fair and tolerable burden, that he should still lay claim to a little of what was mine.

I've been living in the gourd lady's tidy cottage since we sold Mama's house. Technically it's mine, but I always think of it as the gourd lady's. She's had to move to Fairway Meadows, Regina's new assisted-living community, and is so tickled her house isn't sitting empty. I always stop in and see her when I go to Fairway Meadows on *Progress* business; they're a major advertiser. I wonder sometimes if Mama would have been happier in a place like that after Daddy died, but I can't imagine her agreeing to it— nor, for that matter, can I imagine how I would have fared without having her home to run away to.

I've considered buying Zephra's property, to get back closer to town. William has held on to it, renting it out through a local realty. Whenever a tenant moves away, he comes and spends a couple of weeks in it painting and repairing damages. The realty could handle that, too, but he prefers to do the work himself. Daddy taught him well, if not gently. He'd sell the place to me in a minute if I asked, but I never want to take away his excuse for coming to Regina or eventually retiring here. He's as proud a man as he is practical, and so long as there's property to maintain, he won't have to credit sentiment for his return.

About Saul. It's hard for me to feature being a pastor's wife, but it may come to that. He can't live with me openly, so he keeps his old apartment, though there's nothing left in it but a set of weights, maybe some canned goods, and he's compelled to sneak out at dawn from the bed we share. He's not thriving in this furtive, adulterous air; he feels unfaithful to an entire congregation. He jokes that we can marry or burn, but I can see that he's straining the seams of his own propriety. I've warned him I don't fit the profile; I'm not enough of a helpmeet and can't promise I'd attend services consistently enough to make a decent impression, though truth is I go more often than not these days. There's something I've been praying for.

To be worthy, I stay sober and eat decent food and get a full night's sleep. I do an honest day's work and sometimes more. I am helpful to people and kind to animals. If marrying the pastor will clinch it, that's no hard bargain—I do love him.

I count the days and take my temperature and look for signs.

Being ready is a sort of prayer, being hopeful, being open. If a child can weather this inhospitable chamber, trace the scars that chronicle my errors, and still opt to be born, I'll know I am forgiven.

If not, I will forgive myself.

acknowledgments

Many thanks to Cindy Spiegel and Nicole Aragi for their patience and trust.

My very best regards to the good people of Berry College, who housed and fed me as their writer-in-residence and got me through an early draft. Thanks also to Bowling Green State University, the University of North Carolina, and Vanderbilt University. To my students: I learned so much from you. I know it's supposed to be the other way around—I got the better end of the deal, and I'm not sorry.

Big love to the Barbour Girls: Ellen, Rita, Hilda, Ozella. Betty, too. I heard your voices the whole time. Barbour Girls, second generation: Nancy and Brenda helped me to know Ila, some of whose spirit, I hope, resides in these pages; Dale helped me get the medical stuff right (where I'm off is my own stubborn fault).

Mom! Forgive me for making you wait. I wanted it to be perfect.

Bottomless gratitude to my husband, Scott, for going through this with me (sometimes walking me through, sometimes carrying me) and wanting to get married anyway; I love you so.

about the author

June Spence's stories have appeared in *The Best American Short Stories,* *The Southern Review, Seventeen,* and *The Oxford American.* The winner of the Willa Cather Award, she lives with her husband, writer Scott Huler, in Raleigh, North Carolina.